WORSHIP THE KING

Books by the same author
available from Marshall Pickering

Feel So Real
Survivor – A Tribute to Cliff

WORSHIP
THE KING

*Prayers and readings for
contemporary worship*

TONY JASPER

Marshall Pickering
An Imprint of HarperCollins*Publishers*

Marshall Pickering is an Imprint of
HarperCollins*Religious*
Part of HarperCollins*Publishers*
77–85 Fulham Palace Road, London W6 8JB

First published in Great Britain
in 1992 by Marshall Pickering

1 3 5 7 9 10 8 6 4 2

A catalogue record for this book is
available from the British Library

ISBN 0 551 02550 6

Printed and bound in Great Britain by
HarperCollins*Manufacturing* Glasgow

To

Stella Wiseman and Paul Eggerton
Catrina Nelson
Karen Unsworth
Bridget Louvion, and son Jerome
Hilary Jones
Harry and Winn Baxendale

Contents

Introduction

Worship the King follows two collections with Myra Blyth, namely *In Unexpected Places* and *At All Times And In All Places*. Previous to this I put together *Living Words For Now*. There have also been visual-word meditative books, *The Illustrated Family Hymn Book*, *The Illustrated Family Prayer Book* and *Rejoice*, as well as two school assembly books for Junior and Secondary levels.

The positive response to these volumes, especially the general worship anthologies, has encouraged me in my continuous gathering of material.

As previously, there is considerable variation in style, language and level of spiritual awareness, but the assumption once again is that the material is to be used in a wide variety of circumstance, and it is to be spoken.

Here, as before, my concern is not with a writer's denominational trappings, or lack of them. I have been guided by asking such basic questions as: What does this extract say? Does it possess life, passion and the Spirit? Does it surprise? Does it open new avenues and awarenesses? Does it seem true to Scripture and orthodox Christian tradition? And if not, particularly if coming from a seemingly non-Christian source, does it possess a genuine quality of disrespect, irreverence, pain and despair that reflects the questioning, pain and despair that are part of people's lives, and indeed the protest that runs through Scripture itself? In a way, if nothing in this collection annoys you, then to some degree I have failed.

There are too many areas of our human experience for which few (sometimes no) prayers have been written. But at least the growing and powerful input of material from women writers has added a freshness and vitality to the sometimes stern, stodgy and unyielding language of worship. Much use is made of feminine contribution in this volume.

The outline of the book is simple. Here are 'words' on a number of basic themes which, apart from those on the Trinity and those which preface and end worship, focus on our current experience of self and world. At the end of each section there is a list of other apposite material that can be found elsewhere in the book.

Other than my own perpetual desire to provide material for worship, an overriding factor in making this collection has been the encouragement from certain British Methodist quarters. There has been tremendous response to the worship anthologies with a welcome shout of 'more'. Those voices have also called for more material that lends itself to dramatic use and congregational participation.

The Bishop of Birmingham, Mark Santer, said it so well: liturgy essentially is 'The Praises of God'. It would be easy in the current surfeit of new words, ways and songs, to postulate the notion that worship is about pleasing ourselves, and then, ridiculously, add God as an afterthought or After-Eights. In our current religious climate there are songs and faith which denote a God pleased with me, a Jesus seen as mate and friend, and both adore and approve me.

The modern axing of *mysterium tremendum* was well illustrated in a letter that appeared in *Third Way* where the writer penned: 'In our group (we do not call it a church any longer as this puts people off) we just find Jesus at the door when we arrive. With open arms he just tell us us to have a good time with him!'

The same writer continues: "We do not worry about metre, rhyming, harmony – did Thomas when he called out, "My Lord and My God"?'

Apart from wondering what Paul might think of substituting 'group' for church (one of the Greek words for church means 'assembly of citizens called out'), I suppose Thomas was speaking with sheer spontaneity. But when he spoke his majestic words he broke through the circle, the limits, the borders he had drawn around himself. He saw beyond, behind and through.

The Thomas 'break-out' was *not* to a good time until the next time. For Thomas that sheer spontaneous moment was manna from heaven, but real discipleship would come from hard discipline, crafting, praying, walking with a Jesus who is sometimes a stranger, and at moments *is there* at a meal, breaking bread, and is *known*.

So may this worship anthology help us to sing and live His praises in unexpected places and at all times and in all places, for in a crowded world there are people gasping for unpolluted spiritual air.

TONY JASPER

How to use this book

Each section is preceded by a list of relevant Scripture passages. These are not an exhaustive biblical guide to the theme, but may prove useful for the Bible readings in a worship service based on that topic. Mostly the references follow the biblical order, but on occasions an Old Testament passage is placed alongside a New Testament reference where it seems relevant.

An introductory note in each section either explores the theme title or explains the whys and wherefores of both title and material. Obviously choice of content is broadly based, and with contributions from so many writers, uniformity of standpoint would not be possible, even if it were desirable.

Words of praise,
adoration and thanksgiving

Bible passages:

1 Chronicles 16:8–36
Revelation 11:15
Revelation 19:6–8

J. Neville Ward in his memorable book *The Use Of Praying* is right. Thanksgiving is not adoration. It is next door to adoration. He says, 'There is something not absolutely final about thanksgiving'. Yet on the other hand, 'There is something final about praise and adoration'.

Neither 'adoration' nor 'thanksgiving' is easy to define. In essence adoration involves *what God is*, while thanksgiving concerns *what God does*. The God who is the object of adoration embodies the typically Christian paradox of being distant and yet approachable. Our knowledge of Him only serves to tell us how much we cannot understand in this life. True adoration includes anticipation of eternity, for the next life will make clear what is obscure in this.

Thanksgiving is earth-based rather than heaven-based. It embodies the great shout of Scripture that the God who is the Creator, the Source of Life, is also the One who is known in the passion and action of human struggle. No place is free from confrontation with this God seen in Jesus.

Praise is the popular word of the times, especially 'grabbed' by house groups and informal worship gatherings. We are invited to a 'time of praise' or, as the leader of preliminaries says, 'we shall now give praise', but whatever the leader may have in mind the word has been 'debased' to mean merely a particular kind of song, a set of words often noticeable by their twentieth-century obscurity. Praising often becomes cosy. It becomes mistaken for thanking.

Yet in essence praising has gone beyond thanking. To quote Neville Ward once more, when he writes of the believer in worship, 'He is praising and wanting that which he dimly discerns as the ultimate cause, value, giver in all his experience of the joy of life and the productiveness of painful life.'

The best praise songs do express a love and longing to know more and more of Him and His ways, with the proviso set by Charles Wesley that we will praise Him for all that is to come.

Blessed

Blessed are you, O Lord our God,
in the light that shines in the darkness
and which has never been extinguished.
Blessed are you, O Lord our God,
in the light that shines in the face
of our Lord and Saviour Jesus Christ,
and which reveals your glory.
Blessed are you, O Lord our God,
in the light of the Holy Spirit
which inflames our hearts and inspires our worship.
Blessed are you, O Lord our God, now and for ever. Amen.

Norman Wallwork

All glory

Glory to God, glory,
O praise Him, Alleluia!
Glory to God, glory,
O praise the Name of the Lord.

Almighty God, Father, Son and Holy Spirit:
We praise you for all good gifts we have received
and for your promise of peace and joy to all people;
Blessed be your wonderful Name
for ever and ever. Amen.

Byzantine liturgy

Blessed be God, Father, Son and Holy Spirit, now and for
ever. Amen.

Sanctus

Leader: Therefore with angels and archangels
and all the company of Heaven
All: We praise you!
Leader (slowly and with depth and dignity):
Holy! . . . Holy! . . . Holy!
All: Holy! . . . Holy! . . . Holy!
Leader Lord God of time and space
eternal reason for existence
All: Holy! . . . Holy! . . Holy!
Leader: We worship you,
we respond with all our being
All: Holy! Holy! Holy!
Leader: Heaven and earth are full of your glory!
All: Reflecting your life,
mirroring your being,
expressing your truth
Leader and all: Glory be to you,
O Lord most high!

Beth Webb

The leader's voice needs to be strong. The congregation follows in unison.
Physical posture can be important. Try doing this kneeling down.

Always and forever

We believe, O God, that you are the eternal God of life.
We believe, O God, that you are the eternal God of love.
We believe, O God of all the peoples,
You have created us from dust and ashes.
O God, who brought us to the joyous light of this day,
Bring us to the guiding light of eternity.

O my soul's healer, keep me at evening,
Keep me at morning, keep me at noon,
I am tired, astray and stumbling,
Shield me from sin.

As you were before us at our life's beginning,
Be you so again at our journey's end.
As you were beside us at our soul's shaping,
God, be also at our journey's close.

Glory to God, the Creator who gives us life,
Glory to Jesus, the Christ who calls us,
Glory to the Spirit, the Comforter, who empowers us.
As it was in the beginning, is now and shall be for ever.
Amen.

Traditional from Carmina Gaedelica

I AM

Before the world was made, I AM,
Before our time, our space, I AM;
Before the rocks or mountains rose,
The Lord has said I AM.

Before the sun pierced through our night,
Or we could stop and ask outright
The meaning of the dark we felt,
The Lord said I AM the light.

Before we stumbled on rough paths,

Or hid in hollow caves,
The meaning of the life we found,
I AM THE WAY, he said.

Before we knew of death or drought,
Or feared what they might mean,
A life that goes beyond he claimed,
I AM THE RESURRECTION.

William Hewett, S.J.

Glory to you

Glory to you, Almighty God!
You spoke, and light came out of darkness,
order rose from confusion.
WOMEN:
You breathed into the dust of the earth,
and we were formed in your image.
MEN:
You looked in the work of your hands,
and declared that it was all good.
And still you speak, breathe and look on us.
We praise you!
Glory to you, Jesus Christ!
You met us as a refugee, a threatened child,
the word made flesh, born in a forgotten place.
WOMEN:
You called us, by name, to leave what was comfortable,
to be your disciples, companions and friends.
MEN:
You saved us by kneeling at our feet,
stretching your arms wide to take away our sins,
walking through death to life again.
And still you meet, call and save us.
We praise you!
Glory to you, Holy Spirit!
You brooded over chaos,
mothering and shaping God's new creation.

WOMEN:
You inspired prophets and evangelists,
you discovered the right word for the right season.
MEN:
You liberated the early church for mission,
claiming all of life for the Lord of all.
And still you brood over, inspire and liberate us.
We praise you!
Glory to you, God, Three-In-One!
You are surrounded by the song of the saints in heaven,
and you are present with us now.
We adore you!

John Bell

The divine praises

Blessed be God.
Blessed be our Father in heaven.
Blessed be the God and Father of our Lord Jesus Christ.
Blessed be His holy Name.
Blessed be Jesus Christ, true God, very man, the Saviour of the world.
Blessed be the life-giving, the liberating Spirit, the Holy Ghost,
    the Counsellor, the Comforter.
Blessed be God in the splendour of His Angels, in the glories of
    His Saints.

Psalm of praise

My God is in a flight of joy
a shout from the heart.

He is the light in the eye
of one who suffers
yet knows she is not alone.

My praise is a word of life
spoken in the face of nothingness.

My song swells

to carry the faint-hearted
like a feather before the storm.

Safe into the enfolding breast
of God,
my Mother-Father.

Beth Webb

Such variety

Glory be to God for the life-giving differences which enrich our
   humanity
Glory be to God for the rainbow colours – diverse but witnessing
   to a single truth, a single providence.
Glory be to God for landscapes plotted and pieced and fallow,
Glory be to God for races and peoples and nations and languages
   and tribes.
But, Lord, we have created divisions which separate your
   peoples.
We have raised obstacles against each other – classes and fears
   and jealousies. Lord, have mercy upon us.
Respectfully, may we listen to one another; each bringing his own
   story yet needful of the history of others.
Lord, encourage friendship between peoples and make us
into one large family with a new confidence, and with
a vision of the future. Help us towards unity in
spite of our differences. Grant us strength because
of the variety of our experience.

Ecumenical group in Strasbourg

Beyond yet near

O God all-powerful, true and incomparable,
present in all things, yet limited by none,
untouched by place,
unaged by time,
unhurried by the years,
undeceived by words,

not subject to birth
nor in need of protection:
you are above all corruption,
you are beyond all change,
you are by nature immutable,
living in light that none can approach,
invisible, yet you make yourself known to me and you are found
   by all who seek you with their whole heart;
you are the God of Israel
and of all who hope in Christ.

Leader: You are our God.
All: We adore you.

                                                             Huub Oosterhuis

With us

Our Creator God is with us to bless us:
The Risen Lord is with us to bless us;
The transforming Spirit is with us to bless us.

                                                             Tony Jasper

Lord of all blessing

Lord of all Blessing,
As we walk about your world
Let us know ourselves blessed at every turn;
Blessed in the autumnal sun and leaves;
Blessed in the winter wind;
Blessed in rain and shafts of sunlight;
Blessed in the moving stars;
Blessed in the turning of the world beneath our feet;
Blessed in silence:
Blessed in sleep;
Blessed in our children, our parents
and our friends;
Blessed in conversation and the human voice;
Blessed in waiting for the bus or train or traffic lights;

Blessed in music, blessed in singing voice blessed in the song
   of birds;
Blessed in the cry that pierces the heart;
Blessed in the smile of strangers;
Blessed in the touch of love, blessed in laughter;
Blessed in pain, in darkness, in grief;
Blessed in the desert and the frost;
Blessed in waiting for the Spring;
Blessed in waiting and waiting and waiting.

Lord of all blessing
We bless you.

*Gathered by Robert Llewelyn from Hugh Dickinson, Dean of
Salisbury.*

Beyond our limitation

Caring God, you come to us as Mother and Father, revealing
the many facets of your love in the traditions of all peoples. The world is large but you are larger, able to work
by the Spirit's power in every place. Thank you for making
us part of something much greater and very wonderful, loved
members of an extended and varied family. Make us one in
your love.

Anonymous

Graffiti

I went to heaven
and saw God

Wow, would you believe:
She's black

Beyond words

He wanted to talk. The word GOD triggered him. He was trying
to get past the letters of a word.

There is play on words that distorts meaning. Words have been
known to lose their meaning and have become like empty boxes.
To get past the letters and vocabulary to the meaning is like a
box with a gift inside.

God.
G-O-D.
God.
I SEE THREE LETTERS.
LIKE ON THREE BLOCKS.
WOODEN BLOCKS.
God.
THREE BLOCKS IN FRONT OF MY EYES.
THREE BLOCKS IN FRONT OF YOUR MOUTH.
G-O-D.
God.
GOD IS NOT A WORD.
God.
A TOY. A GAME.
God.
YOU HAVEN'T TOLD ME ANYTHING.
YOU HAVE ONLY GIVEN ME THREE
LETTERS. ONE WORD. BACKWARDS
IT SPELLS. DOG. D-O-G.
God.
YOU JUST STAND THERE REPEATING THE
SAME WORD. GOD. GOD. GOD. LIKE
A TAPE LOOP WITH GOD-GOD-GOD HANG-UP.
God.
GOD ISN'T A WORD. HE'S NOT A SENTENCE,
AN ANTHEM, A POEM. GOD IS NOT A BOOK.
God.
HE IS NOT THE BIBLE. GOD IS

NOT JOHN 3:16.
God.
HE IS NOT WORDS AND WORDS AND WORDS.
HE IS NOT THE WORD *LORD, JEHOVAH,*
JESUS, BROTHER, JAVEH, CHRIST . . .
God.
GOD CANNOT BE SPELLED.
HE CANNOT BE PUT IN CAPS OR TYPESET.
HE CANNOT BE PRINTED IN BLACK INK
OR OFFSET.
God.
HE IS NOT THESE SYLLABLES,
THESE SIGNS, THESE SYMBOLS.
God.
GOD IS A SPIRIT.
God.
HE IS THE SPIRIT BEHIND THE LETTERS.
God.
THE FIRST WORD THEY SAID;
THE FIRST THING THEY DID.
God.
THE ONE BEFORE THE WORDS.
God
AFTER THE WORDS.
God.
THE EXPLANATION OF THE WORD.
THE EXPERIENCE OF THE WORD.
God.
THE WORD MADE FLESH.
My God.

> *God, be God.*
> *Be lord of language,*
> *of sentences,*
> *of words.*
> *Take us all the way,*
> *and come to us all the way.*
> *Let there be no words between us.*

> Let words unite us.
> Lord. Christ. Lord.
> Amen.
>
> *Herbert Brokering*

Credo

Voice 1: I believe in one God, the Father Almighty

Voice 2: God, I know you are there, in form unimaginable

Voice 3: in love and compassion, all embracing

Voice 1: Maker of Heaven and earth, and of all things visible and invisible

Voice 2: your hands stretch beyond the universe

Voice 3: to mould a speck of dust

Voice 2: in an empty place

Voice 3: and to hold it lovingly

Voice 1: And in one Lord Jesus Christ, the only begotten Son of God, begotten of his Father before all worlds

Voice 2: your love yearned to take on form

Voice 3: and it was so. Might, perfected in frailty.

Voice 1: God of God, Light of Light, Very God of very God, begotten, not made,
being of one substance with the Father,
by whom all things were made

Voice 2: perfect expression of the unsayable

Voice 3: all that can be known of the unknowable

Voice 2: he, who made everything

Voice 3: was conceived and carried by a woman

Voice 1: Who for us men and for our salvation, came down from Heaven.

Voice 2: Stop!

Voice 3: Contemplate!

Voice 1: He was incarnate by the Holy Spirit of the Virgin Mary and was made man.

Voice 2: *He* took our human form to share *our* pain

Voice 1: He was crucified for us under Pontius Pilate

Voice 3: Injustice!

Voice 1: He suffered and was buried

Voice 2: Let the whole world stand in stunned silence (*long pause*)

Voice 3: in the chill night of the universe (*pause*)

Voice 2: let every sphere hold still
in its eternal dance
God, the eternal Maker,
has suffered human death.
(*pause*)

Voice 1: (*joyfully*) And the third day, he rose again, according to the scriptures!

Voice 2: like catching the wind in a paper bag

Voice 3: death split itself open

Voice 2: quite inside out!

Voice 3: Now Christ is alive!

Voice 1: He ascended into Heaven and is seated at the right hand of the Father

Voice 2: for all to see, and know, and behold

Voice 1: When he shall come again to judge the living and the dead

Voice 1, 2 and 3: God's Kingdom shall have no end!

Voice 1: And I believe in the Holy Spirit

Voice 2: the breath, the breathing

Voice 3: inspiration of life!

Voice 1: The Lord, the giver of life
who proceeds from the Father and the Son

Voice 2: your essence poured out

Voice 3: like fire

Voice 2: like wind

Voice 3: burning

Voice 2: cleansing

Voice 3: filling

Voice 1: With the Father and the Son together,
the Spirit is worshipped and glorified

Voice 2: before our God, whose love is community
Voice 3: we respond
Voice 2: we become your single body of many parts

Voice 1: The Spirit spoke through the prophets
Voice 2: speak through us now
Voice 3: so we may remain one universal church
Voice 2: the church of apostles
Voice 1: Acknowledging one baptism for the forgiveness of sins
Voice 2: looking for the resurrection of the dead
Voice 3: and the life of the world to come
Voices 1, 2 and 3: Amen

Beth Webb

(*Voice 1 deeper, possibly a man's voice. Voices 2 and 3 lighter, women or teenagers.*)

Eternal and loving God

ETERNAL and loving God
wonderfully creating us in your own image,
striving with our reluctant wills,
renewing us in Jesus when we fail to love,
so fill us with your Spirit
that as he came to share in our humanity,
we may come to share in his divinity;
who is alive and reigns with you and the Holy Spirit,
one God, now and for ever. Amen.

Christ, who by your incarnation
gathered into one things earthly and heavenly,
fill us with your joy and peace,
now and for ever. Amen.

Jim Cotter

More words of praise, adoration and thanksgiving:

Words to lead into
and close worship

Bible passages:

Psalm 78:1–8
Psalm 115
Psalm 117
Psalm 150
Revelation 15:3a–4
Revelation 22:12, 13

The concern of this section is simple. It is not with the kind of prayer and preparation that should be done well ahead, nor with the vital attention that should be given to decor, visual, acoustics, sound system, greeting of people and proper provision of accompanying worship materials.

Rather, this section provides some powerful words that may well preface and provide the right setting for worship in mainstream gathering or a less formal service.

Too often, the beginning of a service is treated with no more respect than a hurried first course of a meal. Often words are rushed, sometimes because of the nervousness of the officiating person, occasionally because of poor or no preparation. 'First' words are not always seen as those that largely determine the mood and feel of the ensuing worship.

The end of a service may receive no better treatment, as though it doesn't matter, like the sealing of an envelope. But the right use of 'end' words can gather together all preceding material. They can give the opportunity for a new commitment, discipleship and call for service. They can remind worshippers that the Lord has gone ahead, waiting to be met and known

I hope this section will dispel any notion that the beginning and end of worship are subservient to the larger things that take place in between.

Beginnings

Beauty overwhelms us
Wonder silences our endless chatter and worries
We can begin to
Worship

Making right

We and God
have business with each other;
and in opening ourselves to his influence
our deepest destiny is fulfilled.

William James, Varieties of Religious Experience

Divine musical underpinning

In the rhythms which our people love – with the simple and direct words of the Psalms and of the Gospel, in expressions of solidarity, of love and of consecration, we believers sing of our hope, of the security of the Lord's presence and of our trust in the power of the Holy Spirit. It is a time of pain, but it is also a time of song. As it was for the Churches of the New Testament, as it has always been whenever the Holy Spirit has renewed the Church.

Slightly adapted from Sign of the Times, *CLAI, South America*

Introt

Narrator: God is here
People: His spirit is with us
Narrator: We are the people
People: The people of His Spirit
Narrator: We are the people
People: The people of His breath
Narrator: Breath of Life
People: Breath of Hope
Narrator: Where His Spirit is
People: There is Life and Hope!

Narrator: God is here
People: His Spirit is with us
Narrator: We are the people
People: The people of His dance
Narrator: Dance of Life
People: Dance of Hope
Narrator: Where His Spirit is
People: There is Life and Hope!

Narrator: God is here
People: His Spirit is with us
Narrator: We are the people
People: The people of His word
Narrator: Then let us be still!
(Stop dancing)
People: Let us be silent! (*Stop bongos*)
Narrator: And Listen to our Lord.

Beth Webb

(*End in silence with everyone kneeling.*
After a few minutes, have a scripture reading.)

This is for the begining of a service. Read it quickly, preferably with a bongo drum beat or rhythmic clapping, and perhaps also a fast walking dance around the church or up the aisle.

Glory

Voice: Let this day be a day of glory to me
All: The glory of Bethlehem
One from the company: Your coming to earth
All: The glory of Cana
One from the company: Your sharing in mirth
All: The glory of Galilee
One from the company: Your bringing of calm
All: The glory of Bethesda
One from the company: Your saving from harm
All: The glory of Calvary
One from the company: Your sacrificial love
All: The glory of Easter
One from the company: Your rising above
All: The glory of Ascension
One from the company: Your presence to see
All: Let this day be a day of glory to me

David Adam

Say this with due spirit and vigour.

Laying it all down

Lord God, we worship you; creator, sustainer, Living God.
Lord Jesus, we worship you; Christ, Son of the Living God.
Holy Spirit of goodness and truth we worship you; Power of the
    Living God.
Lord our God, we remember how great you are. We think of your
    perfect goodness, purity, truth, love
    and justice.
We confess our imperfection. We say and do unpleasant things
    without always even meaning to. We make others and ourselves
    unhappy.
We come to Jesus our living Saviour who takes control of our
    divided lives, to bring good from evil, light from darkness,
    peace from conflict.

Jesus we bring to you:
> our lives for healing
> our sin for forgiveness
> our sadness for you to share
> our happiness and laughter for you to complete
> with your joy.

West Yorkshire Methodist District

Today and more

This day will we praise thee, O Lord;
This day will we thank thee, O Lord;
This day will we love thee, O Lord;
This day will we serve thee, O Lord.

Prayer from an Indian theological college

Psalm 96

Verse 1 – two men and two women:
> O sing to the Lord a new song; sing to the Lord, all
> the earth!

Verse 2 – add two further men, two women:
> Sing to the Lord, bless his name; tell of his salvation from
> day to day.

Verse 3 – all eight say:
> Declare his glory among the nations, his marvellous
> works
> among all the peoples!

Verse 4 – one woman:
> For great is the Lord, and greatly to be praised;

Verse 4 – one man:
> He is to be feared above all gods.

Verse 5 – two of the readers:
> For all the gods of the peoples are idols; but the Lord made
> the heavens.

Verse 6 – further one man and one woman to make four voices:
Honour and majesty are before him;

Verse 6 – add further man and woman to make six voices:
Strength and beauty are in his sanctuary.

Verse 7 – add remaining two voices to make eight:
Ascribe to the Lord, O families of the peoples,

Verse 8 – ascribe to the Lord glory and strength! Ascribe to the Lord the glory due his name;

Verse 8 – one woman:
Bring an offering and come into his courts!

Verse 9 – one woman:
Worship the Lord in holy array;

Verse 9 – tremble before him, all the earth!

Verse 10 – one woman, one man:
Say among the nations, 'The Lord reigns!'

Verse 10 – add one woman, one man to make 4:
'Yea, the world is established, it shall never be moved';

Verse 10–11 – add remaining four voices:
'He will judge the peoples with equity.' Let the heavens be glad, and let the earth rejoice; let the sea roar and all that fills it;

Verse 12 – two women:
Let the field exult, and everything in it!

Verse 12–13 – two men:
Then shall all the trees of the wood sing for joy before the Lord, for he comes,

Verse 13 – two men and two women making four
for he comes to judge the earth.

Verse 13 – all eight voices:
He will judge the world with righteousness, and the peoples with his truth.

From an arrangement by Clare Davidson – Psalm 96 (RSV translation) read by 8 people.

Ahead of us

We draw near to the Father
He gives the gift of eternal life
We worship Him
In Jesus' name we do so
Jesus is Lord
Jesus is the Risen One
Jesus goes before us
He is known where we are

Tony Jasper

Claimed and wanted

Through God our Father
in the name of the Son
through this same Holy Spirit
we are the sons and daughters of the Living God
in love created
destined for life.

Glory be to you, Father,
through Your Son, Jesus Christ,
with the Spirit who brings life and blessing
forever and ever.

We take each other in a lovely embrace

We gather in the glorious freedom of the sons and
   daughters of God
You are very near
We come with prayer and thanksgiving

This moment the dawning of new surprises
As we believe, so let us live

Today and all days
You are to be praised

Tony Jasper

In all places

We stand before you today to thank you for all your gifts.
All that is, is yours, and you have given all to us.
We thank you.
We thank you for the wonders of human invention
for the love and caring from friends,
for the gift of your loving Spirit.

We come together in the name of Jesus your Son;
may we come to know Him better.
He showed us we can find you everywhere.
He taught us that your love makes it possible for us to be
    ourselves,
to be free from sin,
and free to love.

The Spirit He has given us makes us confident
that we can serve you.

We praise you for His presence.

All glory and honour is yours,
For ever and ever.

Amen.

Vision

Lord, as we worship today give us vision,

Move us by your Spirit.

Bring good news to us all.

Freedom to broken people.

And Heaven, here on Earth.

Open our eyes to see you as you really are,
and open our hearts to praise you.

Give us a vision that will carry us through
our disappointments and our failures,
our anxious and unhappy times,

and the monotony of boring routines.

Give us a vision that will lift our lives
and lead us to new ways of service.

Help us to dare to dream of love
in a world that speaks of hate.

Help us to dare to dream of hope
in a world that speaks of despair.

Help us to dare to dream of peace
in a world that speaks of war.

In our worship today, Lord, give us vision
through Jesus Christ our Lord. Amen.

(From MAYC London Weekend Worship)

Your Spirit

Risen Christ,
today, tomorrow and always,
Your Spirit lives in us.
Sometimes we feel we understand so little,
But remaining in your presence, wherever we are, is prayer.
And perhaps close to you, O Christ,
silence is often everything in prayer.
And then we sense that, our whole life long,
we advance when trust in you guides every step,
when a trusting heart is at the beginning of everything.

from Taizé

United in need

Lord God, we who have come together to worship you are very
different people. We are at various stages in our life, and our
circumstances vary. We are conscious of widely differing needs.
It is difficult for the words of one of us to convey what we are all
feeling.

And yet we are united by our common humanity. As we look

at each other, we see what we were in days gone by, or what we shall be in days to come. We see the kind of person we might have been, or the kind of person we should like to be. And we could not do without each other. We need one another to talk to. We need to help and be helped.

And we are here because we have all sensed something of life's mystery and wonder. We feel thankful, and we reach out to the author of all good things. We feel responsible, and we want to give account to our maker.

We believe that we have seen something of the pattern for our life in Jesus Christ and those who have followed Him. Help us to understand that pattern more fully and enable us to come nearer to it.

The Jesus prayer

Lord Jesus Christ,
Son of the living God,
have mercy on me,
a sinner.

Take and use

O God, take all our sorrows and use them to show us the nature of Thy joy.

Take all our sins and, forgiving them, use them to show us the way of true pleasantness and the paths of true peace.

Take all our broken purposes and disappointed hopes and use them to make Thy perfect rainbow arch.

Take all our clouds of sadness and calamity and from them make Thy sunset glories.

Take our night and make it bright with stars.

Take our ill-health and pain until they accomplish in Thy purpose as much as health could achieve.

Take us as we are, with impulses, strivings, longings so often frustrated and thwarted, and even with what is broken and imperfect make Thy dreams come true.

Through Him who made of human life a sacrament, of thorns

a crown, of a cross a throne, even through Jesus Christ our
Lord. Amen.

Leslie Weatherhead

Gospel realities

Lord Christ, you take us
with our hearts just as they are.
Why should we wait for our hearts to be changed,
in order to go to you?
You change them, day by day,
without our knowing how.
You have all that is needed to heal us:
prayer, hymns, forgiveness,
and the springtime of reconciliations.

Praised be the living God
for the multitude of women, men and children
who throughout the world
are searching, striving, and giving their lives
in order to be bearers of reconciliation.
Through the repentance of our hearts,
and the spirit of simplicity of the beatitudes,
you clothe us with forgiveness, as with a garment.
Enable us to welcome the realities of the Gospel
with a childlike heart,
and to discover your will,
which is love and nothing else.

Brother Roger, Taizé

He is Lord

All say together and with force:

Lord of the world
Lord of the heart
Lord of the universe
Lord of creatures

Lord of all
Lord of life
Lord of light
Lord of knowledge

pause, then all shall say:

We take refuge in you

Unexpected Spirit

Spirit of God, powerful and unpredictable as the wind, you came upon the followers of Jesus on the first WhitSunday and swept them off their feet, so that they found themselves doing what they thought they never had it in them to do.

It is you who through all ages have fired men (and women) with enthusiasm to go about telling the good news of Jesus and serving other people for His sake.

Spirit of God, powerful and unpredictable as the wind, come upon us as we worship and become the driving force of our lives.

Let us adore the Holy Spirit, who was there at creation sweeping the emptiness and bringing the universe from God's will to birth.

Let us adore the Holy Spirit, who brought about the greater creation, when the Word was made flesh for us in Jesus.

Let us adore the Holy Spirit, who came to disciples like fire and a wind, so that the power in their lives was then God's power.

Are we thankful?

Paul said: 'Always give thanks for everything.'
Do we ever give God thanks that we can see?
That we can hear?
Do we thank Him that we can walk and run and laugh?
Feel the wind and the rain,
Enjoy the warmth of the sun,
Enjoy a good meal.
That we can close the door and be safe and cosy in our
   own house.

For the warmth of our beds on a cold night.
Do we ever give God thanks that we live in a free country?
That we have never known what it is like to flee in terror from
   our homes.
Do we ever give God thanks that He lives in us,
That God sent His Son to die for us,
That Christ is with us today,
That His Spirit dwells in us and gives us strength to live,
That God has forgiven us?
Do we thank God for the love of Jesus?
For Christmas,
For Easter.
For the summer holidays,
For the weekend break.
Outings to the seaside,
Runs in the country,
For flowers and trees,
For friends,
For neighbours.
Do we ever give God thanks for our family,
For children?
For a bed when we are tired,
For a meal when we are hungry,
For water when we are thirsty,
For a fire when we are cold.
Do we ever give God thanks?

A litany of thanksgiving

Give thanks to God, for He is good. His love is everlasting!
For the gift of Christ the Lord:
Thanks be to God.
For the truth of the gospel that routs the cynicism and pessimism
that assail us:
Thanks be to God.
For the power through grace to discern the goodness of the world
   and rejoice in it:
Thanks be to God.

For joy in beauty, in splendid sights, in glorious sounds:
Thanks be to God.
For joy in truth and love and all things of abiding quality:
Thanks be to God.
For the call of God to replenish the earth, and the challenge to
   share constructively in His creative work:
Thanks be to God.
For the mystery of the sacraments and the privilege of prayer:
Thanks be to God.
For the right to become the sons of God through Christ our
   brother:
Thanks be to God.
For the heritage of faith enhanced by the passing of time and by
   every new experience of the Holy Spirit:
Thanks be to God.
For the call to share with Christ in His continuing ministry of love,
   and the challenge to work with Him in redeeming the times:
Thanks be to God.
For the friendship of Christ and the companionship of all
   His saints:
Thanks be to God.
For the blessings of every day and the hope of glory:
Thanks be to God.
Give thanks to God, for He is good: His love is everlasting!

A litany of supplication

If the Son sets you free, you will indeed be free.
Enable us, O God, gratefully to believe what the Scriptures openly
   declare.
The Jerusalem above, which is the mother of us all, is free.
Teach us, O God, to love that Jerusalem as the greatest of
   our joys.
From the evils of this world and the subtleties of sin:
Lord, set us free.
From what is artificial, shoddy, and insincere:
Lord, set us free.
From what is lazy, cowardly, and slack:

Lord, set us free.
From what is compromised and second-rate:
Lord, set us free.
From what is dishonourable and mean:
Lord, set us free.
From hatred and prejudice:
Lord, set us free.
From arrogance and pride:
Lord, set us free.
From self-indulgence and self-pity:
Lord, set us free.
From casualness about the things of God:
Lord, set us free.
From all our secret sins:
Lord, set us free.
Bind us to your service, O God, and we shall be free.
Give us by grace the rewards of your kingdom and keep us in life
    eternal;
through Jesus Christ our Lord. Amen.

Prayer of thanksgiving

By your creative word, O Eternal Wisdom,
you established us and all things living in your saving Presence.

You sent Moses to free your people from slavery in Egypt,
and he drew courage from your promise: 'I will be with you.'

To Mary your promise was: 'Hail, favoured one, the Lord is
    with you.'
And by the overshadowing of the Holy Spirit the World became
    flesh and dwelt among us.

Therefore with the whole creation, existing for your glory,
with the minds you have filled with your purpose;
with the bodies you have given us as women and men
and the hearts you have inflamed with love;
with Eve, the mother of us all,
with Sarah, Deborah and Miriam and all who lived by faith in
    the promise of freedom;

with Mary who bore your son and Anna who recognised him,
with Mary Magdalen who found his grave empty,
with prophets, apostles and saints of every generation,
we proclaim your great and glorious name,
forever praising you and saying:

**Holy, holy, holy, God of power and might;
heaven and earth are full of your glory;
Hosanna in the highest**.

Consultation of Methodist women ministers, Oxford, 1984

In His presence

Knowing God is here –
We are freer in our interaction,
more daring in the sharing of our personal visions,
loving in our confrontations,
deeply silent in consideration and
accepting in the choices that help us
to define our actions.

In God's presence,
We meet to order ourselves anew,
to consider where we stand
and who we are.

from a service at Kerrisdale Presbyterian Church

Go down

Go down
into the plans of God.
Go down
deep as you may.
Fear not
for your fragility
under that weight of water.
Fear not
for life or limb

sharks attack savagely.
Fear not the power
of treacherous currents under the sea.
Simply, do not be afraid.
Let go. You will be led
like a child whose mother
holds him to her bosom
and against all comers is his shelter.

Helder Camara

His ways

And those whom we, through ignorance or forgetfulness or the number of names, have not remembered, do Thou O God remember them, who knowest the age and the name of each one, who knowest each from the mother's womb. For Thou, O God, art the help of the helpless, the hope of the hopeless, the saviour of the tempest-tossed, the harbour of mariners, the physicians of the sick. Be Thou Thyself all things to all men and women, who knowest each and their petition and their dwelling and their need.

Liturgy of Basil the Great

Letting go

You are searching for God. Are you aware that what matters most is the welcome you extend to Christ, the Risen Lord? By His presence, always offered to each person, by His forgiveness, he brings you to life. By placing your confidence in Him and by forgiving you will break out of your inner prisons to dare to commit yourself as a pilgrim of reconciliation, even in the diversions of the Christian family and even in those which tear apart the human family.

Brother Roger of Taizé

End and begin with Him

And now unto Him who is able to keep us from falling and lift us from the dark valley of despair to the bright mountain of hope, from the midnight of desperation to the daybreak of joy; to Him be power and authority for ever and ever.

Martin Luther King, his last words as he left his church at Montgomery, Alabama, before accepting his wider role in the movement to combat racism.

May He

May the Lord bless us and keep us; may Christ smile upon us and give us His grace; may He unveil His face to us and bring us His peace. Amen.

Fathomless

Deep peace of the running wave to you;
Deep peace of the flowing air to you;
Deep peace of the quiet earth to you;
Deep peace of the shining stars to you;
Deep, deep peace of Christ to you;
Deep, deep peace of Christ to you.

> *Based on a traditional Gaelic Blessing.*
> *The music for these words can be found in*
Celebrating Together *(Corrymeela Community).*

The Lord

We thank you
for this unforgettable person
who has fulfilled everything
that is human –
our life and death.
We thank you.

Your name will be made holy,
Lord our God.

Huub Oosterhuis

Strength in risk

Holy Spirit, why are we so afraid of silence? Why do we fill our lives with talk, and people, and work, and action, until we feel guilty if we sit still and do nothing? Because we do not want to hear God who often speaks through dullness, emptiness, stillness, loneliness? Make us brave enough to try.

Monica Furlong

The confident Word

Thank you, God, that you have given us the Bible for the enlightenment of our minds, the quickening of our imaginations, and the renewal of our lives. Help us by your Spirit as we read it and explore it not to impose on it the opinions we have already formed, nor yet to be afraid of any new truth which shocks us and shakes us, but to be open at all times to your word as it is shown to us. Through Jesus Christ, our Lord. Amen.

Prayer: The Bible Guide

Prayer for preservation and protection – Numbers 10. 35–36
Prayer for a sick child – II Samuel 12
Prayer for understanding of affliction – Samuel 21. 1–12
Prayer in national danger – II Chronicles 14. 11
Prayer as intercession – Job 42:7–10
Prayer for preservation here and hereafter – Psalm 16
Prayer for confession and a broken heart – Psalm 51
Prayer for peace – Isaiah 26
Prayer for the oppressed – Lamentations 5
Prayer as taught by Christ – Matthew 6.1–13
Prayer habits of Christ – Mark 1. 35
The intercessory prayer of Jesus – John 17

Tony Jasper

Up-dating the Psalms

(*For two voices*).

1: (*Reading*) 'The Lord is my shepherd, I shall not want . . .'

2: Just a minute. Isn't it about time we brought that old-fashioned language into the twentieth century?

1: You mean like 'The Lord is my Star-Wars defence system – I shall never be blown up by nasty Russian rockets'?

2: No, that's far too political.

1: Then how about 'The Lord is my British Rail high-speed train – I shall always arrive on time'? (*Pause*) No, perhaps we ought to stay closer to reality. All right, if you're so full of bright ideas, how would you start it off?

2: Well, you have to open it out a bit – use more technical phrases. How about this? 'The reading this evening is from David Lyric Two Three. The Lord and I are in a shepherd/sheep situation and I am in a position of negative need . . .'

1: Negative need?

2: I suppose you could say 'Positive sufficiency' . . .

1: But noone's going to understand that.

2. You don't have to understand it. You just listen to it. That's what happens in churches most of the time.

1: All right. Then what about 'He makes me lie down in green pastures'?

2: 'He prostrates me in a green belt grazing area.'

1: 'Your rod and staff'?

2: 'Pastoral walking aid and quadruped pick-up unit.'

1: 'My cup runneth over'?

2: 'My beverage utensil experiences a volume crisis.'

1: Ah, I've got you with this one! 'I will dwell in the house of the Lord for ever.'

2: 'I will possess tenant rights in the housing unit of the Lord on a permanently open-ended time basis.'

(*Silence*)

1: Well, I'll tell you one thing – you'd feel totally inadequate saying 'Amen' after that!

2: Ah, I'm glad you mentioned that. When it comes to 'Amen'
   there are several interesting possibilities . . .
(*They leave*)

Peter English

His presence

O Lord hear my prayer
O Lord hear my prayer
When I call answer me
O Lord hear my prayer
O Lord hear my prayer
Come and listen to me

Psalm 102

*Say as a group or congregation, or go along each row or circle with each
individual saying 'O Lord hear my prayer' and all saying 'When we call
answer us'.*

*More words to lead into and
close worship:*

Words about Jesus

Bible Passages:

Ephesians 5:19
John 1:1–18
Acts 2:36
Romans 1:4
1 John 1
2 Thessalonians 3:16

Praise, adoration and thanksgiving words in the first section have spoken of God, Jesus and Holy Spirit, for here the fullness of Christian faith is realized. Material to lead into and close worship assumed that all worship is prefaced and ends in the spirit of the oldest form of the doxology, 'Glory be to the Father, through the Son, in Holy Spirit'.

This section gives words that are descriptive of Jesus. Some are devotional, others speak of His Person, life, teaching and presence. As with the past two sections there is a mix of traditional and formal together with new language and unexpected approaches. There is more in the sections that follow – on Birth and Christmas, on Cross and Resurrection.

The witness is straightforward – Jesus lives. We speak of the past, of one moment in time when God came, but not as precious memory, rather as now. This testimony is explored in other sections, for instance under Faith and Conversion. Here we have powerful affirmations of why Jesus strides our culture and our world with increasing relevance.

Never say die

Christ lives! Let's celebrate
and wait for this great gift;
Holy Spirit divine,
come to our heart.

Tony Jasper

Be assured

In Christ, dear friends, all our need is fulfilled.
Would you be healed? Christ is the healer.
Are you weighed down by your sins? It is He who clears you.
Are you in need of help? It is He who comes to your aid.
Has night overtaken you? Christ is the light.
Are you lost? He is the way.
Would you be delivered from lies? Christ is the truth.
Are you afraid of death? Christ is life.
Happy is the person who puts his trust in Him.

> *From 'Cinque Projets de Liturgie' of the Reformed Church
> of France, with the word 'person' replacing 'man'.
> The first statement is said by the leader. Let one side of the assembly
> ask the question, and the other answer. All say the last line.*

He is beside us

Our relationship with Christ is one of friendship. And just as
all friendship knows periods of indifference, in our life there
are times of indifference to Christ. And then we wonder: have
we left him?

No friendship can grow without new beginnings, reconciliation.
When we are reconciled with Christ, we discover Him as if for the
first time: the love of all loves, maltreated, wounded, rejected by
many, and yet never tired of accompanying us.

Brother Roger of Taizé

True peace

Christ our hope:
We give you the glory
For the great grace
By which upon the Cross
You stretched out your hands in love
To us all.
By that same grace
Come, risen Saviour,
Into every gesture of unity and fellowship
We make toward one another.
May the peace we share
Be your peace.
Amen.

Jamie Wallace

Such consistency

The whole life of Christ was a continual passion; others die mar-
tyrs, but Christ was born a martyr . , , His birth and death were
but one continual act, and His Christmas Day and His Good Friday are but the evening and the morning of one and the same day.

John Donne, 1626

True recognition

Saviour Christ, we greeted you as a baby in a manger,
We knew you as the one who welcomed sinners into God's
    Kingdom,
We wept with you, a dying man on a criminal's cross.
Now we hail you King of Kings, Lord of Lords.
The lowly has indeed been lifted up.
Praise be to you, our Lord Jesus Christ,
whose greatness is to be humble,
whose freedom is to be obedient,

and whose power is the power of love.
To you be all honour and praise, all glory and might,
From this day forwards, and through all eternity. Amen.

The unrecognised

You who loved all
You who died for all
You whose rose for all

Give men and women their true freedom
If only they knew

Tony Japser

His offer

We believe in life
life that Jesus brings
life that has no bounds
strong as eagle's wings.

Tony Jasper

Prayer of St Anselm

And Thou, Jesus, sweet Lord,
Art Thou not also a mother?
Truly. Thou art a mother,
The mother of all mothers,
Who tasted death,
In Thy desire to give life to Thy children.

Eleventh century

Creed of the radical Christ

Leader: Let us declare our trust in Christ
All: I trust myself to Jesus Christ

Group One: *Group Two:*
Son of a carpenter   Calling God Father

One with His people	Creating a new family
Draining the old wine	Fermenting the new
Open to everyone	Narrowing the gate
Delivering the captives	Binding the free
Bringer of peace	Stirring up strife
Creator of unity	Dividing asunder
Hope for the hopeless	Destroying our hopes
Crucified for all	Compelling cross-bearers
Emptying the tomb	Going ahead of us

All: I trust myself through this Jesus
To the Kingdom He points to
To the Father behind It
In the Spirit who sustains it
With disciples everywhere
Who live for it

John Vincent 1982

Hymn to love

1: I may be able to chatter in a dozen languages, but if I have no love what I say is no more important than a pop song that hasn't made the charts.

2: I may be a TV star – like Terry Wogan – so that everyone switches on to watch me

3: Or know more amazing things than Patrick Moore and David Bellamy put together

4: I may have such faith that I can do things like Superman –

2: Or Wonderwoman –

2, 3, 4: (*together*) But if I have no love – I am nothing.

1: I may support Christian Aid, Oxfam, Save the Children – even finish up being a volunteer worker – but if I have no love it adds nothing to my worth as a person.

5: Hang on. Hang on – why is this love so important? What's it like?

1: It's like Jesus.

2: Jesus had time for the sort of people everyone else avoids.

3: He was never toffee-nosed or pompous.
4: He didn't stereotype people.
1: He let them be themselves.
2: Jesus was never prickly.
3: He didn't bear grudges.
4: He didn't enjoy seeing people spoil their lives.
1: He knew too much about real joy.
2: He was tough. He went on believing in the power of love right to the end.
3: He believed that love is what life is about –
4: What we are born for.
1: All the knowledge, science and technology are useful but are only little bits of the truth.
2: Our love for one another is a reflection of God's much greater love.
3: We just know bits about God – like a jigsaw not properly joined up.
4: One day we shall see the whole picture, and understand the truth of love.
1: In the meantime we have three things to go on – faith, hope and love.
5: But love is what it's all about.

Rosemary Wakelin

A little word of encouragement

He had it coming to him, didn't he?
Know what I mean?
Mr Mental, Mad Lad, up there, saving the world.
Compassion, friendship, justice, love, peace –
no chance . . . especially nowadays.
It's a good time for me – nowadays.

I watched the whole thing
from start to finish.
My only complaint was, it didn't last long enough.
He went too quick . . . couldn't take it.
There were people crying and wailing . . . usual stuff,

usual humanitarian response.

He got talking to this fellow next to him . . . as you do
when you're being crucified . . . know what I mean?
Yak, yak, cross-talk . . . cross-
examine . . . cross-your-heart-bra . . .
See, got you laughing, didn't I?
Got you mocking.
Eh, Peter, I can see your house from here.
It was a good joke, that one, wasn't it? One of my best.
Got you laughing.
Got you mocking.

He was talking to this fellow about forgiveness.
No chance . . .
that's like getting through to Directory Enquiries first
time . . .
can't be done.
No one can be forgiven.
Believe me, I know what I'm talking about.
I'll always tell the truth.

Stewart Henderson

More words about Jesus:

Words about birth and Christmas

Bible passages:

Psalm 137:1–6
Luke 1:26–35
Luke 2:19
Romans 8:22–25
2 Corinthians 6:2
1 Timothy 2:3–4
Luke 1:68–71
Basic narratives in Matthew 1:18–2:23; Luke 2

'Make ready for Christ,' writes Thomas Merton, 'whose smile, like lightning, sets free the song of everlasting glory that now sleeps, in your paper flesh, like dynamite.'

In this section there are cries of birth, at times painful, songs of new life underpinned by the promise of Presence. New life supposes possibilities. Bonhoeffer in his book *Ethics* wrote 'In Christ we are offered the possibility of partaking in the reality of God and in the reality of the world but not in the one without the other.'

Christian worship must continually celebrate birth, the embryonic, lest it forget that the marvellous things of God constantly appear in new clothing. A community denied the cries, smells and breathing of children being born will soon die.

Christmas, following upon Advent, stretches beyond itself, for it is intrinsically linked with Easter. If the Child to be born is *It*, the sign, the pledge, the promise of God to take flesh and 'live among' us, it is also true that new life can be lost as quickly as it comes, with pain and suffering.

Always possibilities
The Lord has seen me

The Lord has seen me and to my surprise
he gave my heart new life, my eyes new sight.
I was reborn and came to life again
and in the dark he kindled a new light.
For he accepts my weakness as it is
and overcomes me with his silent might.
The Lord our God knows every one of us
and he has written our names in his hand.
He wants to live in us as in his house,
to plant his life in us as in his land,
to play with us and take us as his bride
and what we are he has already planned.
You visit us, your loved ones, on our dreams
and while we're sleeping sow your name like seed.
Just like the rain that falls upon the earth
or like the wind you come in word and deed.
You seek us out and make us live again
and open to receive all that we need.

Huub Oosterhuis

For the darkness of waiting

For the darkness of waiting
of not knowing what is to come
of staying ready and quiet and attentive,
we praise you O God.

For the darkness and the light
are both alike to you

For the darkness of staying silent
for the terror of having nothing to say
and for the greater terror
of needing to say nothing,

we praise you O God.

For the darkness and the light
are both alike to you.

For the darkness of loving
in which it is safe to surrender
to let go of our self-protection
and to stop holding back our desire,
we praise you O God.

For the darkness and the light
are both alike to you.

For the darkness of choosing
when you give us the moment
to speak, and act, and change,
and we cannot know what we have set in motion,
but we still have to take the risk,
we praise you O God.

For the darkness and the light
are both alike to you.

For the darkness of hoping
in a world which longs for you,
for the wrestling and the labouring of all creation
for wholeness and justice and freedom,
we praise you O God.

For the darkness and the light
are both alike to you.

Janet Morley

The Scrap

He stood there in the shop. Clearance Sale. The rustle of wrapping
paper and dollars at the head of the line. His turn.

'Two inches of God, please', he said.

'Can we make that four, sir? I have a scrap of goods here, just four by four. Then I won't have to cut any.'

'Right. Just wrap it up, please.'

He paid the usual price.

Outside again, he stepped cautiously over the slippery ripples of frozen snow, mumbling to himself, 'What shall I do with this scrap? It's too small to sleep on, too soft to build a house on, too expensive to make clothes out of. But just for fun, I could easily send it to somebody to use as a Band-Aid. Or send it imprinted with a kiss, or with something written on it about someone I love, maybe.'

Still mumbling, he took care not to slip on the ice. And he walked, year after year, took to the sky now and then, while his eyes asked the light, his feet asked the ground, and his hands asked each other, 'What shall I do with this scrap?'

Huub Oosterhuis

The shepherds' journey

For us it was but a short journey
down our familiar hill,
past landmarks we had always known.
We should not have been
surprised by the angels –
we had always sensed their presence;
known, especially at lambing,
and when the snows melt up in the hills
and new blades of green thrust upward.
God is born in every living thing –
this special babe was something we understood.
That God should choose this way
lit up the dark with glory –
the silence of the stars bursting into song.
What was it, peace to those of goodwill?
Yes, for us it was a simple journey;
only the wise have far to travel.

Cecily Taylor

Be filled

Divide the gathering into three with each section saying a verse at a time. Do this in the chosen prayer position. Then repeat but this time will everyone standing. The last verse is to be repeated by the whole assembly.

All things growing skyward, heavenwards
Wheat is celebrating life
Wine poured out in death remembered
So much pain and sacrifice
Bitter-sweet and touched by terror
God and man are reconciled
Drink and fill your thirsty hearts
Eat and fill your emptiness

Breathe upon our world completeness
You have charged us with its life
Pierce the dark with lasar brightness
Touch the secrets of the heart
Pain and joy are bound together
Touch His hands and touch His side
Laugh with Him, the chains are broken
Love will never be denied

Breath by breath, your life was given
The cry was heard throughout all time
Thunder raged, all earth was shaken
Death the final sacrifice
Rescue for a fallen universe
Love and life, unending days
Miracle of empty graveside
For the least of us He died

All say: Gloria in excelsis Deo, Gloria in excelsis *(twice)*.

Charity Quin

Annunciation

She sat on the ground in the middle of a small clearing, and spread a handful of pebbles out in front of her. The stones were smooth from years of rolling water. The stream which had shaped them was not far from where she sat, not far from where she lived. It was a source for her. Water for drinking, for washing, but also water for watching, water which came from a place she had never seen but understood. Water which came from higher places, but could also well up from deep in the earth. It took part of her away as it rolled past her, but it brought to her much more.

The pebbles in front of her were also smooth from handling. They were never far from her. Her hands found them easily in a pocket or tied in the hem of her skirt. Smooth, not from worrying although there was plenty of opportunity for that, but from remembering. The touch of the stones reminded her of the past – of choices and decisions. But she remembered too a future which she saw in her mind and felt in her body. It was strange but not unusual for her to see and feel beyond the place and time of the present moment. She found it exciting, the excitement at the edge of fear. She felt alive.

The pebbles laid out before her shifted with her touch. She arranged them in a row as straight as you can create with objects which are alike but so different. She made a small circle with just a few and then took four more and placed them at four corner points around the circle to form a box. She pushed them in a pile in front of her. They tumbled over each other as she forced them together, and then with a single quick movement, the pile was dispersed. They could be scattered as easily as they were gathered.

But then she took the stones one by one and placed them in a wide gentle arc next to her body, each one just as far away as she could reach with her left hand. It looked like she had charted the position of the moon as it crossed the night sky, its arc matching the inner curve of that mysterious light.

But she could reach each stone as she would never touch the moon, and saw in their path the shape of her life. Could she follow the grace-filled curve the stones described or must the pebbles be pushed into a different shape?

She remembered the future she saw in her mind and felt in her body. It was life she felt in her body – life that couldn't be there but clearly was. A life that beat with her own heartbeat. To accept that life – no, to welcome it – what would that mean to this smooth arc of stones? She pushed a small stone out of place and felt a sudden breath rush through her body, like a wind that catches you unaware in the middle of a clearing. There was power there and pain. She felt excitement, but now, clearly, the excitement was tinged with fear. To take this path – to follow this arc in the stones that surrounded her body . . .

She placed her hand gently on her belly. There was life there. It couldn't be, but clearly was. To choose that life was to choose difficulty and pain, but could she expect otherwise from any life she chose? Beyond that difficulty and pain was a joy as boundless as it was a mystery. Not the happiness of a family gathering or a kind word, but a resonance a vibration that changed the beat of her heart and the rhythm of her breath until it matched the pulse of the earth and the melody of the wind in the trees above her. Could there be any greater clarity in this song that rang through her body and the earth? This question spelled out in the stones in front of her – to welcome, embrace, the joy, the pain, the melody, the pulse:

Yes. The answer could only be. Yes.

Phil Porter

The not yet born

Volcano – Volcano.
Bubbling rich red.
Steaming.
Spirit – creation
Bursting. Bursting
For release and life.

And I must
Carry you
Hot and aching

Within me
Until your time
Is come.

Mysterious,
Lonely gestation,
Formed in darkness.
Fed and nurtured
By a life and spirit
Breathing gently, powerfully
In my soul.
Hush. Silence.
The time is
Not yet.
Now is only
Slow murmurings and
Gentle stirrings.
Oh! Not yet born!
But how you live!

I love you, Volcano.
I love Your
Sweeping pain and
Thrusting, tentative movement.

I love you, Volcano,
As you sleep and wait
Within me

For your life.
And for your death.

Edwina Gateley

Cloud-baby

Cloud-baby
rocked in the cradle
of two strong mountain arms –
matronly

veined with snow
so white!
Rockaby
rockaby baby . . .
Sing slow
swing low:
Goodnight.

Look, baby:
a mirror in the elbow
of the rocks, a lake –
reflecting you.
Your head
Grows like a mushroom, fast
and bright!
Oh, look away,
look away, baby.
You blow
embittered kisses. Sing a last
goodnight. Goodnight . . .

Kate Compston

Gift of God

John, the gift of God
when we looked for none.

Last,
by no means least.

Life's little celebrant
on rusty bike with buckled wheel
enjoying every moment to the full
as you wear your mother out.

Gift of God
with freckles and big teeth
you broke the bank.
Now we are skint.

But in laughter,
we have riches
Beth Webb

Christmas angel

Gabriel, my Christmas angel,
at 5 am
announcing a great nativity:
'The mouse has had quads –
no quins, come *on*, Mum!
Come and see!'

No one can blame you, little one,
for your enthusiasm at crack of dawn.
Eager to tell the good news.
It cannot wait,
it *must* not wait.

And had your namesake felt unwell
that Christmas morn,
You would have spoken up all right:
'A Baby's born this chilly night,
Oh, come and *see!*'

May you never lose that sense
of urgent joy belonging to your name
and may your listeners always love
your news
better than their beds.
Beth Webb

Epithalamial sonnet

Come tender-free, soft-naked to our bed, my gentle dove;
no clothen garb gap-making 'twixt myself and thee.
Then together shall our entwined limbs our constancy
and, in full healing clasp, our oneness prove.

Leave the lamp burning, so that we – mouths enwoven
each from other nothing hiding, flesh as we be,
yet faith-keeping, true-trust-telling – open-ey'd shall see
each other down-stripped, yet Christ-transfigured by our love.

Taking-taken and tender; eager caressing-playful feet;
boldly and softly, our heart-mind-soul barriers drop. Heart
warms,
so each-other-enfolded, thus are we opened to enfold,
sinking closer together in fullness, fallen-heavy in each other's
arms.
Solemn and ridiculous, we, new Adam's son and daughter,
are made one by sensuality – and Heaven's laughter!

*'For I saw very surely that our substance is in God, and I
also saw that God is in our sensuality . . .' (Mother Julian of
Norwich)*

R. Akerman

No.El

The word was made flesh
and marked as a statistic
in the imperial register:
– one more birth,
one more indigent,
displaced and homeless,
soon another refugee.

A figure that did not add up,
like an odd half penny
carried on, persistent,
a marginal intruder,
later becoming one more
unemployed, a native
vagrant and religious
dissident, altogether
one more suspect,

source of agitation,
trouble-maker.

An awkward number that recurred,
annoyingly defiant,
breaking the order of the columns,
till there was only one resort
which was to cross the number out
and cancel its existence.

The which was promptly done,
correctly justified, except
the number would not go;
it reappeared and multiplied,
defying ruler and eraser,
threatening the bases of security.

Such numerology now
smacks of an unprogrammed age,
long shut within the safety
of old ledgers. But as
the needle jumps awry,
and the unscheduled blip
cavorts across the screen
to crumble theory in
a hundred questions, we
may guess God's awkward number
dances still, upon
the data bank and through
the circuits of computers,
to defy our certainties,
and unbalance the account;
a shift of the horizon
that will nag at tidy minds
the way a crying child
may nag a restless night.

Eventually,
for the sake of clear accounting,
a whole new mathematics was

devised around this figure
to contain it. Even then
it would get out of hand
from time to time,
upsetting calculations.

Tony Lucas

God with us

Christmas time.
Sunday newspaper. Glossy magazine.
On the cover is
the face of a suffering child.
The title:
'This child is eight.
He carries three tons of bricks a day.'
Inside is a colourful brochure.
Dozens of expensive toys
and Christmas gifts.

Bricks and toys.
What is wrong with the world?
How is it that some children
are laden with toys
while others have to carry bricks?
Perhaps these are symbols
of our unjust world.

But this is Christmas time.
A time of joy: God is with us.
What are we going to communicate
to the suffering children of our world?
Words of compassion are not enough.
We need to offer acts of solidarity.
We need to commit ourselves,
as communicators,
to denounce injustice and oppression
and to take our stand

with 'the least important ones'.
We need to commit ourselves
to the One who begins His life
by receiving gifts in Bethlehem
but who finally chooses
to carry bricks to Golgotha.

In the suffering face of any child
Christ is present with us
calling us
challenging us
to work boldly for genuine
community.

Carlos A. Valle, WACC general secretary

The Wise Men and the Shepherds

Lord, when the Wise Men came from far
Led to Thy cradle by a star,
Then did the Shepherds too rejoice,
Instructed by Thy angel's voice;
Blest were the Wise Men in their skill
And Shepherds in their harmless will.

Wise Men in tracing nature's laws
Ascend into the highest Cause;
Shepherds in humble fearfulness
Walk safely, though their light be less;
Though Wise Men better know the way,
It seems no honest heart can stray.

There is no merit in the wise
But Love (the Shepherds' sacrifice);
Wise Men, all ways of knowledge past,
To the Shepherd's wonder came at last
To know only wonder breed,
And not to know is wonder's seed.

Sydney Godolphin, 1610–43

New Testament Lesson: Luke 2

Person 1: In those says a decree went out from Caesar Augustus that all the world should be enrolled.

Persons 1 and 2: This was the first enrolment, when Quirinius was governor of Syria.

Person 1, 2, 3: And all went to be enrolled, each to his own city.

Woman's voice: And Joseph also went up from Galilee, from the city of Nazareth, to Judea, to the city of David, which is called Bethlehem, because he was of the house and lineage of David, to be enrolled with Mary, his betrothed, who was with child.

Man's voice: And while they were there, the time came for her to be delivered.

Woman's voice: And she gave birth to her first-born son and laid him in a manger, because there was no place for them in the inn.

Man's voice: And in that region there were shepherds out in the field, keeping watch over their flock by night.

Man's Voice: And an angel of the Lord appeared to them, and the glory of the Lord shone around them, and they were filled with fear. And the angel said to them:

Boy's voice: Be not afraid, for behold, I bring you good news of a great joy which will come to all the people; for to you is born this day in the city of David a Saviour, who is Christ the Lord. And this will be a sign for you: you will find a babe wrapped in swaddling cloths and lying in a manger.

Man's voice: And suddenly there was with the angel a multitude of the heavenly host praising God and saying:

Everybody: Glory to God in the highest, and on earth peace among men with whom he is pleased!

Woman's voice: When the angels went away from them into heaven, the shepherds said to one another:

Three men: Let us go over to Bethlehem and see this thing that has happened, which the Lord has made known to us.

Woman's voice: and they went with haste, and found Mary and Joseph, and the babe lying in a manger.

Man's voice: And when they saw it they made known the saying which had been told them concerning this child, and all who heard it wondered at what the shepherds told them.

Man and woman's voices: And all who heard it wondered at what the shepherds told them.

Man's voice: But Mary kept all these things, pondering them in her heart.

Everybody: And the shepherds returned, glorifying and praising God for all that they had heard and seen, as it had been told them.

Adapted by Clare Davidson

In the stable

Mary and Joseph walked into the untidy deserted stable, brushing thin sticky cobwebs off their hair. Straw lay dead and asleep on the ice cold limestone floor. Rats and shrews pranced around in the straw, squeaking loudly. Something furry caught Mary's eye. It was a sheep, white fluffy wool covering a smooth skin. There were other animals lying looking sad and forlorn. Owls hooted, bats hovered.

Evening passed and the pitch black night-time came. Mary and Joseph made the best sort of bed they could out of spickly prickly straw.

In the middle of the night Joseph was awoken. Mary was in very bad pain. Sweat trickled down Mary's face. She was screaming. Joseph went outside to fetch water for Mary He had found a rusty old tin, good enough to hold water. Joseph went out into the ice cold air. Mary gave one great shout, screaming for help. Joseph dropped the rusty old tin. It shattered. He was too late. The baby Jesus had been born.

Tears of happiness filled both their eyes. Joy filled the little stable and an old barkwood manger was Jesus's bed.

Jane Thompson

God with us

There was no room in the inn
For a pregnant woman and her partner.
There was a stable at the back,
They could stay there if they wanted.
Anything was better than sleeping out on the street
To be the objects of abuse
To be trodden upon by drunks
And spat upon by the ignorant revellers.
The straw in the stable was clean,
The innkeeper had checked it,
It smelt good,
Offering softness and comfort
After the long, long journey.
Mary and Joseph lay down to rest,
Satisfied they had reached their destination,
Content in their loving commitment to each other,
Proud in their forthcoming parenthood.
Then the dull ache in Mary's back increased.
At regular intervals she tensed up with excruciating pain.
Joseph held her close, mopped her forehead.
Should he get help?
He didn't know the local midwives.
Should he stay with Mary himself?
His religion taught him
That birthing was for women only,
Men should not allow themselves to be defiled by contact,
But they were alone.
The innkeeper had given them some water.
It was cold but clean.
Mary needed Joseph there,
She would not let him go.
His words and caresses eased her anxiety.
He encouraged and urged,
He waited and responded again,
At the final moment he gently helped

The blood covered baby
Into the world,
Holding the baby boy with care.
Within minutes mother and child were asleep.
Joseph cleared the birthing straw aside
And spread fresh around.
He was amazed at the whole experience.
Elated he too lay down and slept
Knowing throughout the whole of his being
That God is with us – Immanuel.

Janice M. Clark

Advertiser's Christmas

(*For two performers. Bounce and Dazzle are go-ahead advertising people.*)

B: If you can spare a few moments, we would like to have a word.

D: We're in advertising – Bounce and Dazzle, at your service.

B: And we feel this Christmas business was badly handled, right from the start.

D: Someone should have called in the professionals. It's always a mistake, leaving it to amateurs. (*Looks up.*) No offence, of course.

B: For instance, look at the place they chose for the launch! Bethlehem! I ask you, who had ever heard of Bethlehem? If they were looking for maximum impact – and, after all, you don't start a new religion every day of the week – what was wrong with Temple Square in Jerusalem? Preferably on market day.

D: Or even Herod's Palace. I'm sure he'd have been all in favour if someone had made it worth his while with a couple of bags of shekels.

B: Then, to make it worse, who in their right minds would decide to use a stable? I mean, I'm all in favour of the simple rural touch with a couple of straw-chewing rustics and a half a dozen cows if you're trying to sell dairy butter, but it's definitely not right for the Saviour of the World. Well, is he important or isn't he?

D: Then there's the timing – would you believe it, the middle of the night? About the only thing you'd try to get off the ground in pitch darkness is a luminous frisbee! Surely Mary could have been persuaded to hold on till daylight when there would be a few more people about? Even a Pharisee or two to give a bit of local colour . . .

B: . . . And a few impressionable women organised to cry their eyes out and then spread the news round the local wells.

D: The build-up was appalling, too. Arriving on a donkey, for goodness sake – not the most reliable means of transport – and not a sign of a reception committee.

B: Yes, they could at least have laid on a cheering crowd and a few palm branches in the road.

D: And then, on top of all that, what do we find? Nobody had bothered to book any accommodation!

B: Census week, too! I hope somebody lost his job over that.

D: Of course, with all this incompetence it's not surprising that things got even more out of hand.

B: Mind you, I've nothing against the angel idea. Makes a change from the 'Red Arrows', anyway.

D: Yes, make a good show, attract attention, set people talking.

B: But look what happened – they lost their way and finished up on top of a hill, frightening sheep!

D: Probably homed in on the wrong star.

B: Mind you, I like that 'Glory to God' jingle – very catchy.

D: All the same, there was a good idea wasted on a handful of illiterate shepherds.

B: Even those Wise Men didn't seem to know where they were heading for. Finished up having to ask directions in Jerusalem!

D: Then those gifts! Gold and incense are all right, I suppose, but myrrh was a bit tactless, to say the least.

B: Yes, the whole thing had real possibilities, if only it had been properly handled. An opportunity missed.

D: Well, thank goodness the whole thing is now in the hands of experts like us.

B: By the way, I've had a tremendous idea for next year. An ashtray shaped like a stable – when you stub out your cigarette a baby's head pops up and says 'Merry Christmas' . . .

(*They leave*)

Peter English

The baby had a birthday

The baby had a birthday –
we made the brandy sauce,
we drank his health
and spent out wealth
upon ourselves, of course.

We had a lovely party
and brightened up the place:
profusely strung
the tinsel hung –
you couldn't see his face.

Then when the feast was over
and we'd run out of cheer,
we packed him in
the trimmings tin
till Christmas time next year.

Cecily Taylor

The Three Spectral Kings

He stumbled through the gloomy suburbs of the town. Shells of houses loomed up against the sky. The moon had not risen. The silence was startled by footsteps so late at night. He found an old board. He kicked it until a rotten piece broke off. The wood smelt sweet and mellow. He stumbled back and there were no stars shining.

When he opened the door his wife's tired, pale blue eyes turned towards him. It was so cold that her white breath hung suspended in the air. He bent his knee and broke the piece of wood. Everything smelt sweet and mellow. He held a splinter of it under his nose. Smells almost like cake, he laughed softly. Don't, said the woman's eyes, don't laugh. He is sleeping.

The man pushed some of the sweet, mellow wood into the small oven. It flared up and cast a handful of warm light around the room. It lighted up a tiny, round face and lasted for a moment. The face was only an hour old, but it already had everything which belonged to it: ears, nose, mouth and eyes. The (s were large, almost too large. The mouth was open. It breathed out softly. The ears and nose were red. He is living, thought the mother. And the little face is asleep.

There are some porridge oats left, said the man. Yes, answered the woman, good. It is cold. The man broke some more off the sweet, soft wood. Now she has her child and has to freeze, he thought. But there was no one whom he could hit in the face with his fist for it. As he opened the oven door, another handful of light was cast on the sleeping face. The woman said softly: look, can you see? Just like a halo. A halo, he thought, and there was no one whom he could hit in the face with his fist.

There was someone at the door. We saw the light from the window, they said. We would like to sit down for ten minutes. But we have a child here, the man said to them. They said nothing more but walked into the room, breathing out through their nostrils. Then the light fell upon them.

There were three. In three old uniforms. One had a cardboard box, another a bag. And the third had no hands. Frostbitten, he said, and held up the stumps. Then he turned out his coat pocket. Tobacco and some thin paper. They rolled cigarettes. But the woman said: Don't, the child.

So the four went out of the door and their cigarettes were four spots in the night. One had thick, bandaged feet. He took a piece of wood out of the bag. A donkey, he said, I have been carving it for seven months. For the child. What's wrong with your feet? asked the man. Water, said the donkey-carver, from hunger. And the other? asked the man, examining the donkey by feeling it in the darkness. The third was shivering in his uniform. Oh, nothing, he whispered, it's only nerves. He had only been frightened rather too much a short time before. They trod out their cigarettes and went back inside.

They looked at the little sleeping face. The one who shivered took two yellow sweets out of the cardboard box and said: These are for the lady.

The woman opened her pale-blue eyes when she saw the three spectral men bent over the child. She gazed at them in awe. But the child kicked her with its foot and cried out so loud that the men got up and crept to the door. They stopped, nodded and went out into the darkness.

The man gazed after them. Mysterious holy men, he said to his wife. Then he shut the door. They are wonderful holy men, he mumbled and saw to the oats. But there was no face for his fist.

But the child cried out, whispered the woman, it cried out quite loudly. They are gone. Look how alive it is, she said proudly. The face opened its mouth and cried out.

Is he crying? asked the man.

No, I think he is laughing, answered the woman. Almost like cake, said the man smelling the wood, like cake. Quite sweet.

Today is Christmas Day, said the woman.

Yes, Christmas, he mumbled. And a handful of light from the oven fell on the small, sleeping face.

By a pupil of Kingswood School, Bath

More words about birth and Christmas:

Words for Easter and Resurrection

Bible passages:

Isaiah 1:4, 18; 2:4–5
Mark 14:33–36
Romans 6:8–11
1 Corinthians 1:18, 22–24
1 Corinthians 6:14
Revelation 3:7–8
Basic narratives in Matthew 26–28, Mark 14–16, Luke
22–24, John 18–21

The Provost of Coventry Cathedral in the book *Ruined and Rebuilt*,
writing of the war-time destruction of the Cathedral and its
subsequent rebuilding, says this is an immortal truth: 'In all
human experience united with Jesus Christ, painful and sorrowful
crucifixion will issue in joyful and glorious resurrection.'

So, with this in mind, comes this section with its mix of despair
and hope, its words testifying to death and rebirth. As later
sections show (see Pain and Suffering, Waste, Liberation), life
triumphs over death.

This worship anthology specifies only two areas of the orthodox
Christian calendar, Advent-Christmas, and the Easter period with
a little of Palm Sunday, but mostly Good Friday to Easter Sunday.
But as other sections indirectly show, the year belongs to the
Lord – the Risen Lord.

The triumphal entry

Leader: Jesus, King of the universe
1: Ride on in humble majesty.
2: Ride on through conflict and debate.
3: Ride on through sweaty prayer and betrayal of friends.
4: Ride on through mockery and unjust condemnation.
5: Ride on through cruel suffering and ignoble death.
6: Ride on to the empty tomb and your rising in triumph.
7: Ride on to raise up your Church, a new body for your service.
8: Ride on, King Jesus, to renew the whole earth in your image.
All: In compassion come to help us, Amen.

Say each line by pew or small groups then speak it through again with the first pew/group becoming Leader, and so on.

The man in a tree

There was once a strange man in a tree. He stretched himself on limbs and looked at people below. Now, the man was deeply perturbed, because life in a tree is tough. He had been in that tree for a long time and only a few had offered him food or water. But from the tree, he could see both sides, whereas on the ground, Truth was divided into halves. Preferring sight to blindness, he stayed there.

But terrestrials do not like a man in a tree, for they are clearly seen by such a man and the arrangement affords no privacy. This is why two groups, formerly estranged by conviction, gathered on either side to convince the man that life in a tree is an unnecessary strain.

'Come down from the tree', cried a group on one side. 'If you are looking for gods, we have one; he lives in our church – we will show him to you.'

'Come down from the tree', cried the group on the other side. 'If you are looking for gods, there are none.'

'If you come down,' said the first group, 'you will be made a part of the biggest, most rapidly growing organisation in the land. You will have the privilege of working under our god, a most kind and merciful man. Serve him as we do and you will be greatly rewarded.'

'How do you serve him?' asked the man from the tree.

'We serve him by obedience', answered one. 'We serve him by praise', another said. 'We serve him by expansion', answered a third.

'Which of these is the greatest service?' asked the man from the tree.

'Our love!' they answered in unity.

'But no one has said love', the man responded.

'Obedience is love', said the first. 'Also praise', said the second. 'And growth, too', added the third.

'No', the man whispered. 'These are not love. . . . They are results of love. You are divided and call yourselves one', and he turned to the other group.

'Wait', cried the first group. 'You have questioned and we have answered. Now, we will question you: what is Truth?' The group waited attentively, but the man turned again to the other side.

'You have discretion,' said a voice from the second group. 'You have turned away from dogma, from creeds, from lies. Come down to us – it is we that search for Truth, not for gods or fantasy.'

'There is no God?' the man asked.

'There is no god,' they answered as one.

'You are searching for Truth?' the man asked. 'Why do you say that there is no God?'

'There is no evidence for such an essence,' answered one. 'Because, we see, as you do, the contradictions in thoughts of those on your other side,' another said.

'We cannot know that there are gods,' a third said. 'Contemplation of Spirit is a beautiful jewel, but it is a stone too small for our minds to stumble on.'

'Every one,' responded the man in the tree, 'who falls on that stone will be broken into pieces, but when it falls on any one, it will crush him.'

'And what is this stone, strange man in the tree?' The group waited patiently, but the man turned to the other side.

'You are wise to turn away from unbelievers,' said a member of the first group.

'Why am I wise?' asked the man from the tree.

'Observe our churches,' a voice answered. 'Look what our belief has done: beautiful, ornate structures of worship – golden bowls of baptism, silver trays of communion, and an air of comfort so that nothing can distract our devotion. We are a group blessed for faithfulness.'

'Observe a suffering world,' said the man from the tree, 'then look at your beautiful buildings. There will not be left here one stone upon another, that will not be thrown down.' He bowed his head between the groups and whispered: 'I thirst.'

'Then come down from the tree,' said the first group. 'We'll give you water.'

'We also will give you drink,' cried the second group.

'I thirst,' repeated the man in the tree.

'He'll come down,' murmured the first group. 'He's thirsty.'

'He'll come down,' murmured voices of the second group. 'Only a fool stays out on a limb.'

'We'll wait,' agreed both groups. 'All come down from the tree. We'll wait.'

And they waited, all day they waited for the strange man in the tree to come down, but in the evening he was still in the tree.

'The fellow is sacrilegious,' said one of the first group. 'Criticism is acceptable, but he talked of our churches being destroyed. We must be open to truth, yet blasphemy should not be condoned.'

'This man is sick,' said one of the second group. 'He is withdrawn and disorganised. Only a dangerous mind mutters of people being crushed by a stone.'

The shadow of the man in the tree grew longer on the ground. By night, the sounds of voices intermingled until the groups could no longer be distinguished.

'It's bad to have someone above us while we sleep,' said a small voice.

'Yes, it is bad,' answered a multitude of whispers.

'He is a strange fellow. What about our children? They are easily persuaded to climb trees.'

'Yes, what about our children?' echoed the whispers.

'His mind is irrational,' said the small voice. 'We must do something to preserve tranquillity.'

So, in order that they might sleep, they nailed him there.

John Somervill

Ordinary transfigured

Rejoice, the wood of the cross, wood three times blessed and deified, light of those who are in darkness; you anticipate in your splendour the rays of the resurrection of Christ, corresponding to the four dimensions of the world.

Orthodox Matins, Third Sunday of Lent

Forgiveness

Find the cross where you live
    when the sky has turned black
      and the man who was dead
      and who said
        down the track
        of time
          'Forgive'.

Hope for all you can be
    since God opened a grave;
      by His life you are freed
      from your need
        to deprave
        the good
          you see.

There is peace for your soul
    in the depths where you failed,
      for a man's touched your heart,
      healed the part
        that was nailed
        and now
          is whole.

Lois Ainger

No other cry

Lord God,
then I would see, in my mind,
how he was pushed and lashed
through city streets to Golgotha
and see there how he died for us . . .
Then Easter
when he rose from the dead.
Rejoicing, dancing and clapping
I would shout:
He is risen!
He is risen!

An unknown Ghanaian Christian

Risen – yes

All: He is risen, he is not here,
He goes before us into Galilee.

Leader: Death cannot contain the Life of the World. Jesus has passed from death to life. Despair and Sorrow give birth to hope. The stones cry out and the faithful rejoice.
All: He is risen . . .

Leader: Death cannot contain the Life of the World. Peace you bequeath to us. A peace the world does not know. Nations search and do not find peace in their defence systems, their national securities, their plans for war and their power to destroy.
All: He is risen . . .

Leader: Death cannot contain the Life of the World. Understanding and compassion can alone break barriers, overcome hostilities, create the way of justice and freedom. The forces of repression surround us.
All: He is risen . . .

Leader: Death cannot contain the Life of the World. You call us to wholeness, to harmony with ourselves and one another and all creation. Each of us reflects in our own inner divisions and dis-ease the separation and sinfulness of our society and world.

>*All*: He is risen . . .

Leader: Death cannot contain the Life of the World. You invite us to life, to let go of our plans, to learn the ways of gratitude and grace, to live as witnesses of your truth. We pray for courage and faith.

>*All*: He is risen.

Spring thoughts, 1986

And again
While the sun shines
It draws forth the sap
Secretly secure within
Nests of translucent green;
And springing forth
The tenderest of shoots
Strive for a brief moment
Of ecstasy
Before they can rest
In their glory . . .

And what will the human spirit attain?
To what noble acts be inspired?
What divine design
Will be carven, created
Crisply new,
Warmly moulded, once minted?
Will it transcend the weight
Of dulled drudgery,
The dross of the sloth of soul,
Self-pity's pathetic whine
Which withers the shooting spires,
Longing to pillow the sky
In patterns of peaceful canopied shade?
Arching, lifting,

Soar the sublimest
Of the sword-thrusting,
Swimming shoals
From the source
Of the song of the spheres –
The summons,
Trumpeted loud to the sin-laden,
Spanning the chasm,
Bridging the shores –
A highway, the Father's joy.

J.R. Brooke

Christ has died and is risen

Christ has died and is risen
Death has been destroyed in his victory,
That is our guarantee that we shall triumph too.
We know and acknowledge the Lord who is active in history
as he has always been.
Our God is the God of the people
and in their present weakness
he is weak too:
But in the display of their strength,
he is strong.

Christ through whom we know the Father
is present with us here today
and calls us to action.
Our faith is fed by his triumph
over death.

That is the guarantee of our victory.
Brothers and sisters, what else remains
for us to do,
except to take up with resolution the
task to which he calls us,
realising at each step his liberating
presence among us.
With Christ, by him and with him,

the people will be the victors.

Christ is alive
Christ is risen
Our faith is not empty
In him is to be found the deepest
meaning of history,
of our people and of our own lives.
In him death is defeated decisively.

In him all comes true –
the immeasureable vitality of our people,
their potential for liberation,
their capacity to revolutionize history,
to put down oppression
and to put the Easter victory into effect,
which is nothing else but passing
from the rule of necessity to the rule of freedom,
out of a society of injustice and
exploitation into the society of
justice and brotherhood proclaimed by the Kingdom.

Lord, before your greatness in the potential
of your people
we see clearly how puny we are.
Before the reality of the resurrection
there are exposed the different ways in
which we remain in death,
in sin, traitors to the cause of the poor.

Our understanding cannot grasp you,
you cannot be reduced to our faith.
We cannot possess you.
You gave yourself over to death
totally, definitely.
Before that we can only, hesitantly,
respond with equal devotion.
But nonetheless we ask your forgiveness.
We want to offer to you this way we follow,
with such hesitation,

the story of our faith and devotion
from the first time we were called,
from our joining this community we love,
from the moment we committed ourselves.

If we believe today, Lord, it is because we
have experienced you
in our feeble but growing identification with
the people.
As we affirm our faith
we do so totally devoid of triumphalism.

We believe in God who exists in the poor.
That is all.

But our faith is riddled with hesitation,
carelessness and fear,
and our confession of faith becomes a prayer
to the Lord
and to our people:
We do believe but our faith needs to be strengthened.

At this moment of time
the ordinary people suffer oppression and misery,
hunger and crises.
The last of the oppressors is upon thier shoulders,
the shoulders of the poor and exploited
bowed down by the toil of every day.

We have to retreat and take up defensive positions
we are still weak in the face of the oppressor
but we have the infinite security provided by our
stronghold in the future,
our great and glorious victory.
On this April day we acknowledge that the Lord is present
and at the head of his people.

The Lord is in command:
who can defeat us?

A prayer for Easter Day in Peru.

But what words, what acts and deeds shall we produce from where we find ourselves? What bites and gnaws at the community in which we live, or do we come from afar to worship at halls and churches that have no real bearing on the lives of men and women who live nearby? What does it mean for us to shout, 'He Is Risen. He is alive in the people'?

Tony Jasper

Easter Intercession

Leader: Let us pray for the whole world, for which Jesus lived and died and rose again.
In your mercy –
Gathering: Risen Lord, hear our prayer.
Leader: Let us pray for growing unity between the churches.
In your mercy –
Gathering: Risen Lord, hear our prayer.
Leader: Let us pray that this Easter may be a time of reconciliation for all who are estranged or at enmity with each other.
Lord in your mercy –
Gathering: Risen, Lord, hear our prayer.
Leader: Let us pray for those who live in fear and doubt, that they may be comforted.
Lord in your mercy –
Gathering: Risen Lord, hear our prayer.
Leader: We pray that by our words and in our lives we may be pointers to your living presence in the world.
In your mercy –
Gathering: Risen Lord hear our prayer.

Easter prayers (John 20:11–18)

Mary stood weeping.
Lord Jesus Christ,
we know only too well
the tears and pain

when someone we love has died.
You too know the sufferings
of this world,
You too wept.
You understand.

She saw two angels in white
God my Father,
  I do not understand angels,
  messengers of God,
  signs of Your presence.
  But I know
  that You have been with me
  when I needed You most,
  even at the tomb.
  I trust You.

She did not know that it was Jesus
Lord Jesus Christ,
  I too have been blind to Your presence
  because of sorrow.
  I have missed Your presence
  because I did not expect You
  to be in the ordinary things of my day.
  May my eyes and ears be open to You,
  my mind and heart ready for You.
  You have promised
  to be with us always.

'Mary' . . . 'Rabboni'
Lord Jesus Christ,
  what love and trust,
  what indescribable hope and glory
  are behind these two words.
  You know my name,
  You call me by name.
  Here and now I respond again.
  You are my Lord and my God.

I have seen the Lord

Lord Jesus Christ.
  what must it have been like
  for Mary,
  experiencing for the first time
  Your living presence,
  this miracle beyond explanation.

  I too have glimpsed You,
  in the worship of the Church,
  in the lives of good people,
  in my own experience
  of being guided, healed, and blessed.
  I have seen the Lord.

A congregation's prayer

Our God,
  this day
  with the whole Church
  in heaven and on earth,
  we sing the Easter hymns with joy,
  we hear the Easter story with faith.
  We believe that evil is not for ever,
  that death is not the end.

  Help us to see in our ordinary days,
  Your power and Your glory,
  Your love,
  as we see them today,
  this day of Christ's rising,
  His living presence with us all,
  for ever.

Victim who wins

Sing, my tongue, the glorious battle,
Sing the ending of the fray,
Now above the Cross, the trophy,
Sing the loud triumphant lay:
Tell how Christ, the world's redeemer,

As a victim won the day,
> *Venantius Fortunatus, AD 530–609*

The gospel of Rod

Rod's gospel's not for the questioning few
Rod has a gospel to keep all in their pew
Rod's eyes-down-gospel will assimilate you
And this is the gospel of rod

Rod has a gospel that hushes debate
Rod has a gospel that prays 'Don't rile the State'
Rod's nighty-night gospel will not stay up late
And this is the gospel of rod

Rod has a gospel for laissez-faire brains
Rod has a gospel of stringed, soothing refrains
Rod's short, sharp gospel clamps its women in chains
And this is the gospel of rod

Rod has a gospel of men being men
Rod has a gospel that detests 'Tony Benn
Rod's cowering gospel is the size of a wren
And this is the gospel of rod

Rod has a gospel of very few qualms
Rod has a gospel that dare not sound alarms
Rod's tidy gospel is not showing Christ's palms
And that is the gospel of rod

> *Stuart Henderson*

Only at Easter

Whips circled and crudely landed
to lash life out of him,
or so it appeared.
Spikes were summoned
to close the stone vault,
and the sky growled.

Haughty robes of passing power
flapped through women wailing,
towards, unknowingly, the chasm of pride,
the parched well of no comfort.
How much those perished priests,
like us, didn't know.

Rising, he rose.
Risen, he remains.
His remains, apart from some ruby drops,
he took with him.
They became our passport out of death,
our living ascent from a
lifeless climate.
His scent of wounds,
in which we are now wrapped,
carried us out of that petrified place
into the calm city
where even the dust has been healed.

Stuart Henderson

*More words for Easter and
Resurrection:*

Words about faith and conversion

Bible passages:

Job 11:15–19
Acts 3:1–10
2 Corinthians 5:14–15
1 Peter 1:8–12
Hebrews 1:1–2

From the first small expression of thanks to the positive silence of being 'lost in wonder, love and praise' (Wesley's line in his powerful hymn Love Divine, All Loves Excelling), there are testimonies for the telling.

An early Christian expression from the fourth century, the Liturgy of St Mark, Anaphora, puts it: 'lips that keep not silence, and hearts that cannot be still.' That statement centres on worship as a whole, but testimony is surely no less an act of praise, thanksgiving and worship. It was the mystic Ruysbroeck who once exclaimed, 'I must rejoice without ceasing, although the world shudder at my joy,' and testimony is often defiance against the alien forces arrayed against the believer.

But testimony, whether it is open proclamation by individuals of their delight in God and of Christ's love for them, or of the ways God has touched and redeemed their lives, has not fared well in recent times as an intrinsic part of informal worship, although somewhat restored by churches of a more charismatic disposition.

The American writer Harvey Cox, in his book *The Seduction of the Spirit* (Wildwood), suggests that in the past famous theologians and thinkers such as Augustine, Wesley, Kierkegaard and Newman were quite willing to give a 'tumultuous account' of their inner and outer struggles. Cox remarks how ordinary conversation is studded with personal statements and testimonies, yet much of conventional and mainstream expression is emotionless. He urges the restoration of testimony.

It is doubtful if Cox has in mind the 'testimony spot' of his youth, when 'people week in and week out' would tell of the marvellous things God had done for them. Yet his central point remains. It is good that people say what they feel and how it feels, and that a person's autobiography is seen as important and valuable in a gathering.

So, here is a chapter of testimonies.

Weights lifted

They were taken by coach to Jerusalem and then to the birthplace of Christ. Glenn was aware of a feeling he had never before experienced. It was of peace and calm. 'I sensed that this story of Christ coming down to earth – because it was only a story to me till then – was real. It was true!'

'I came away from that place with a completely different outlook on life. I began to talk to other Christians. I read the New Testament. It clicked. I understood everything. I couldn't put it down.'

Suddenly, the tabloids were on to it: Glenn Hoddle had become a Christian . . .

'Someone told me I'd been pretty brave speaking out about my faith the way I had done, but all I could reply was that I couldn't keep quiet about something that has changed my life like this. Before, I was going down a narrow road. It wasn't that I was a terrible person or anything, more that, like everyone, we'd got cued into our selfish ways.

'Now, that narrow road's broadened. It feels as if I've been walking around blind all those years, but now the scales have been lifted from my eyes.'

Glenn Hoddle, Gerald Williams

Mike Peters

For many years Mike Peters was lead singer with The Alarm, a rock band that found considerable success on both sides of the Atlantic. He has made individual appearances at Greenbelt. In the early days of the Alarm, he wrote a song entitled 'Shout to the Devil' which was his attack on religion, the Bible and Jesus. When the song appeared on the group's first album, *Declaration*, in 1983, the words were changed. He was beginning to see real truth in the very faith he had once condemned.

I received through the post a book that was called 'Countdown', which set out the case for Christianity. I was going to Liverpool for the weekend, and I just remember something in my head saying, 'You musn't leave that book behind. You've got to pick it up and take it with you.' I did and it was a decision that I will remember for the rest of my life.

All I remember is that the book said, 'Do you want the gift of everlasting life?' I knew I did. The book explained about belief in a series of questions and answers that you couldn't deny. And I remember having a massive feeling of release and an overwhelming joy deep inside and I knew I could no longer deny the existence of Jesus. I was sitting in the middle of a crowded train, crying my eyes out and deeply happy.

Tony Jasper

Mouthings

Everywhere and nowhere;
everything and nothing.

Years ago, a small child,
I mouthed your name in Sunday School.
You spoiled my sunny freedom,
kept me from my sunny games.
I left you lying in a prayer book
presented for good attendance.

What can I do to know you now,
what words to break
the years of unbelief?

I have been in the dark too long,
lived off my brain too long;
worshipped the craven
images of the mind,
cerebral madness,
intellectual arrogance;
I think and I am not.

Father of light,
healer of pain,
I re-open the book,
speak your name.

Dennis Reid

The way it happens

Lord, teach us to see you
and reveal yourself to us
when we seek you,
for we cannot seek you
except you teach us,
nor find you
except you reveal yourself.
Let us seek you in longing,
let us long for you in seeking,
let us find you in love
and love you in finding.

The innkeeper decided

The innkeeper decided.
Herod decided.
Peter decided.
Mary Magdalen decided.

The rich young ruler decided.
John decided.
Judas decided.
Pilate decided.
Stephen decided.
Paul decided.
The innkeeper decided to leave Him outside.
Herod decided to kill Him.
Peter decided to follow Him.
Mary decided to worship Him.
The rich young ruler decided to hold on to
   his money and leave Him.
John decided to love Him.
Judas decided to sell Him.
Pilate decided to try and wash his hands of Him.
Stephen decided to die for Him.
Paul decided to live for Him.
And you decided . . .

And . . . you . . . decided?

Kairos Group

The touch of a hand

I feel the touch of a hand
   stretched out to calm
      my inner storm
         to make alarm
           die down.

I feel the touch of a hand
   stretched out to heal
      the blind disease
         that fights to seal
           me down.

I feel the touch of a hand
   stretched out to me
      that men have nailed

but cannot be
   nailed down.
      Lois Ainger

Lord of the absurd

O Lord of the absurd,
why did you birth me into being
with not enough answers
to fill my questioning heart?

I am a pilgrim, Lord.
I'm looking for a home.
I'm death in search of life.
I'm life searching for death.

O Lord of the absurd,
empty me of the meaninglessness
that stands between
death and life.
Empty me of all this unbirth.

O Lord of the absurd,
teach me how to die
so I can truly live.
Amen.

Macrina Wiederbehr

Crazy

What are you trying to tell us, Lord?
If you're a shepherd
surely you should know
that leaving ninety-nine
to look for one,
is really crazy . . .

Is your love for us a little bit crazy?
Is that what you're trying to say?

I just wanted you to know, Lord,
that everytime I feel lost
I remember that story.

You can leave ninety-nine
to look for me
any day
even if it is a little bit crazy.
Amen.

Anonymous

A snow-covered gospel

Winter God
God of hidden face
I have been so angry
at your coldness.

I wanted to welcome you home.
But you wouldn't come.
We used to be friends a little.
That was when you came
in just the *right amounts*.
But now, you are too much for me.
It will take a warmer heart than mine
to hear a snow-covered gospel.

Anonymous

Touch my eyes again

I see men as trees walking.
Twilight shadows
Half seen
Half heard
Unknown.
Fearing, I stand alone.
Love's hands have touched my eyes

As through a darkened glass I see
Shapes pass me by
But still am I
Alone.
Humbly I kneel.
Lord touch my eyes again.
That I may see
　　　　　And love
　　　　　And live.

Francis Uren

Amy Grant's story

Popularity does change things in some ways. People do stare at
you but I can go out and not be mobbed, and I can go to a movie
and be relaxed, though sometimes it is hard. All of a sudden, when
you become somebody, people start making value judgments and
sometimes they find you are not the person they think you are.
I don't think I would like someone to try to make me into a
superstar. I think they would fail miserably. I think you have to
have a certain flavour to your personality to be a superstar, and I
just don't think I have that. I get frightened when someone thinks
they have a corner on my life. I get worried if I think people are
asking more of me than they're asking of themselves. I have to
admit, though, that since I'm in the public eye and have chosen
to be there, my life will be lived under a magnifying glass, at least
in some respects.

It hasn't been easy taking myself from a religious music world
to the music scene as a whole and at very least trying to convince
some people that I've not forgotten my past. When I signed with
A & M I asked why they signed me. They said they signed me as
an artist. They said 'We want you to be you' and 'so long as you
pay the rent, you can have time to write songs!'

I'm fortunate that I'm a songwriter, although of course I do
sing other people's songs. When it comes to choosing my songs
there are five of us who vote! We sit around and play tapes of
demo songs that are submitted by others or simply ones we have

come across and I sing my songs. All in all it means a lot of work. It helps, of course, that I know some songwriters well, such as Michael Smith whose music I like a lot. You know sometimes it can be just me who wants to do a particular song, and this was the case with one song that has proved so popular, 'Saved By Love'. On the demo, it really hadn't sounded too good. The song meetings at the farm are fun. Sometimes when there is doubt about a song I stay with it for a bit and then we might all agree that it's okay.

All these moments have made life so precious. It is so precious to have found such love from my husband, too. But, of course, I had the right start in life. I had a Christian upbringing in a closely knit family and I've always been led into good ways. I was aware of Jesus from an early age.

I thank God for allowing me to sing. I've experienced so many marvellous things. Once in Atlanta five thousand kids lit candles, then got up from their seats and sang together. I have had so many moments of truth, but there is one very precious and special moment which happened in 1973.

Like I said, I grew up among Christian things. I heard and I sang about Christian faith from my very early years, and I didn't ask questions. It all seemed so right and true. Then, there does come the time when you ask what it means and I knew I must know Jesus for myself.

So it was that in 1973 I was baptised. I just let go and went down on my knees. It was my finding and my commitment, so I was moving from learnt faith to knowing faith. For me, it was another few years before I was really swimming. I'm still with Jesus, praise His Name!

In many churches 'testimony' has become a forgotten form of worship. Here is one person, Amy Grant, telling her story. As it happens, Amy has become a major figure in the pop world, and not merely in the Jesus Music area.

Books such as Rock Solid *(Word) and* Feel So Real *(Marshall Pickering) contain many testimonies from music people who are Christians, and there are various other books that bring together a panoply of people with their story.*

Best, of course, is not retelling the story of someone who is known in the public arena, but the hearing of experience and faith from amongst the local gathering.

This extract is from Moments Of Truth *(Marshall Pickering).*

Tony Jasper

Amazing Grace

Amazing grace, how sweet the sound,
That saved a wretch like me.
I once was lost, but now I'm found,
Was blind, but now I see.

'Twas grace that taught my heart to fear,
And grace my fear relieved.
How precious did that grace appear,
The hour I first believed.

Through many dangers, toils and snares,
We have already come.
'Twas grace that brought us safe thus far
And grace will lead us home.

When we've been there ten thousand years,
Bright shining as the sun
We've no less days to sing God's praise
Than when we first begun.

Amazing grace, how sweet the sound
That saved a wretch like me.
I once was lost, but now I'm found,
Was blind, but now I see.

This has long been a Christian expression of joy and trust in its Lord. The words were sung by John Newton when his ship reached America and show his thanks for a safe voyage.

The basic assertion rests on the claim that God's Love is shown in the life and resurrection of Jesus Christ. The singer knows he is loved, that his life has meaning. He feels like someone who having wandered aimlessly, having been frightened and confused, is found.

Write about any experience of yours where you've been up against the wall, full of uncertainty and suddenly you've been aware of some light or insight being shed on your experience.

What does it mean to love and be loved, accepted? How do you feel when someone says they love you?

Is there such a thing as having one's life transformed? What

conditions are likely to cause
this to happen?

What makes us able to say 'yes'
to ourselves and to someone
else? Why do we seem willing
to put up with someone let-
ting us down, making mistakes,
annoying us as continually we
once more accept them?

When we feel at peace with ourselves, how does this increase
our potential and ability to
handle situations?

Originally, this extract appeared in Sound of the Seventies *(Galliard)
and as is evident from the opening of paragraph three, it is directed to
the school and group study situation. But the song is popular with most
Christian groups, and its assertion and accompanying study questions are
surely applicable at any time.*

*Within a group worship situation, the song can be sung verse by verse
with the question paragraphs spoken between them. It can then form the
basis of a discussion sermon. The same process can be enacted with other
songs or hymns.*

Tony Jasper

Inward narrow lanes

I will be still
And learn of you.
I will, I say I will, be still.
Impatience gnaws, and nags 'til peace be gone.
'Birds build, but not I build, no.'
Frustration builds
Like anger in a skin tight boil.
And so the teacup storm within me rages on
Until I sleep,
To wake before the day.

Your soul is in my hands
And shall no torment touch you.

Not righteous I,
But still I hear,
And still
I am.

Francis Uren

Visions never sleep

I have lived it myself:
A life of no love
Only passion
A life of no reason
Only cause
A life of no substance
Only death.

'My life was created by the big bang.'
These words have come from my very lips
And all that time, you were calling me.

I have lived myself:
A life of no safe haven
Save my ego
A life of no knowledge
Only pretence
A life of no temptation
Only ignorance.

I have become one of those I have
Always feared
And now I have
Accepted God
My life is no easier
But stronger.

Simon Law

Don't you believe me?

(For two performers)

1: Faith? I don't believe in it. Take my word, the only way to a peaceful life is to doubt everything. If someone makes a statement to me, I always say 'Are you sure?' or 'I doubt it.'

2: Sounds quite an interesting philosophy. (*Puts glass on table.*)

1: Philosophy – now there's another thing. The whole meaning of existence. Take that table, now.

2: Why? Don't you want it any more?

1: No, I mean, ask yourself – is that table here or isn't it?

2: Well, of course it's here.

1: How do you know?

2: I can see it.

1: Are you sure? Perhaps it's only in your mind.

2: But why should my mind tell me there's a table there if there isn't?

1: Well, if it didn't, wouldn't you wonder why your glass didn't fall on the floor?

2: I suppose so.

1: There you are, then.

2: Where?

1: You can't cope with the idea of your drink going all over the floor, so your mind tells you there's a table there, just to keep you happy.

2: (*Picks up glass*) Well, I do know I'm holding this wine glass.

1: Are you sure?

2: Of course I am . . . Oh, I see. If my mind didn't provide a wine-glass, then I should have wine all over my trousers.

1: You're getting the idea. Then, of course, there's God.

2: (*Startled*) Where?

1: I don't mean he's here. In fact he isn't anywhere. He doesn't exist. He's been invented because he was needed.

2: You mean, like that table and this glass.

1: That's right. Human beings have to have somebody to blame for everything that goes wrong, don't they? Apart from the Government, I mean.

2: I suppose so.

1: Religion is all like that. I ask you, walking on a lake and turning water into wine – I'm surprised we don't have any stories about bending spoons.

2: Not that spoons really exist, of course.

1: What? No, that's right. Anyway, talking about wine has made me thirsty. It's your turn to pay.

2: Are you sure?

1: Of course I am. I paid last time.

2: No, that was just in your mind . . .

1: I tell you, I'm absolutely certain. Don't you believe me? . . .

(*They leave.*)

Peter English

Charismatic prayer

Holy Spirit,
in whom I lose myself,
grasp me now with the force
that hooped
a thousand planets
down the Milky Way
and sent the stars
spinning through space,
that gave new words
to baffled fisher folk
for ever mending nets
a throw away
from miracles
drawn from the Sea.
Throb now in me
and let my tongue
make plain
to every eye
one mystery
caught in the glare
of truth.
Teach me to run

to jump
to sing
lost in the words
of another time.

Anonymous

Number One

The tune is composed
the words written
the hits can come
we are the artists
He has signed us
we sing for Him
always and forever.

Tony Jasper

---

*More words about faith
and conversion:*

Words of wholeness

Doubtless, some will see this section as rummaging in the dubious world of 'New Age' philosophy.

And probably little can be done to change the mind of anyone who thinks so, but that is not my intent. Rather, these words for worship shout that there is no radical distinction between the sacred and profane. These are words that suggest our total selves are worthy recipients and vessels of God's gift of life.

We pray quite happily, 'Out of love you fashioned us human,' but many see this as no more than that God gave us 'minds', and if some do pray that in creation 'we find traces of love' they fail to see this in terms of the bodies they possess: emotions, affections, imagination, feelings, responses, urges, let alone the sheer joy of taste, saliva, skin, hair, and so forth. Should you see some of this as errant nonsense then talk with someone who has had radiotherapy for cancer of the throat, and you will soon be humbled by your taking taste and saliva for granted.

For spiritual happiness and well-being, even for acceptance of ourselves on an honest and open level, we must let worship be unhampered by our ridiculous self-imposed restrictions.

Listen

LISTEN
to your life.
See it for the fathomless mystery that it is.
In the boredom and pain of it,
no less than in the excitement and gladness;
touch, taste, smell your way to the holy and hidden heart of it
because in the last analysis all moments are key moments
and life itself is
GRACE.

Fredrick Buechner

How does it taste? smell? feel?

For a small group, assemble on a table a number of basic items that have taste, smell and feel, e.g. some newly baked bread, a partly peeled fruit such as an orange, a free range egg boiled and put back into its shell.

In groups of two or three, let each give to the other. The recipient could have eyes closed, with all taking their time in very slow motions.

If total silence seems awkward, play appropriate music softly in the background as the group tastes, smells and feels.

Ask the group to imagine what it might be like if they could never taste, smell and feel.

Then line the objects on the table, and ask the group to walk slowly past, focusing on the colour of each object, and to think of a word that describes how this colour makes them feel. Then with people sitting, perhaps in a circle on the floor, ask each to say the word that describes how they felt. After each word, let all shout Yes in affirmation of that person's feeling.

Turn to familiar hymns about nature and harvest. Read some of them. Talk of what is missing from them. Sing any ones that seem true to the experience of that moment. Ask for prayer arising from these experiences.

Tony Jasper

The amazing day

I thank You, God, for this most amazing day:
for the leaping greenly spirits of trees
and a blue dream of sky; and for *everything*
which is natural which is infinite which is yes.

e. e. cummings

This is our life

The kingdom is within you
You carry it about wherever you go
And it is either a joy or a burden.
Perhaps sometimes a joy
Sometimes a burden.
You can't cut it out and throw it away
You won't find it in any mass X-ray
It is your life
Life pulsing through the senses
Life delighting in colour and in light
Life struggling for truth and understanding
Man made in the image of God.
This is your life
The power and the glory
The shame and the suffering
This is the Christ within you
And with Him in His Bethlehem.

Canon R. E. Hougham

Inspiration

Rock and metal: these are the basic materials of which the earth
is built. What do we do with them?

The exploration of the world's resources for our own purposes is
something that today we take for granted. We have lost the habit
of looking at things for their own natural qualities. To enable us

to see the world as a gift, to be accepted with gratitude and used with reverence, we need the artist.

Barbara Hepworth was born and brought up in Yorkshire. 'Moving through and over the West Riding landscape with my father in his car, the hills were sculptures; the roads defined the form. Above all there was the sensation of moving physically over the contours of fullnesses and concavities, through hollows and over peaks – feeling, touching, seeing through mind and hand and eye.'

Long ago the Christian Church took some of the basic elements of our day-to-day life – water, bread, wine – to symbolise certain spiritual realities. Art is not meant to be a substitute for the sacraments, but perhaps a sculptor who uses in her work the common materials of the everyday world – stone, metal, glass – and explores their possibilities, can help us to have through them a new sense of the transcendent. We may even begin to find these simple forms expressing for us deep levels of experience that we find difficult to put into words.

Born in Wakefield in 1903, Barbara Hepworth went on to study at Leeds College of Art, where Henry Moore was a fellow student. Later, after travelling in Italy – 'Florence, Siena, Lucca, Arezzo, basking in the new bright light' – she settled in London with her husband Ben Nicholson and a group of fellow artists, which at one time included Naum Gabo. From there she moved (in 1939) to St Ives in Cornwall, where she died in 1975.

Cornwall, with its long curves of moorland, its standing stones and caves coiled into cliffs, provided new imagery; so did the rhythms of the sea, the spirals in shells, the pattern and structure of crystals. Forms and relationships, spaces between forms, the space inside caves, holes and hollows in rocks became very important. For her they were 'A piercing of the superficial surfaces of material existence'. It is as though we are invited to climb into these sculptures and explore them, and so to look out with fresh vision on earth and the mystery and meaning within it.

In these new experiences of the world around her she found inspiration for work which may have little to do with traditional religious symbolism but often expresses, in her own words, 'a rhythm of form which has its roots in earth but reaches outwards towards the unknown experiences of the future'.

Brenda Lealman and Edward Robinson

Our God

God of after-sunset,
God of half-light and almost night,
God of quiet and stillness,
God of coolness
that drifts up from the river,
God of silhouetted leaves
against a silvered sky,
God of singing crickets
and blinking fireflies –
God of these, be my God, too.

Anonymous.

Other contact

Dr John Hull is Professor of Religious Education at Birmingham University. Now 56 years old, he registered as a blind person in 1980. So much beauty is visual but now he would claim beauty in aesthetics.

'We had a rain porch built. We told the builders to make it as noisy as possible – no carpet, no double-glazing, metal panels on the roof. I don't sleep much. Now I can get up at three o'clock in the morning and nip downstairs. I've got a little camp bed in the porch, and I lie there listening to the rain teeming down. I don't need to analyse it any more: I live in it.'

From an interview by Clive Davis with Dr Hull on his book, Touching The Rock: An Experience In Blindness (*Arrow Books, 1991*), *in* The Guardian.

Read this, then try to gather other expressions of beauty from those who use senses that people with full faculties neglect.

Read appropriate psalms. Sing songs and hymns that make use of nature and senses, for instance, 'All Creatures of our God and King'.

Tony Jasper

Football

Not so long ago
when footballers played football
instead of
opening discos, recording LPs, and having their hair tinted
my father would take me to Anfield
his hand squeezing mine like an affectionate vice
boyish, joyous, inarticulate excitement as we neared the Ground
cold day
scarf rubbing like a Brillo pad against thin-necked skin
stopping off at the newsagent's on Anfield Road
one packet of Spangles
one tube of Trebor mints
Not so long ago
when hooliganism was classed
as dropping your sweetpaper on the floor
and when a writhing centre forward on the turf
usually meant at least a broken leg
my father would take me to Anfield.
Not so long ago
I would look at the names in the match programme
and savour the syllables
caress the vowels
and know that they would still be there for the next Home
    game.
Not so long ago
when a contract dispute
was something that happened to people buying houses
when you could almost smell the Brylcream
on the opposing fullback's head

before Burgess's horrific prophecy of roaring hordes
of vandalous mutants
came true
my father would take me to Anfield.
Not so long ago
when television commentators were informative
and did not resemble a town-crier having a nervous breakdown

my father would take me to Anfield.
Not so long ago
when losing a game was only rather annoying, instead of
one sacked manager
'The lads couldn't get it in the back of the net, Brian,
that's why we didn't score'
removal of sponsorship
and several written transfer requests.

Not so long ago
football was fun
footballers played football
my father was alive
and he would take me to Anfield.

Stewart Henderson

A prayer for feasting

For those who love You, O Lord,
   is not everything holy, everything prayerful?
As I prepare to celebrate any feast,
   give delight to my heart and arouse my taste buds.
May I truly realise that happy are those times
   when we can pause in the midst of our labours
   and share good food and drink,
   joyful song and story with one another.

From the first day of creation
   Your children worshipped You
   in the act of eating and drinking together,
   and beheld therein Your divine presence.

Each feast is meant to be a taste
   of that eternal celebration at Your table
   in the cosmic feasting hall.

I thank You, Lord of the Feast,
   for holidays and holy days,
   for anniversaries and victory celebrations,

for homecomings and weddings,
for all these times and many more
when we can pray with food and drink,
in the company of candles and conversation.

I thank You, my God,
that in the holy feast of Passover
and especially in the Last Supper of Your Son, Jesus,
You gave to us holy signs
of Your eternal presence at our tables
and a promise of the great feast
that awaits us in the life to come.
May every feast in which I share,
be praise, honour and glory
to You, my Lord and my God. Amen.

Edward Hays

The marvel of a car

O God,

I thank thee for the marvel of a car – alive and powerful
at the touch of my hands and feet – a thing of tremendous
possibilities – wonderful or terrible!

Help me to achieve the skill that will control it completely
and wisely, like a tool, shaping a better life for me and those
around me.

I thank thee for the promise of adventure that is mine each time
I slip behind its wheel: the thrill of the open road . . . far places
. . . strange sights . . . new 'neighbouring'.

Make me aware, as I drive the streets of my town – signalling,
stopping, waiting, turning, and zooming ahead – that

I do not have to do merely with trucks, taxis, cars,

bicycles, and pedestrians, but with PEOPLE!

People such as I know and touch as I walk the sidewalks and enter
the homes of my neighbourhood; people such as I am – making
mistakes, perhaps, but not really wanting to.

Because I like people and know how important their happiness
and how precious they are to thee . . .

Let me be alert, courteous, patient, considerate of the rights of
    others on the road, gracious enough to give up some rights of
    my own, and always . . . careful, realising that:
    another's pain would destroy my pleasure,
    another's loss would rob my gain,
    and the life I save is just as precious as my own.

Amen.

Ernst H. Nussmann

Daily thanks

God is great; God is good;

God is great; God is good;
and I thank Him for
ribbons of lace.
Ribboned, crocheted-lace traces in pretty pastel.

For white wool and nylon.
For mint-flavoured cotton corduroy.

I thank Him for tiny buttons.
Wrinkle-free buttons. Braided-leather buttons.

For collars and cuffs of lace.
For stand-up collars
and for bewitching stockings.

For thin-heeled date shoes
and two-toned snake charmers.
For pale-beige suede strapped and block-heeled.

God is good, and I thank Him
for the no-sleeved dress with yes-striped top
and the maybe-striped hat.
For the low-waisted dress.

For plaids in pink, sparked with lace and velvet.

God is good. I thank Him
for pink and green plaid wool cut on a slant,

stopped by a swashbuckled velvet belt.

And a dress with baby-doll touches of ecru lace.

By His hands we all are clothed.

In neon stripes of lilac and green topping off
electric-green stem-legged pants.
In zany wool and mohair fabric.
In aqua, worsted-wool jersey bonded to acetate.

Give us, Lord, exotic print,
lush with splashy jungle flowers.

Give us print of coral roses, blue daisies,
and moss-green leaves on white petticoat.
Printed on the slant, scalloped, and side slit.

Satiny as skin.

God is good. I thank Him for
fine wool skirt of colour-matched plaid,
herringbone, heather.
For blue, gold, raspberry, ecru, pink.

Plus deep, vivid, bold colours. For colours vibrant.
Fabric sleek and snappy.

God is great.
The soft-textured sweater knitted to perfection
is great.
White with black.
Beige with chocolate is great.

Mint with olive.
Pink with cranberry.
Blue with navy.

God is great, and I am vivacious. Lustrous.

Audacious.

Herbert Brokering

Praise him in the dance

Praise God in the admiration of beauty,
in the delight at companionship,
in the appreciation and valuing
of the fullness of another's being;
in the comfort of bodily contact.

Praise God in the pleasure of caresses;
in the mutual response of love;
in the movements in and out;
in the joys of fulfilment.

Praise God in the respect for another's body;
in care for another's feelings;
in reticences as in frankness;
in the meeting of two minds in love.

Praise God in the courtesies each partner shows
of restraint and consideration,
of care in times of illness or strain,
of forgiveness after times of difficulty;
praise God for love which grows and endures.

Praise God, who is love,
for giving us this love as his gift,
so that we may indeed love one another
as he has loved us:

As fully, as freely,
with our whole selves,
possessing here on earth
a foretaste of God's own love in heaven.

Daphne Fraser

Lead us through

SPIRIT of Wisdom,
take from us all fuss,
the clattering of noise,
the temptation to dominate by the power of words,
the craving for certainty.
Lead us through the narrow gate of not knowing,
that we may listen and obey,
and come to a place of stillness,
of true conversation and wisdom.

Spirit of Love,
take from us all lust,
the battering of force,
the temptation to dominate by physical power,
the craving for control.
Lead us through the narrow gate of loneliness,
that we may be chaste and let others be,
and come to a place of intimacy,
of deep communion and love.

Spirit of Freedom,
take from us all rust,
the cluttering of things,
the temptation to dominate by the power of money,
the craving for comfort.
Lead us through the narrow gate of constriction,
that we may let go of possessions,
and come to a place of simplicity,
of glad conviviality and freedom.

Jim Cotter

Let us be fools

Let us be fools for Christ's sake:
in facing the truth, may we be set free from illusion;
in accepting our wounds, may we be healed and made whole;
in embracing the outcast, may be know ourselves redeemed;
in discovering our child, may we grow to full stature;
in seeking true innocence, may we no longer harm;
in yielding to dying, may abundant life flow into us;
in vulnerable risk, may we know love's pain and joy;
in the folly of the Cross, may .we see the Wisdom of God.

Jim Cotter

Words about ourselves and faith

Bible passages

Psalm 73
Luke 11:33-36
Ephesians 4:15-16
1 Corinthians 9:24
1 Peter 1:8-12

Corporate prayer, no less than personal, can be akin to ordering goods and expecting immediate delivery. Reciting a list of wants in the end is a charade that resembles a spoilt child who desires more and more. This is not the scenario of this section.

There is no denial that Christianity is about happiness and our struggle for it. It is not wrong to 'want' happiness, nor is it wrong to desire good for oneself, although some who call themselves Christians have a proclivity for misery. But true prayer moves within the context of the Lord's Prayer and is set against a vastly wider backcloth.

This section has an underlying theological aim. In its breadth and width of subject matter it insists that there are no categories where God might come into His own – *every* aspect of our life has significance and can find transformation.

Fogged
Our generation is remarkable . . .
for the number of people
who must believe something
but do not know
what

Evelyn Underhill

Death of a stranger

My heart is burdened
with another's grief,
   A father and mother are crying
   because their son/daughter is dead.

Dear God, sometimes You are so heavy,
Your will so difficult to understand.
   I do not know these people.
   They have no faces that I call to mind.
   no voices that are familiar,
   no shared memories.
   They do not live nearby –
   I cannot touch their hands
   and feel their tears drop on my fingers.
   I have no bond with them
   except our common, human
   fragile hold on life.
Father, You know their grief;
You had to say, 'My Son is Dead.'
Help them to remember this,
help them to give themselves up.
Help them to let go,
so that they fall into the pit of Your love.
   I pray for them, Father.
   I pray You will stay with them;
See that someone will come to them;
some person who will touch their hands
and gather up the tears;
some person who will hold them
with such a love
that they will hear You say:
'For you My Son was dead.
            For You My Son now lives.
            This is your peace
            and your life.'

Stay with them, Father.
Be there
when they are ready
to give this terrible burden
back to You.

Anne Springsteen

In public worship, someone might preface by reading a relevant extract from a newspaper.

Death lib.

The liberating thing about death
is in its fairness to women,
its acceptance of blacks,
its special consideration
for the sick.

And I like the way
that children aren't excluded,
homosexuals are welcomed,
and militants aren't banned

The really wondering thing
about death
is that all major religions
agree on it, all beliefs
take you there, all philosophy
bows before it, all arguments
end there.

Con men can't con it
Thieves can't nick it
Bullies can't share it
Magicians can't trick it.

Boxers can't punch it

Nor critics dismiss it
Don't knows can't not know
The lazy can't miss it.

Governments can't ban it
Or the army defuse it
Judges can't jail it
Lawyers can't sue it.

Capitalists can't bribe it
Socialists can't share it
Terrorists can't jump it
The Third World aren't spared it.

Scientists can't quell it
Nor can they disprove it
Doctors can't cure it
Surgeons can't move it.

Einstein can't have it
Guevara can't free it
The thing about dead
Is we're all gonna be it.

Stewart Henderson

Body fusion

May sex be an expressive act.
May our sex not be a necessary or compulsive one.
May we in sex offer to the other our feeling of life.
May we share our personal histories.
Make our sex not be divorced from the rest of life's activities.
May our sexual act be a celebration of life together.
May our sex be pleasing to each other.
Forgive us for reducing sex to the trivial.
May we have trust,
May it be enjoyable,
Whether in embrace,
  in the kiss,

in deep penetration.
May all express the wonderful gift of sexual feeling and desire
that we have.

Tony Jasper

Unknown soldier

For the most part the majority of western peoples do not live
with war as an everyday reality, but even so, the recent conflicts
involving Western powers have meant some loss of life.

> Was he old?
> No, not old.
> Twenty or so,
> no more.
> An officer?
> A private,
> no stripes,
> front line.
> Decorations?
> Stone over
> his body,
> medal for
> his mother.
> Was he famous?
> No,
> but he went at
> the bidding
> of the famous.
> What say
> the records?
> Only
> that his records
> were lost
> in the world's next war.
>
> *Steve Turner*

Mortal foil

Cancer couldn't get me
Cancer wouldn't dare
Cancer doesn't scare me
Hate to lose my hair

Cancer's got no manners
Cancer lays you flat
Cancer's like aerobics
Stops you getting fat

Cancer is an addict
Cancer's full of drugs
Cancer is a tantrum
Won't respond to hugs

Cancer stalks the playgroup
Comes from who knows where
Dolly's now an orphan
Cancer isn't fair

Cancer is religious
Urges you to pray
In such numb devotion
A reverent display

Cancer is remedial
Never sees the fun
That even if it kills you
Doesn't mean it's won.

Stewart Henderson

As I am

World, I am Youth, unsettled and searching
Exploring the heights and the plain.
I wander your deserts, thirsty and pale,
I weep in the beating rain.

Ascend I the mountains with eagerness,
Hungry, and seeking my goal.
Then into barbs of stinging thorns
I fall with deluded soul.
In your shadows of dusk I tremble,
I fear death and even life.
Tomorrow I laugh, and confidence
Pervades my daily strife.
World, I am Youth, the hope of your day,
I'm bewildered and young in this land.
I'm searching your paths for a vision called truth
– Give me your hand.

Ellen Bryan

Growth

Growth is encouraged and enabled when we:
— ask the question 'Who am I?'
— are able to question
— establish a personal faith about *life* and *death*
— explore the meaning of life
— appreciate other people's philosophies and beliefs and values
— experience the sense of belonging (whether to small groups or large organizations)
— develop a firm commitment, within which discovery and exploration take place
— are valued as a person
— are listened to with respect and care
— express feelings and explore feelings (anger, joy, resentment, happiness, etc.)
— face pain and cope with isolation and alienation
— experience achievement and fulfil potential
— understand and cope with our own sexuality, and value the sexuality of others
— are at one with the environment
— value silence
— are loved and express love

Reflections

I sometimes wonder
if you see me the way
I see me?

Even when I look into a
mirror I don't see myself
as I really am because
my face is not symmetrical.

I don't know how I really
look.
Only you know.

I want to creep up
on a two-way mirror
But I've never had the guts to do it
because I will shatter
all my notions of how
I thought I looked.

But this revelation
does not worry me
that much.
I feel safe in the knowledge
that you know
how I really look
and you think I'm
beautiful.

You have not run
away from me
the way I often do.

St Mark's Sunday Club

Sin

Have you ever smelt nail varnish,
And longed to taste that same smell on your tongue?
Not clever enough to hold your nose?
Not having the strength to anyway?

Well, the smell may drive you mad,
Like the voice of the sirens,
But the taste is more foul than the
Most rotten fruit
And it in turn eats away at you
As you devour it.

An apple with a rotten core
May look sweeter than
An apple without.
But you will always tell which is more
Wholesome.

Do not fear though, for our condition
Is not permanent.
And you are by no means alone.
Love will wash away the dark
And love is God.
Just know this;
Some of us are so burnt by the acid
That we no longer feel
The pain. Help these people
To feel that pain.
So they can also feel love.

St Mark's Sunday Club

Time possesses

Time is stealing forward
        and dreams are left behind
Time I started calling

through this darkness in my mind
But life don't wait
    I'm struggling in this pain
And love is very distant
    and this day looks just the same

I've gambled with my feelings
    and not listened to my heart
I've tried to use my reason
    and lost before the start
Giving in is easy
    when I believe it's true
But simple things are hardest
    when I can't get through to you!

I think I saw you yesterday
    with hope in your eyes
I saw your hands were bleeding
    through the shreds of my disguise
Take away the fantasies
    and leave me with the pain
Then I'll look up
    and face you once again

Graham Claydon

Holy bodies

God of creation: you have given us bodies and made us for love. We pray for those who are overwhelmed by flesh or frightened by desire. Chasten all our loves, but set us free to be who we are, so we may affirm one another in bodily covenants, approved by Jesus Christ the Lord, your word and our flesh. Amen.

The Jesus Claim

Because we are human,
Because we are in need,
Because we hope,
Because we want to be different,
Because we want to change the world,
Because we look for a better country. . . .

We trust ourselves to Jesus,
We hold out our lives to Jesus,
Jesus the New Humanity,
Jesus the Converter and Healer,
Jesus the Hope of all Humanity,
Jesus the Bringer of New Wine,
Jesus the Bread of the Kingdom,
Jesus the Embodiment of God's Way.

Because God loves it all,
Because the Spirit upholds it all,
Because the Church lives for it all . . .

We bind unto ourselves this day
The strong arm of the Trinity.
We hold ourselves into this way
From now into eternity.

John Vincent
from Prayers of Methodist Conference of Britain 1989

When Maddy is good

When God made Maddy she
was as cute as can be.
and when she was seven she was
as cute as can be
and when she was helpful
she was as good as can be.

Maddy Ralls

Everyone laughed at me

I messed it all up, Lord,
and everyone laughed at me.
Why can't I say what I mean without
getting my tongue all tangled up?
I know what I mean,
but it just doesn't come out that way.
I'm being very serious
and to other people I'm funny.
Help me to choose words well,
so people will take me seriously.
One more thing, Lord –
help me laugh at my own mistakes!

Jane Graver
Based on 1 Corinthians 1:21–2:5

Rooted Joy

My heart is bubbling over with joy;
with God it is good to be woman.
From now on let all peoples proclaim:
it is a wonderful gift to be.
The one in whom power truly rests
has lifted us to praise;
God's goodness shall fall like a shower
on the trusting of every age.
The disregarded have been raised up:
the pompous and the powerful shall fall.
God has feasted the empty-bellied,
and the rich have discovered their void.
God has made good the word
given at the dawn of time.

Phoebe Willetts

Rebecca's rage

Becky is mad, with tantrum in her eyes,
fierce looks, and a hanging of her head.

She curls up tight,
ignoring my advances.

Although I am innocent of all harm,
she holds *me* accountable for her rage.
I must suffer because *she* has lost her shoe
the new one she's been using as a boat.

Oh little Becky, how like you are to me
when I in anger blame my loving father
for my sin,
and for the mess that *I* am in.

Beth Webb

Do they understand?

I know I'm not perfect,
My limbs don't obey,
Muscles in spasm,
My body a statue.
Do they understand?

Meal-time a knife slips,
Bread crushed in tense fingers,
A misjudged drink,
I drown in tea.
They must understand!

Speech so tiring,
A mumbled mass of syllables
My English,
They reply – 'What did he say?'
Don't they understand?

You might think me an imbecile
Because of these faults,
My disability is worn like a cloak:
You'll find me within.
You've got to understand!

Chris Antcliff

Fooling about in the Kingdom

As we grow we go to be educated
    we learn to analyse,
    to rationalise,
    we become reduced to our hands.
Two and two makes four
    and God is dead.
    Right is right
    and left is wrong.
We have become
    stuck
    in a sterile mind,
    dry as dust.
Part of us has died,
    The child inside
    has become repressed,
    silenced
in an alien adult world
    that is embarrassed
    by the spontaneous
    reaching out
    of love.
We live with only part
    of ourselves.

Clowns
    do not now
    nor have they ever
    obeyed
    'no trespassing' signs

that have been laid
across
forbidden places.

They come crashing
smashing
planting their feet
in the hallowed flower bed.
O unreasonable
irrational
illogical God
You who come
to fill us
with
abundant life,
Have mercy on us.
O child-like God,
Let us not
reason ourselves to death.
O God
who walked on the water,
We thank you
who make no sense to us
that you defy explanation.

Clowns
do not now
nor have they ever
obeyed
'no trespassing' signs
that have been laid
across
forbidden places.

They come crashing
smashing
planting their feet
in the hallowed flower bed

Conway Barker

What sort of woman this is

Now when the Pharisee who had invited him saw it, he said to himself, 'If this man were a prophet, he would have known who and what sort of woman this is who is touching him, for she is a sinner' (Luke 7:39:RSV).

For a number of years now
I have come to terms
(man that I am)
with the woman who is part of me.
I have learned to love her
and to say, 'Welcome, sister-within-me'.
She has a tender heart
and would rather be hurt
than hurt another.
As a priest,
I lean on her intuition,
for I have learned never to enter
a situation that does not 'feel right'.
She will not force her way in
and she rejects confrontation,
instead she will ask a sideways question
or pluck at the sleeve of one who is passing
to swing him alongside.
She has lived with me many years now
for she was, is and always
will be part of me.
When my Bishop stretched out his hands,
how much of me received the Spirit?
Some – or all?
So then,
Was she also ordained to the priesthood?

Roy Akerman

Naming names

We bring (name) who finds life hard
We bring (name) who has been made redundant
We bring (name) who has been mugged
We bring (name) whose property has been burgled
We bring (name) who never feels well
We bring (name) whose child keeps missing school
We bring (name) who has been in an accident
We bring (name) whose mother/father/child has died
We bring (name) who has heard they have a major illness
We bring (name) whose witness to truth causes suffering
We bring (name) who is wanting a partner
We bring (name) whose drug taking is taking their life
We bring (name) who hangs around with no motivation
We bring (name) who is dying
We bring (name) who needs sleep

We bring (ourselves) for strength
We bring (ourselves) for healing
We bring (ourselves) for renewal
We bring (ourselves) for today
We bring (ourselves) for tomorrow
We bring (ourselves) for always.

Tony Jasper

Other offer

All the things that make up the 'good life' – cars, clothes, records – don't keep me from dying. In fact, they don't necessarily make 'life' all that 'good'. There is more to it than that – and You offer that more.

Slightly adapted from Discovery in Prayer

Perfect peace

Others delight in length
of days;
but I –
I wait for the lover that I
long for,
Death!

prayer of Shirano, a Japanese leprosy Patient

Century mishap

In the nineteenth century
the problem was
that God is dead;
in the twentieth century
the problem is
that man is dead.

Eric Fromm in The Sane Society

Fish and chips

I like fish and chips.
They are nice and warm.
And they are nice and crunchy.
And I like the smell of salt and vinegar.
You make the chips out of potatoes
And you peel the skin and
Then you chop them up.

Paul Mettham (age six years)

True ones

(*Leader*: Let us hold before God in confidence:

the ones who laugh when we are funny,
and the ones who make us smile at ourselves;
the ones for whom we weep,

and the ones who, in joy or sorrow, weep for us;
the ones who worry that we may be lonely,
and the ones who ensure that that does not happen;
the ones who feed our minds and our bodies,
and the ones with whom we share faith and break bread;
the ones who reveal in themselves what is hidden,
and the ones who, unasked, tonight will pray for us.

And let us praise God
for the one from whom we are sent,
the one to whom we are summoned,
whose image we are,
whose flesh we share,
whose love is all.

All: Amen.

Two people could read this prayer, with all saying the lines after 'And let us praise God'.

A psalm of lament

God of the upright and forward looking
Hear the prayers of those whose lives are bent over
Listen to those who look only at the ground.

For women who are given away by their fathers
As though they owned them
And then become the property of another man
Taking his name
And losing their identity.

For women who succumb to advertisements
Of glamour and fashion
Of slim figures and sweet smells
Of expensive make up and stiletto heels
Looking for acceptance
Hoping to attract their man
and find happiness

Remove the weight of guilt

From women who considered motherhood
As the only way of finding fulfilment
To discover that it can be oppressive
Mentally stunting, physically trapping.

Lift up the women
Who thought that housework
And an immaculate home
Equalled acceptance by their husband
Admiration by their neighbours
And satisfaction for themselves
Only to discover that it can be drudgery
Boring, petty and that people are far more important.

Relieve the women whose backs are bent
By churches which do not listen to them
Or Christians who quickly label their questions and opinions
As emotional
Or feminist
Or going over the top.

Encourage those women
Who do not want to be called men
Who know they are human beings and not mankind

Who are daughters and not sons of God
who are sisters and not brothers

Offer the sight of the sun
To those women
Who understand you as mother
Who relate to you as lover
Who find joy in your partnership.

God of the upright
Lift up your daughters
To see the faces
Of their sisters and brothers
Who offer them
Your love.

Janice M. Clarke

Hair

On average we grow 120,000-odd hairs on our scalps (blondes have most, redheads fewest), nourished by the bloodstream and oiled by sebaceous glands. When we feel well our hair has the gloss of a thoroughbred horse's coat; when we feel ill, or frightened or tense it lies limp or stands on end, and stops its usual process of replacement.

Guy Mascolo and his Italian brothers have established a worldwide reputation in caring for hair. Their salons and cutting training schools are part of an overall philosophy that says hair is beautiful.

Gone are the days when a haircut was just a cut, for the new breed of hairologists talk of transforming clients, making them more beautiful and more than that, by using a psychological approach, they aim to make a client feel good as well as look good. The Toni & Guy world-famous Academy of Advanced Hairdressing at St Christopher's Place, London, tells its clients from all over the world: 'As a painter uses colours and a poet uses words, we as hairdressers use hair to create a picture of beauty.'

Guy Mascolo loves every hair of your head. You feel he looks at your crowning glory first and foremost. His customers become deceived by his easy genial manner without realising that as they pass the time of day before the so-called practicalities of shampoo, cut and blow-dry get under-way, this equable Italian is running his hands through their hair and looking at the texture, seeing whether there's a lack of life, if there's curl and bounce. He admits frankly: 'You're just chatting, she thinks anyway! What cloth is to a tailor so hair is to the real hairdresser.' He is from a family of five brothers and his father was a hairdresser so it's almost inevitable the hairdresser's son would one day think big and so he did when he and brother Toni left Italy and the Toni & Guy hairdressing world was born.

They see how hair goes with face, body and deportment. They think of the client, his or her aspirations, background, employment, even fantasies occasionally. It's not just a question of cutting with skill to get rid of split ends!

Guy says: 'You can have a hair style which is common to anyone from 15 to say 65. Of course there's a difference, maybe a little more elaborate for the younger person. But whatever is the case I talk always to people about their life-style and try and build a profile. I mean a nurse may come in and she wants the latest style but we would try and moderate it for she has to remember the hat she wears and of course she isn't allowed to wear hair down on her shoulders.'

He recalls a lady solicitor who persisted in having what she knew was contemporary for her age-group but who rather forgot the job she did.

'She had a spikey hair-style, it stuck out all over the place and looked different, shall we say! But she found herself refused admission to court. So what good was it?'

He may cut the hair of someone who is at school and then to his amusement he finds the teacher wanting similar. He says: 'Well, we do change it, a little.'

Over the years he's seen hundreds of styles come and go and seen the media create a particular style which everyone wants. Once it was the Purdy look after Joanna Lumley in the Avengers TV series. These days it's someone like Princess Diana who sets a popular fashion style.

'Some people actually produce a picture of her and say that is what they want. Others beat around the bush before they come to the point!'

Guy has particular pride that his clients vary socially. He does see the rich of London's Mayfair and there are those who can spend a few hours every day having their head attended. Models and media personalities come and so do those who party in London's clubland and want something very striking. But he also gets secretaries, shop-workers, nurses and others of average wage, for his prices are reasonable. But it is possible to spend a considerable sum of money.

So his world consists of what the trade calls dealing with controllable, shiny, lacquered, permed, full feminine hair. But these days the male is becoming very concerned how his hair looks.

Guy says: 'Men have always been concerned about their hair or at least making sure they have some up there. They can be very vain.'

Guy says there are certain basics for keeping hair well. It should be washed once a week. He warns against sprays and pleads you should read the instructions carefully and especially when colour is entertained. He says: 'Some people have seen their hair fall-out or seen horrendous colours appear.' It's not a desire for trade that makes him say, 'Go to a professional if you want a colour change.'

He suggests a cut every four to six weeks. He is a fan of the new hair gels and also has time for mousse. For Guy, as with Tony and the two other brothers involved with the business, Bruno and Anthony, every hair of your head is numbered.

That's a line culled from Jesus. Guy, his brothers and many others believe hair is beautiful, a gift to be respected as much as the body. A dowdy individual with glum face and unkempt hair is poor advertisement for a God who is associated with so much beauty in creation.

Tony Jasper

Beatitudes

Happy are those who know they are spiritually poor
– who are aware that they don't have ready answers to the big questions and are prepared to keep looking.

Happy are those who mourn
– who know that there are millions who are suffering physical or social deprivation and who ensure policies are framed primarily to benefit them.

Happy are those who are humble
– who don't see themselves as superior to others but give each person and each people an equal standing.

Happy are those whose greatest desire is to do what God requires
– who are prepared to walk by forgiveness and change their minds and ways; who look to the longer term and to the interests of all.

Happy are those who are merciful to others

– who don't see others as a market to be exploited but as partners from whom we learn.

Happy are the pure in heart
– who by concentrating on God's larger purposes are freed from   the worries and jealousies of immediate quarrels and conflicts.

Happy are those who work for peace
– who make justice and fulfilment for all their steady concern.

Happy are those who are persecuted because they do what God requires
– who are prepared to be awkward and unpopular among their peers and to let their own national interest come off second-best if that can serve the long-term good of all.

Martin Conway

The Lion Dream

Racing, the lion,
    (powerful and male, but a she)
Crosses the line into human races.

Pouring across the pavement, a flash of gold tosses
    two-legged beasts on a board of macadam.
She leaps like the sun in the trees; but a vision,
    not a ghost, or the breeze, and so the children
    go cold with fascinated watching.

Over everything she flies, galloping with gathering speed
    and soaring over heads we know and respect.
I in my car must stop at this, brakes slamming.

I am always failing, but I stand and watch her.

She races in sport, her idea of passion being to frighten accidentally.
Because she had to run, had to leap and fly over children's heads
    because she knew they needed protection if only for an instant,
    had to knock over respectable women who never looked up
    in time.

Still in my car I can only stare after her effortless glory.

I watch till my eyes open, till sights of morning steady me and
   stop me from crying out at the sight,
      help me call it only a dream and close my eyes again;
      let me carry on galloping and racing down the highway till
      I disappear.

Carol Short

The fall

This revue sketch, taken from Motive, *has two characters, Adam and the
Devil. The point of this revue is its depiction of man's love of self and his
consequent materialism.*

A: Eve . . . Eve . . . Eve . . . where ar-r-r-r-r-re you?

D: Like hi.

A: Oh! I don't believe I recall your name.

D: I'm a serpent, man.

A: Wait a minute, now I remember, I thought I named you
   'snake'. Yeah, snake. What is this insubordination?

D: Sn-a-a-ke. Ugh! I don't like it. Serpent is more Frenchy.

A: More what?

D: Like sex, man. You dig?

A: You mean Eve?

D: Yeah, she's drinking her supper.

A: Drinking?

D: Metrecal. It's a liquid diet plan – 500 calories per day – all
   measured out – no fuss, no worry – three flavours, chocolate,
   vanilla, butterscotch. She's getting fat.

A: I don't understand.

D: You know – thickening waist, spare tyre round the midriff.
   Like large man.

A: I hadn't noticed.

D: What are you, man, platonic or something?

A: He hasn't been born yet. I'm a God fan myself.

D: God? Good Lord, man, you aren't with it.

A: Why? I like him.

D: Look, since when did *that* have anything to do with the price of eggs? The question is: Is he a ***?

A: God? I don't think he has a last name.

D: It's a cinch he's not a ***. Wise up, man, you gotta consider the image. You gotta be like learned. You gotta read the right books, know the right people.

A: I don't know any people.

D: See what I mean! Leave it to me. Now, next thing is, you must look the part. Uphold the image. All right, let's see one of your suits.

A: I don't need any.

D: I don't need any, he says! Like man, do you ever want to stay here forever? You know, it's not warm everywhere in the world.

A: It's not.

D: Wouldn't you like to go on a ski-ing weekend in Switzerland?

A: I guess so, if God thinks it's okay.

D: Why keep dragging him along? I don't like him.

A: He's a nice fellow. You should get to know Him.

D: Look buster, we are on like speaking terms. So don't bug me. Now, do you shave?

A: Well . . .

D: Use deodorant? talc, vitalis? Man, and you're asking why Eve's not around. Now do you like Eve? Does she send you? Fire you up?

A: Eve is my companion and I love her.

D: But are you compatible? What sex problems do you have?

A: We never thought about it.

D: We? Well, maybe you should do a little thinking on your own. You don't talk about it together, do you?

A: No, we don't have time to talk about . . .

D: Look, man, this is an important phase of life. It is life. Maybe it's about time you started to work a few things out. It's not always money that breaks up a marriage.

A: What's money?

D: That's what you can buy things with. Anything.

A: Is there something I don't have?

D: You don't have a television set.

A: Would I like one?

D: Man, it would complete your life . . . Good for boring hours, educational, entertaining . . .

A: I'd rather talk to Eve.

D: Wait till she gets wrinkled, deaf, and has false teeth. Then we'll see.

A: We'll see.

D: Okay, I give up.

A: You do?

D: Yep. You've got real possibilities.

A: I do?

D: Right. You're a good boy. I mean that seriously, clean cut, honest, dependable, hard working, good.

A: Do you really think so?

D: Do I think so? Man, I could see you in a crowd. You'll be a leader, and yet, well modest and sincere as well.

A: Gosh, serpent (you don't mind if I call you serpent do you?), I really think you're flattering me. I do try though.

D: Sure, you try! And you do a damned good job, if I do admit it myself. I bet God is happy with you.

A: Well . . .

D: Say, Adam, you know that tree . . . ?

Anonymous

The first temptation of man

One burning day
When lilies craned their necks towards the sun
She danced for him with tambourines
Scattering demons
To shadows in the rocks.
Her arms long wrapped him round
Hair hung soft against his heart
The pale, pale neck summoning his lips
As angels watched
Breath-held against the fall of Earth.

Then through the mirage-air
The tree shook
Shedding fruits of disbelief.
Birds sang lamentation
Good and evil
Chased the other's tail around the trunk
As Adam munched.
The sourness made him wince
Her nails drew great stripes
Along his back
A thousand seeds fell into the sandy soil
Moistened by water and blood
Their mouths caverns,
Deep pools with ancient springs.

Hot embers scorched the roots
The hyssop-cup was raised again
Against the sun
The lilies bowed their heads
Afraid to look.

She broke the fall
Catching his body
In a shroud of myrrh.

Martin Eggleton

Common mistake

Men [and women] go forth to wonder
at the height of mountains,
the huge waves of the sea,
the broad flow of the ocean,
the course of the stars —
and forget
to wonder at themselves.

Augustine, Confessions X.15

Perfect grip

Where could I go
to escape from your Spirit?
Where could I get away from
your presence?
If I went up to heaven,
You would be there . . .
If I flew beyond the east
or lived in the
farthest place in the west,
You would be there to lead me,
You would be there
to help me.

Psalm 139: 7–10

Must wait

Lord, all my longing is known to thee,
  my sighing is not hidden from thee,

My heart throbs, my strength fails me;
  and the light of my eyes – it also has gone from me,

I am like a deaf man [woman], I do not hear,
  like a dumb man [woman] who does not open his mouth.

But for thee, O Lord, do I wait;
  it is thou, O Lord my God, who wilt answer.

More words about ourselves and faith:

Words about relationships

Bible passages:

Isaiah 54
Malachi 5
John 17:9–26
1 John 3:13–18

There is nothing in this volume that suggests the Christian can choose to remain uninvolved and distant from the lot of travelling humankind. To be sure, the individual makes a personal response to the Gospel, and has a right to pray for self amid the demands of the Kingdom and the ever-present cry of the Jesus prayer, 'not my will but yours'. But there is much more. Beyond an individual's ever insistent search for true integrity, there is the pressing need for company, the meeting of people as they too struggle to be born, to find meaning, shape and purpose, and so invite participation and sharing.

American Christian educationalist Ross Snyder has said, 'Fellowship is not merely liking each other, but common possession of significant culture!' Perhaps it is the latter that holds some groups together, for often in churches and Christian gatherings people are at odds with people, and mutual love is not an easy practice. Prayer is needed in the community of Christian to develop both levels of relationship.

Making peace through justice

Leader: God of all salvation, through your Son,
Who is the breaking in of your purpose
in time and space,
you have shattered the walls
that divided us as man and woman.
In Christ you now show us there is no male or female.

People: You formed us in your image,
creating us male and female.
You shape our union and harmony.
In this wondrous way you call us
to share the fullness of your own being,
your knowledge and your bliss.

Leader: Having all been made one through our peacemaker
People: Let us live together in peace and justice.

Peace plan

Lord, make our hearts abodes of peace
and our minds harbours of tranquillity.
Sow in our souls true love for you and for one another
and root deeply within us friendship and unity,
and concord with reverence,
that we may give peace to each other sincerely
and receive it beautifully.

Anonymous

Open arms

In your open arms,
The love of God shines.

St Hippolytus, third century

Nearest tensions

We pray for our families,
with whom we live day by day.
May this most searching test of our character
not find us broken and empty.
By all that we do and say
help us to build up the faith and confidence of those we love.
When we quarrel, help us to forgive quickly.
Help us to welcome new members
into our families, without reserve,
and not to neglect those
who in our eyes have become
less interesting or demanding.

Caryl Micklem

Kids warning

For all children in danger from poverty – Lord, hear our prayer.
In danger from homelessness or bad housing – Lord, hear our prayer.
In danger from committing crime – Lord, hear our prayer.
In danger from drug and solvent abuse – Lord, hear our prayer.
In danger from unemployment – Lord, hear our prayer.
In danger from sickness and handicap – Lord, hear our prayer.
In danger from inappropriate custody – Lord, hear our prayer
In danger from battering Lord, hear our prayer.
In danger from abduction – Lord, hear our prayer.
In danger from sexual abuse – Lord, hear our prayer.
In danger from alcohol – Lord, hear our prayer.
In danger from neglect – Lord, hear our prayer.
In danger from marriage breakdown – Lord, hear our prayer.
In danger from violence – Lord, hear our prayer.
In danger from running away from home – Lord, hear our prayer.

From Prayers for the National Children's Home

A litany

Lord God, hear our prayers for all people:

> For those who feel betrayed by their friends and abandoned by their families, and for those who feel abandoned by You.
> For those who wait with uncertainty for the results of tests or diagnoses,
> For those who as a result of HIV infection are ostracised, unemployed or homeless,

Lord, in your mercy . . . *Hear our prayer.*

> For those who seek to comfort and care for those with AIDS,
> For loved ones who share risk, alienation and loneliness,
> For those who grieve,

Lord, in your mercy . . . *Hear our prayer.*

We give you thanks, O God, through our Lord Jesus Christ who, though He was rich, for our sakes became poor, taking our nature upon himself, humbling himself, being obedient to death, even death on a cross;

We thank you that, as we accept His love and forgiveness, through His grace,

> Though we are broken *we are made whole*,
> Though we have fallen *we are lifted up*,
> Though we have sinned *we are forgiven, loved and free*.

Though we have nothing, in His name we have all things; for You have exalted Him to your right hand in glory and we trust that You will also raise us up,

> from sorrow *to joy*,
> from doubt *to certainty*,
> from pain *to peace*,
> from death *to eternal life*.

For in the depths of our deepest betrayal you have identified with
us, in Christ, and we thank you.
Amen.

Andrew Pratt

God, you are Love

God, you are Love,
and reveal yourself through loving relationships,
you make women and men in your own image,
and invite them to bear your own likeness.
In motherly love you bring us to birth,
nourishing, sustaining us before we comprehend,
so you teach us the depth and strength of love.
From the protection of fatherly love
you teach us to use the amazing gift of life
and we learn that power is for caring.
In sisters and brothers you are beside us in all our explorings,
deepen our longing to be at home with you.

Rosemary Wakelin

Bring us together

Lord Jesus Christ!
We have lost contact again –
a husband and wife
who love and live
together –
sit, speak, eat, sleep
together –

we have disconnected ourselves
and left each other alone.

We push words at each other,
but there is no response.
We eat our food together
for the sake of habit and health,

but there is no communion.
We perform our duties and services
for those who depend on our activity,
but there is no blessing.
We give ourselves to each other,
and even this is a complaint,
and it is difficult to sleep.

Lord Jesus Christ,
forgive my foolishness,
my pride, my silence.

I will go to him now and touch him.
I will put my hand in his,
and I will say the difficult words,
'Forgive me,' and, 'I forgive you.'

I need love to do this, Lord Jesus,
the kind of love You give me.

It will not be enough this time
to remain silent,
to take these words for granted.

Lord Jesus Christ,
this is the word You gave us to say
aloud – to each other –
'by Your command and in Your stead.'

Praises be! I don't have to depend
on my undependable moods and feelings.
Your love covers us and connects us again.

Anne Springsteen

More words about relationships:

Words of forgiveness

Bible passages:

Isaiah 53:11–12
Mark 1:14–15
Luke 7:37–38, 48–50
John 20:21–23
Colossians 3:1–2
1 Timothy 6:11–12, 14
1 John 3:18–20

We pray each day, each week, year by year of our lives, as individuals, as a community, the words Jesus taught: 'Forgive us our trespasses'. There are words for just such moments in this and other sections of this book.

We know how often we fall short of the life we would lead, how we fail to witness to the demands and ultimate partying of the Kingdom. Some would intensify things much more by reminding us, as Evelyn Underhill expressed it in her book *Worship*, of God 'the Wholly Good, setting a standard of holiness, and convicting man of sin: and a step forward is taken in that total sanctification and redemption of experience, which is the manward aim of worship. Before Him the seraphim veil their faces; yet He asks for the willing and open-eyed co-operation of imperfect men.' But this is language rarely heard in mainstream evangelical preaching and witness.

Gerard Hughes in his memorable book *God Of Surprises* is hardly the first, nor will he be the last, to pose the deeply felt dichotomy between what we know and see in ourselves, and the words we pray. Praying people can be intolerant, inhuman and cruel, and this, Hughes would argue, is mainly because such individuals are

afflicted by the temptation of pride, of wishing to create God in
our own image.

Most of the aspects of faith covered in this volume can suffer
from this and other temptations, for we can suffocate belief in
God, Jesus, Holy Spirit; may kill life at birth, hinder another's
faith, stifle hopes for wholeness. Always we need grace to forgive
others who surely are hardly worse than ourselves.

Unlimited Amens

All: If we blunder many times
Males: Bless us and forgive us
Females: Bless us and forgive us
All: If we fight or sulk or even yell
All: Bless us till we change

All on left of pulpit/lectern: Bless us everywhere
All: At home or in the world at large
Males: Help us see the cross of Christ
Females: And help us that cross to bear
Males: And help us that cross to bear

All: And if we sneeze in Jesus' name,
Males: Bless us just the same
Females: Bless us just the same

All: Amen, O Lord, and then
Once more, Amen, Amen!

Prayer of confession

God our Creator,
we come to confess that we have failed:
we have not made room for sisters
and brothers to be themselves;
we have rejected the space you have
made for us,
and clung to the narrow limits
imposed by false expectations;

we have treated with distaste the
delicate, beautiful workings of our bodies.

For our failure to accept what we are,
our refusal to allow our bodies to
speak to our minds and our spirits,
our inability to cope with being
made in the image of God –

Gracious and accepting God, forgive us.

For our failure to accept the pain of others,
our refusal to stand alongside the
hurt of other women,
our timidity and cowardice in the
face of opposition and evil.

Gracious and accepting God, forgive us.

Help us to start again,
accepting with
joy our whole humanity, made in
your image,
so that we may offer our
mind, spirit, and body
to be a living
sacrifice to your glory. Amen.

Consultation of Methodist women ministers, Oxford 1984

Plea for non-economical integrity

Heavenly Father,

Please forgive us for those times when we have been insensitive, inconsiderate, sinful and un-Christlike in our treatment of other people.

Please help us always to see people as being made in your image, unique, special and of immeasurable value.

Please help us to reflect that truth in the way we behave to others, the way we act in society, and the way we use our time, our energy and our possessions.

Prayer at Spring Harvest, 1987

My body

I know You created my body
and it's good.
Holy, even.
But those kids at school make bodies seem dirty.
I don't know what to do when they talk that way.
Sometimes I find myself joining them
thinking as they do
making a dirty joke out of something that should be clean
and beautiful.
Forgive me, God.
Fill my body with Your Spirit.

Jane Graver
Based on 1 Corinthians 6: 18–20

Thick skins for instant peeling

O God our father, who has made us to live together in love as
brothers and sisters; we confess that we have failed to love one
another. We have seen our brother's our sister's success as our
own failure and their fulfilment as our own despair.

Wrapped up in ourselves we have been afraid to reach out,
and we have been afraid of our brother's response because we
don't have faith in our brother's love. Forgive our disobedience,
O God, and help us be courageous enough to believe that we can
love and help produce love in others, so that we may serve you
and live together. Through Jesus Christ our Lord. Amen.

Mistaken flouting

God of mercy, hear us!
We have betrayed you,
And have not listened to your voice,
Nor followed the laws you gave us;
We have become a byword among all around us.

But now, Lord, listen to the prayer for your
servants.
For your own sake, Lord,
Let your face smile again on your desolate people.

Listen, Lord!
Lord, forgive!
Hear, Lord, and act!
For the Gospel's sake do not delay,
Because we bear your name,
We are your people.
God of mercy, hear us!
Through Jesus Christ our Lord. Amen

Power to forgive

(*For four speakers*)

Bearer: All round the house the crowd was thick;
             all round the house the lame and sick.
Paralytic: Capernaum village buzzed with talk;
             the deaf could hear, the lame could walk.
             Forgive us, heal us, make us whole.
Bearer: Jesus' followers packed the place,
             hung on his words and left no space.
Paralytic: No space for sick men, anywhere near.
             Waiting and longing, we strained to hear.
             Forgive us, heal us, make us whole.
Bearer: Four of us carried the paralysed man;
             swinging the litter, we eagerly ran.
Paralytic: Baulked at the front door, one of them spied
             stairs to the roof-top, round at the side.
             Forgive us, heal us, make us whole.
Bearer: Straining, striving, jolting him there,
             step by step we climbed the stair.
Paralytic: Up on the roof, the Master's voice
             sounded a gentle, murmuring noise.
             Forgive us, heal us, make us whole.
Bearer: Down below, the expectant crowd,

the simple souls, the learned proud.

Paralytic: All absorbed, till the roof gave way.
Down I went, and there I lay.
    Forgive us, heal us, make us whole.

Lawyer: Helpless there in the dust he lies;
fastening Jesus with his eyes.

Paralytic: How will he treat this shameless one?
Listen:

Jesus: Your sins are forgiven, my son.
    Forgive us, heal us, make us whole.

Bearer: Consternation to the proud!
The learned lawyers gasp aloud,
Quibble, grumble, take it amiss.

Lawyer: It's blasphemy to talk like this!
    Forgive us, heal us, make us whole.

Jesus: Which is the easier thing to say:
'Your sins are forgiven'? or 'Go away,
you paralysed man, pick up your bed
and walk'? Isn't it easily said?
    Forgive us, heal us, make us whole.

Lawyer: Truly, easier said than done.
Sin can be secret; sickness is known.

Jesus: You know you're forgiven. Listen to me:
pick up your bed. Go home. You're free.
    Forgive us, heal us, make us whole.

Paralytic: I stood on my feet in front of them all,
rolled up the litter and walked from the hall.

Jesus: Now you see that the man can walk,
you know he's forgiven; it's no mere talk.
    Forgive us, heal us, make us whole.

Bearer: Simple and learned, all amazed,
we could only stammer:

Lawyer: God be praised!
Such power in men!

Bearer: We were thrilled to the core.

Lawyer: We never saw the like of this before!
    Forgive us, heal us, make us whole.

All: The Lord who set the paralysed free

is the Man of men for you and me.
He forgives our sins; his healing power
is ours for every day and hour.
Forgive us, heal us, make us whole.

Sudden awakening

God
forgive
God
deliver us
God
save us
God stop us
from being so self-centred
when
sometimes life is just
too much of nothing

for how can we say that?
the privileged people
the over-fed people
the over-moneyed people
the over-travelled people
the over-dressed people
the over-loved people
the over-warm people

God forgive
God
deliver us
God
kick us up the backside
right now

Tony Jasper

More words of forgiveness:

Words of pain and suffering

Bible passages:

Psalm 9:10–11, 19
Psalm 71
Psalm 106:20–21
Matthew 10:17–20, 26–27
Romans 5:1–5
Romans 8:38–39
Revelation 21:1–5

Christian worship that is true to Scripture offers to God both a community's joy and the bitterness of sorrow, and a group of God's people will wish to widen its horizons and encompass a larger world.

By its very nature the Christian place is a centre of both celebration and tears. Underpinning the ultimate offering of all life is the Gospel's assertion that evil is not finally and forever itself, but it can and will be made into good. Much joy has already been expressed in preceding sections, but many of these shouts have been laced in varying spiritual alcoholic strength with the awareness that joy is a fragile thing. In reality pain and suffering are often its close companion.

Here are the words of those who have heard, felt, and ultimately survived the numbing effects of our theme. There is little dispassionate expression – how can there be? But our aim is not to push those with pains and sufferings out into a special category, for they belong with those who are well.

Right direction

Living Lord – we cry:
who can interpret the news
who can make sense of the flood of news that comes our way
who can sense what shape history is taking
who can sense the shape of history and see future?

Loving Lord –
within the events of every day there is struggle
each and every day people fight for the right and good
with the time of each day there is so much destruction
each and every day people defy overwhelming odds.

Healing Lord –
Use us to remove brutality, sordidness and impotent
   goodness
Use us to make history and future
Use us to encourage growth and maturity amongst those lacking
   hope.

Living Lord –
remove from us feelings of fatalism
teach us that we can be true to your Gospel where we are
may we express care and feeling for people and life
let us radiate even a quarter of your loving intensity

Living, loving and Healing Lord –
We praise you.

Tony Jasper

Aids victim

Positive, there's no doubt.
The confirmation set him back
Ten years or more
To rendezvous in pubs,
Dark mats and soft lights

Above the fruit machine
Where whisperings and beer
Frothed his downfall.

Trips to see the sea on Sunday,
Waffles and saunterings
Down the cobbled streets
Back to his place.
Touchings, women's gestures,
Strutting peacocks around the television
Until their love collapsed
On the carpet.

The agony came later,
Guilt locked in an earring,
Unsaid sins from childhood
Festooned upon his face,
A sign of love
Pinned on the nurse's breast
Gave him water when he called.
And in the night
She listened to it all.
Like Mary, she had the better part.

Martin Eggleton

Nearness of tears and laughter

God weeps with us
so that we may one day laugh with Him.
You do not have to sit outside in the dark.
If, however, you want to look at the stars,
you will find that darkness is required.
The stars neither require it nor demand it.

In spite of

I understand you, Christ,
because I know betrayal and the spear,
because, like you, I say
I am king and claim my crown.

I ask to be a monarch of my own destiny
and father of all children,
I desire emancipation for myself and brothers.

I demand a sceptre for a poor and earthly kingdom,
but dignified and free,
built by the brotherhood of creative hands
in a community of equality and historic prophecy.

That sceptre is mine and I claim it today,
because what I stand for is greater
than the cross I carry,
because my cheeks are tired of the Pharisee's blows
and my arm is asking for the whip,

And when the 'whip' of the whip is silent
and the temple empty of merchants,
then the thorns, the hate and the vinegar,
the scoffing and weeping will be changed into
a welcome to the repentant centurion,
into kindness, poetry, and work,
because the man brought back to life
is always incarnating himself in his children . . .
and Christian hope has the face of a child.

Poem by a political prisoner in a Chilean concentration camp

Never forgotten

Lord Jesus,
you experienced in person
torture and death
as a prisoner of conscience.

You were beaten and flogged,
and sentenced to an agonising death
though you had done no wrong.
Be now with prisoners of conscience
throughout the world.
Be with them in their fear and loneliness,
in the agony of physical and mental torture,
and in the face of execution and death.
Stretch out your hands in power
to break their chains.
Be merciful to the oppressor and the torturer,
and place a new heart within them.
Forgive all injustice in our lives,
and transform us to be
instruments of your peace,
for by your wounds we are healed.

Amnesty International

Beyond crass nationalism

The blessing of the most holy Trinity
    God unbegotten
    God incarnate
    God among us
Keep us now and for evermore

Spoken at Greenham Common, Women's Agape, August 1985

Painful remembrance

Three long years.
I remember them in my heart.
It was a dark, dark night
Without a single star in the sky.
Intimidation, threat and isolation,
Torture, insult, and sarcasm
Were my constant companions.
Trials were open but ridden with bias.

Rampant in prison was political discrimination,
Dear ones were torn apart north and south.
Blessed that the Lord was my Refuge . . .

Remembering brothers and sisters still in prison,
Sorrow and pain are beyond words.
May the Spirit of the Lord be with them
And rescue them from the pit of suffering,
Enabling them to sing with us hymns of praise
With one heart giving glory to the Saviour Lord.
Wake up, O people of this land!
For our future and our destiny
Let us rouse ourselves and struggle together,
Water our own soil and fields
Bearing fruit of freedom, democracy, and human rights.

*Hsu T'ien-Hsien was pastor of Lim-a-lai Presbyterian Church in Tainan,
Taiwan. He was arrested for his participation in the Human Rights Day
Rally in December 1979, and sentenced to three years' imprisonment. During
a thanksgiving service for his release and return, he read some words entitled
'On Leaving Prison', from which this is taken.*

Another Voice

God whose holy name defies our definition,
but whose will is known in freeing the oppressed,
make us to be one with all who cry for justice;
that we who speak your praise may struggle for your truth,
through Jesus Christ. Amen.

No turning back

O God,
Our suffering sigh in heaven is heard
and faith in you will ease all pain.
We shall not give up!

O Christ Jesus,
We know that you are alive in all of us.

You strengthen us by your own journey to Calvary.
We shall not give up!

O Holy Spirit,
You give us hope and courage.
We shall not give up!
We shall continue to live in hope.
Help us in our struggle to live in hope.
Help us in our struggles for daily bread.
Help us in our struggles for justice and peace.

Gershon Anderson

A city's grief

May 1985 saw a celebration football game turn into an inferno. Fire swept through the stand at the Bradford City football ground. Many died and countless people suffered injury. Groups of rescue workers came from many agencies. This is one account of how some Methodist Christians found the disaster affecting their community.

Later, a massive programme of after-care was offered to survivors.

Prayers were said in Methodist churches throughout Bradford and West Yorkshire as the full horror emerged of the celebration game that turned into an inferno at Bradford City football ground. As the death toil mounted, it became apparent that several Methodists had died in the blaze and others had managed to scramble to safety.

Many more who were at the game found themselves eye witnesses to the horrific scenes which became a conflagration, engulfing hundreds in seconds.

Two days afterwards the words 'tragedy' and 'horror' seemed meaningless and banal to describe the sheer scale of anguish and grief being experienced by the Bradford community, but Methodist ministers throughout the Bradford area met in manses and churches in attempts to co-ordinate the practical and pastoral help necessary to comfort the bereaved and help the injured.

The Chairman of the West Yorkshire District, the Rev John Atkinson, was at the football ground in Valley Parade at 9 am on Sunday with a message of sympathy for the club chairman and offers of pastoral and practical help where necessary. 'This is the most terrible and horrendous disaster,' Mr Atkinson told the Methodist Recorder. 'It should have been such a bright day of celebration but instead it ended in anguish, grief and tragedy,' he said. (The game had been in celebration of the Club's promotion to Division Two of the Football League.)

Ministers throughout the Bradford circuits had their own accounts of the horror and of the immense pastoral task now facing the churches of all denominations in the city. There were individual tales of death and injury, of near escape and of heroism in the disaster – the scale of which was still difficult to comprehend the following Monday, when it emerged that at least five people with Methodist connections had perished in the blaze and were unaccounted for, and another had died in hospital later.

A teenage member of the Aldersgate church, Bradford, Moira Hodgson – 16 the week of the fire – was in charge of catering arrangements at the rear of the doomed stand. She was doing the work for pocket money and ran back to the till to retrieve the afternoon's takings. She was not seen again. Her father is a member of the choir at Aldersgate church.

A Girl's Brigade officer at Cutler Heights church in the Bradford (Trinity) circuit, Mandy Roberts, who was in her 20s, was at the match with her mother and boyfriend. They held hands as they began to escape – but Mandy disappeared and was not seen again. Her mother and boyfriend survived.

Two former members of Thorpe church in the Woodhouse Grove circuit – Mr and Mrs Fred Hindley, keen Bradford City supporters, both died in the blaze. Mrs Edith Hindley was a member of the Bradford Women's Luncheon Club, while a member at the Clayton church in the Great Horton circuit, Mrs Francis Crabtree, lost her husband.

Mr Samuel Firth, whose daughter attends Ebenezer church, Bradford, died in hospital on Saturday evening.

Among those known to have scrambled to safety was Mr Harry Briggs, a member of Trinity church, who was in the stand cheering one minute and running for his life the next. He was uninjured. A member of the Great Horton church, unnamed but known to be in his 70s, was pulled out of the blaze to safety by the police.

A member of the Bradford police force and on duty at the ground was clearly seen on the television screen running across the pitch with his hair on fire. He is David Britton, a member of St Andrew's church, Undercliffe, thankfully, he was later reported to be without serious injury.

The first Methodist minister on the scene was the Rev Leslie Shaw, Free Church chaplain to Bradford Royal Infirmary. He was returning home from a visit to a local garden centre when he spotted the stand beginning to burn. 'It was absolutely horrific the speed at which the fire moved – in seconds the stand was ablaze from end to end,' he told the Recorder, adding, 'There were over 3,000 people in that stand and it is a miracle more were not killed.'

Mr Shaw went immediately to the Infirmary and spent time with the fire victims in the casualty department and on the wards as they were being admitted and treated. He described the scene: 'People were in a state of shock, desperately looking for signs of relatives known to have been at the match. It was very upsetting to witness their anguish as they searched for their loved ones.'

Mr Shaw said there was also concern for those apparently uninjured in the disaster, but who witnessed the dreadful scenes. 'These people will take longer to recover – they have been internally scarred by the panic and horror,' he said. He went on to pay tribute to the 'magnificent job' done by the police, fire services and hospitals.

The Rev Derek Hoe, if he had not had other commitments, would have been in the stricken stand with his son, Andrew. Andrew went to the game with a friend and his friend's father. They watched from another area of the ground. Mr Hoe, a minister in the Trinity circuit and an industrial chaplain, watched from his study window as the black cloud of smoke billowed in the air. As soon as he realized the full extent of the tragedy, he went to the main St Luke's Hospital, where he spent most of Saturday evening amid scenes of 'unimaginable grief, anguish and distress'.

Recounting the scenes at the hospital, Mr Hoe described the sense of hopelessness felt by many people. 'They were out of their minds with desperation,' he said, 'totally grief-stricken and all

I could do was to be there to offer a shoulder to cry on and to offer love, care and support to all who had suffered loss.' On the following Monday only one person had been positively identified and Mr Hoe said then that there were many families in Bradford who would have to come to terms with the fact that a member of their family had left home to watch the match and had not returned. There was nothing more to go on. Because of the intensity of the blaze identification in many cases was impossible.

Mr Hoe went on to say that ministers were now in the position of having to wait to respond to the needs as they emerged. The whole of the city was in a state of 'stunned shock' at the horror of the weekend events. Nevertheless, he concluded, out of the horror there was emerging a 'real sense of togetherness' in the suffering being experienced.

It was the consensus of the ministers to whom the Recorder spoke on Monday, however, that the pastoral work in the aftermath of the tragedy had not yet really begun. Those injured being treated in hospital were visited through the normal chaplaincy channels but for some time ahead it was foreseen that individuals and families whose loved ones have perished will need love, support and practical help over many months. The biggest problem will be identifying those in need who are unconnected with the churches.

A service was held in Bradford Cathedral on the Sunday afternoon following the fire at which the Bishop of Bradford, the Rt Rev Roy Williamson, said the city was shocked and numbed by grief. The Provost, the Very Rev Brandon Jackson, said that in a small city, everybody knew everybody else. 'All of us will know someone who has been affected by this tragedy. Go, and minister to them, don't leave them in the anguish of their bereavement,' he said.

Avril Bottoms

A litany of intercession

For the reconciliation of humankind through the revolution of
non-violent love: WE CALL ON THE SPIRIT.

For the established churches that they may be humbled, reformed,
and united:

For the global movement of peace and liberation, the church
of Jesus incognito:

For all poor and hungry, migrant workers and hobos, outcast
and unemployed:

For the people of the streets and ghettos, for children unwanted
in their homes:

For the wounded, for prisoners and exiles, all those persecuted
for conscience or resistance:

For victims of discrimination, harassment and brutality:

For the sick and suffering in mind and body, for those freaked out
on drugs or fear:

For all oppressors, exploiters and imperialists, that they may
be confused and disarmed by love:

For the masters of war, N N and N, that they may be given
a new transplant in place of their heart of stone:

For uptight authorities, police and officials, especially N and
N that they may all listen to the voice of
the humble and
meek:

For all whom we fear, resent, or cannot love; for the unlovable:

For the liberation of our twisted lives, for the opening of
closed doors:

For those who are dying and have died, whether in bitterness
or tranquillity:

For doctors, nurses, and social workers, for ministers to the
poor:

For organisers, students, and writers, all who raise the cry
for justice:

For all who are close to us, here and in every place:

That all couples may realize their union with

the universal
flow of love:
That our tables may be spread with the natural
fruits of the
earth:
That our grandchildren may inherit a restored planet:
That we may have desire to study the books of ancient
wisdom:
That people's revolution everywhere may become humanised
and democratic:
That each one who enters our house may receive the
hospitality due the Christ whom he bears:
That with compassion and fidelity we may work for renewal
to our life's end:
In thanksgiving for all who have turned away from
exploitation, especially N:
In thanksgiving for all who have been freed
from the prisons
of this world, especially N: WE CALL
ON THE SPIRIT
Here the leader shall ask for free intercession from the people.
When they are finished, the Deacon shall conclude:
We call on the Spirit to bind us in solidarity with all who are
using their lives to resist evil and affirm community:
WE CALL ON THE SPIRIT.

From A Covenant of Peace: A Liberation Prayer Book

This powerful litany dates from the late 1960s. Establish a rhythm in its
saying and encourage loud shouts of We call on the spirit.

Where the letter N is used, introduce relevant places and people from
current events.

Say what you mean

(For three performers. 1 is a radio commentator, 2 is a man/woman in the street, 3 is an expert.)

1: Today the latest unemployment figures were published. In the last month they have risen by over 15,000, which is an increase of about half a percentage point – if my pocket calculator is to be trusted. Of course, these figures have to be seen in their proper perspective, bearing in mind seasonal adjustments, year on year trends, regional variations, and the overseas trade balance . . . all of which leaves me a good deal more confused than I was before.

2: Me too – and I'm one of the 15,000.

1: Well, perhaps we should turn to our expert in these matters. Can you help us?

3: I shouldn't think so for a moment, but I'm prepared to try. You see, the best way to look at it is not to consider the rise as a rise, but as a negative fall. Then you look at that negative fall and realize that the rate of negative fall is actually falling, and that the fall in the rate of negative fall is falling faster than the falling rate of comparative negative fall recorded between periods of positive fall, especially when the statistical data is adjusted to take into account similar falls in the barometric pressure, the thickness of the polar icecap, and the average height of skirts above the knee in the suburban districts of Greater Manchester.

2: Excuse me – does that mean I'm unemployed or not?

3: If you'd been listening, you would have heard me just now conclusively proving that you can't be.

2: Thank you very much. I'm sorry to be a nuisance – I was just confused by the fact that I don't have a job. (*Leaves.*)

3: You know, it's people who confuse things. It's so much easier when you can keep your mind on the figures and forget about all these individuals who keep getting in the way and complicating the issues.

1: Perhaps it might help if we presented a brief glossary of commonly-used phrases and their real meanings. Here goes. In this time of economic crisis . . .

3: I've got the figures wrong again.
1: The spirit that made Britain great . . .
3: Things are getting worse.
1: At this particular, present moment in time . . .
3: Now.
1: When the economic recovery curve makes an upswing . . .
3: Never.
1: We intend to make a significant contribution . . .
3: Be thankful for small mercies.
1: I have it on the very best authority . . .
3: A little bird told me.
1: It is absolutely clear to all intelligent people . . .
3: In my opinion.
1: I can see your point of view . . .
3: You're wrong.
1: The future is full of hope . . .
3: We're as confused as you are.
1: The under-privileged of our society . . .
3: (*Turning to 1*): Who?
(*They leave.*)

Peter English

Graffiti

I believe in the sun
    even when it is not shining.

I believe in love
    even when I feel it not.

I believe in God
    even when he is silent.

(*found on a concentration camp wall*)

Junkies at the circus

sickness of loving and life drifts misunderstood
blanketing the everlasting frustration of our dreams –
red orange then green
slowly it grinds to a start again
into the darkening London night . . .

my heart moans on the pavement
nauseous the needle drives its course
bliss of oblivion rises up to sweetly submerge once more –
junkies at the circus are all alone
and the London dead crawl on

The forgotten people

They found the body of a traveller today
in the boiler-house of a school;
they found the body of a tramp today
huddled beneath a railway arch;
they found the body of an alcoholic today
lying flat out on a park bench;
they found the body of a missing teenager today
still wrapped in its cardboard box;
they found the body of an old woman today
in the corner of a multi-storey car-park;
they found the body of a young prostitute today
behind the screens of the cricket pitch;
they found the body of a drug addict today
surrounded by needles and sugar-lumps
and polythene bags;
they found the body of Christ today
hanging on a Cross.

And some of these bodies they carried away
and some they left undisturbed.
A few of these bodies showed signs of life . . .
They had not died yet; they meant to arise . . .

And to haunt those who worried
only when they moved . . .
and those who passed by
when they didn't move.

O God, when *You* found our bodies
were our hearts already frozen?

Godfrey Holmes

God of whoever

God of the city, God of the tenement and the houses of the rich,
God of the subway and the night club, God of the cathedral and
the streets, God of the sober and the drunk, the junkie and the
stripper, the gambler and the faithful parent: dear God, help us
to see the world and its children through your eyes, and to love
accordingly.

Monica Furlong

God-in-a-box

She passed the convent every day,
and genuflected outside the chapel,
for God was in there,
in a gilded box.

She passed the homeless every day
but did not genuflect.
She did not notice
that God was there,
in a cardboard box.

Beth Webb

Urban aid

Lord of our city, we bring you its pain,
The muggings, the dole queues, the lifts bust again,
The fear of each stranger and nowhere to play,

The waiting for buses at the start of each day.

Lord of the homeless, we bring you their cry,
The waiting on promises – pie in the sky –
The red tape and questions and sent on their way,
The sense of frustration at the noon of the day.

Lord of all peoples, all colours of skin,
Please make us fight racism, help us begin
To see how our prejudice colours the way
We treat friends and neighbours at the end of the day.

Lord of our whole lives, we bring them to you,
We're powerless, defeated, 'til you make us new,
Then powered by your Spirit, we go on once more
With news of your wholeness, Good News for the Poor.

Jane Galbraith

*Although written as a hymn (sung to the tune 'Slane'), this serves well as
a prayer for saying by all; or precede each verse with a visual (slide, poster,
set of photographs), then all present pray the verse.*

Papering over

These high echoing chambers
Hold dusty references to
A thousand paper wars;
It is surprising to find
These white papers so clean,
These revolutions so pristine,
So unmarked by their contents . . .
All so quietly and logically marked,
Discussed, deplored, voted on, and
Filed away.

*The passing and shuffling of papers has become part and parcel of many
people lost in bureaucratic structures, often with deadening impact upon those
whom the system should serve. This peace poem comes from the Bulletin of
the European Youth Centre.*

Putting a figure on it
A story from the last days in Jerusalem.

And Judas, the one called Iscariot, who kept the disciples' purse, came to Jesus that evening.

'Master,' he began, 'I was struck by what you said in the Temple. Do your remember the poor widow who put such a tiny amount in the box for offerings but whom you said gave more than the rest because she gave all she had? Could you not re-tell that story when you are preaching?

'And why should I do that Judas?'

'Well, it would be an excellent way of reminding our richer supporters of their responsibilities. Indeed, in the re-telling, you could make more of the fact that the rich had effectively given less than the widow and needed to give a lot more to bring themselves up to her level.'

'But I only mentioned her,' said Jesus, 'so that you would be reminded not to judge by appearances. So that you would remember to give as much respect to a poor widow as you would to the richest lord.

'Poor widows don't pay the disciples' bills,' muttered Judas. 'I'm not saying anything against poor people, you understand, it's simply that we do need to impress upon our wealthy friends just how large our outgoings are, these days.'

'Are we in debt?' asked Jesus.

'No, but think how much easier it would be if we could find a way, for example, to insist on a minimum contribution just as the Temple can.'

The Lord's eyes seemed to darken a little then and his voice was sad when he spoke.

'What about the new ways, Judas? Where would the freedom be that we have spoken about? If people are not moved by love to give, why should we attempt to move them at all?'

The words were met by an awkward, uncomfortable silence. Outside, some distance away, there was the sound of soldiers marching and a guard changing.

'We have enough to live on,' continued Jesus. 'We have good

friends in spite of all that has happened. Tell me, how much more do we need?'

Judas drew in a short breath.

'It's not easy to put a figure on it but I suppose we could do with an additional, say, thirty pieces of silver.'

Dave Kitchen

Good Enough For Anyone

Look at them? Do they seem odd to you? Do they seem any different from anyone else's hands? A little rougher they may be. A little more calloused and marked than if I were a fine gentleman, I grant you that. But they are ordinary human hands.

You wouldn't think it from the way the people like me are treated. If we had leprosy, I could understand it. If we had any disease that made people frightened and concerned. But we don't. All we have is sheep.

Somebody's got to look after them. The silly creatures would get everywhere if we weren't there to keep an eye on them. If the priests didn't have their lambs for Temple worship there would be all kinds of trouble. They want the sheep, right enough. But they don't want us. We are . . . what is the phrase? – 'ritually unclean'. It means we're not good enough to get anywhere near God. I think it does anyway. I'm certain of what it means in practice. We're shut out: all right for hillsides and market places, no good for worship or the better parts of life.

I ask you: how can the lamb be suitable for God and the person who has cared for it twenty four hours a day be unsuitable?

I know what the priests would say. They'd wave their hands about and declare that they didn't write the Law of Moses and it wasn't their fault. Well, let me tell you, it's the priests who interpret the law of Moses and it's the priests who tell us what it's supposed to mean.

I don't believe there's anything wrong with what Moses said. I say it's what the priests have done with it. I can't read all that well but you don't have to be very bright to understand what has happened in this land. Would Moses, who was a shepherd himself, have excluded shepherds from the most precious and most sacred parts of our faith? Of course, he wouldn't. He would have said that people like shepherds come first.

But we don't these days. We come last if we come anywhere at all. Do I sound angry? I suppose I do. My father Jethro always used to call me his little old radical. He was happy with his lot. Even as a child, I was the one who wanted to change things. I swore that, when I grew up, I would be the one who made the break and went to work in the city. The reality was that I became a shepherd like my father and grandfather before me. On the hillsides I discovered plenty of radical talk, not a lot of radical action. We all knew what was wrong, we were all too busy to put it right. When shepherds were putting the world to rights around a fire of an evening, Manasseh, who was older than the rest of us, would say: 'What do you think God would do?'

Until last year, I had no good answer for him. Then something broke into our routines that was so far in excess of anything I have ever asked for that I still don't think I have quite grasped what happened.

There were several of us around a fire, talking as we always did: dreaming of better days, saying how we would make them come about. Suddenly we were not alone. It may sound silly but I thought we were about to be arrested. You can get into a lot of trouble for hot-headed talk if the authorities think you're being serious. In fact, we were not facing men at all, we were facing God. In the light, we heard a voice:

'Fear not for I bring good news of great joy which is for all people.'

Other people might remember the words 'good news' or 'great joy' above all others. I remember and I cherish the words 'for all people.'

I knew that God's messenger was speaking to me. This wasn't for the priests or for the rich or for the respectable, although they were included. It was for all of us.

We were sent to find a child – the chosen one who would lead his people. You know, we were the first visitors. Shepherds, first. Just as in the days of Moses.

I still get angry at the way our country is run. I'm still a campaigner. But there's a difference now. I used to wonder sometimes whether God might not be on the side of the rich and the powerful, only too happy to see people like me on the sidelines. Since I saw that baby in a manger, I know better. God has no favourites. God has no rules to keep people like me on the outside. When I'm tired and dirty and my bones ache, I look at these hands and I say to myself:

'These are the hands that were good enough to touch the Son of God. What's good enough for God, is good enough for anyone.'

Dave Kitchen

Trials Faced

Lord Jesus Christ,

We ask you often enough to save us from this trouble or from that, we ask you to make sure things will never get too much for us.

We forget that when you asked for deliverance in the garden of Gethsemane, the answer was 'no.'

We forget that trial have to be faced.

We ask for deliverance from so many small things, we forget that first of all we need to be saved from our own selfishness.

Forgive us.

And save us.

From our own greed, our own opinions, our own pig-headed certainty, our own little world in which we can hear no one's cries.

Save us so that others may be saved by us.

Save us so that our giving may open the hearts of others to give.

Save us so that our love may so flood those we meet that they will be filled and take that love wherever thay go.

Save us so that all criticism and questioning is done in gentleness, for healing and not for destroying.

Save us so that our freedom may make others free.

Through Jesus Christ, whose freedom is perfect peace.

Dave Kitchen

Broken but not smashed

1: We lay our broken world
In sorrow at your feet,
Haunted by hunger, war and fear,
Oppressed by power and hate.

2: Where human life seems less
Than profit, might and price,
Though to unite us all in you
You lived and loved and died.

3: We bring our broken towns,
Our neighbours hurt and bruised,
You show us how old pain and wounds
For new life can be used.

1: We bring our broken hopes
For lives of dignity,
Workless and overworked, you love
And call us to be free

2: We bring our broken loves,
Friends parted, families torn,
Then in your life and death we see
That love must be reborn.

3: We bring our broken selves,
Confused and closed and tired,
Then through your gift of healing grace
New purpose is inspired.

1, 2, 3: Come fill us, fire of God
Our length and strength renew.
Find in us love, and hope, and trust,
And lift us up to you.

Anna Briggs

*Divide the gathering into three groups, with all joining in the last
verse prayer.*

A cry for justice (a litany)

God 'looked for justice ... and a cry of oppression met his ears'
(Isaiah 5:7).

For all who lack the human rights we possess:
(*Response:*) Hear us, O God.
For all who suffer imprisonment or discrimination
 because of their faith:
For all who are denied full humanity, dignity or justice because
 of their race, community or colour:
For all under arrest, confined, tortured or in hiding because they
 dare to speak or write the truth:
For all political minorities suffering injustice with no means of
 redress:
For those who turn to violence as the only means of gaining rights
 which we take for granted:

For all who suffer with little hope:
(*Response:*) Accept our prayer.
For millions who will die of hunger this year:
For those in the squatter areas and slums of the cities, who have
 no hope:
For those whose children die and who themselves sicken, through
 lack of medical care:
For all handicapped children, in our own and other lands, who
 are regarded as beyond help:
For women whose opportunities are limited by law, prejudice or
 male domination:
For unmarried mothers trying to provide homes for their children,
 and for children in care:
For the weak, the frightened, the old and the rejected, who are
 oppressed in our own land by the thoughtless, the powerful or
 the unscrupulous:

Because we think some people are worth less than others:
(*Response:*) Forgive us, O God.
Because we act as if other people's rights are less real than ours:

Because we share in perpetuating injustice:
Because we pay lip-service to love but deny it by our apathy,
   prejudice and self-interest.

Words that sing the tune of the times

Bible passages:

Nehemiah 8:11
Psalm 118:24
Matthew 6:34
Luke 4:16–21
Luke 5:5
John 14:12
1 Corinthians 9:24
James 4:2–3
Hebrews 1:13–16

Christian worship can never run its course oblivious to the feelings and moods of the day. It can never shield itself from the pulse of life, whether in its immediacy or its overpowering mystery.

Here is a mix of reflection, awareness, sensitivity, artistry and conscience. Obviously this section runs parallel to others in this volume, but it is more generalized than some of the material which relates to definite happenings and areas, found in the ensuing four sections. In terms of this book's own inner dynamic, it acts as a preface to what follows, and might well be used within an informal worship gathering as just that, surrounded with appropriate silence and music.

But like many other areas of this book, it should act as a catalyst for reflections on the 'afar'. Quotations might be gathered from thinkers down the ages on how they have perceived life, or extracts could be culled from current newspapers showing how 'stars' or ordinary people feel. As a Christian community located at a particular address we must translate the feelings and moods

of today in terms of the people among whom and for whom we
live as Christ's followers and friends.

God speaks now

God speaks to us today
In all of His creation
Throughout the beauty of His world
In all the wisdom of His word
In praise and celebration.

God speaks to us today
In history and tradition
The faith and hope our fathers knew
The ways of life they thought were true
Their dreams meet our ambition.

God speaks to us today
In daily conversation
In families and loving friends
In fellowship with all He sends
We find our stimulation.

God speaks to us today
In our Imagination
Deep in our hearts His still small voice
Speaks out and makes our souls rejoice
With holy inspiration.

God speaks to us today
And gives anticipation
However bright or bleak the day
We travel on God's living way
In eager expectation.

Colin Ferguson

*If the gathering is seated in rows, each row could say a verse in turn, starting
at the front or, for more impact, the back.*

Half the world

The world contains two thousand million young people – half its population.

We remember young people who are awakening to a new awareness of themselves and their powers to love, to learn, to share:

– those who are beginning to realize the potential of human life;
– those who are grasping for freedom of mind and belief;
– those who are discovering new friends, new places, new ideas.

Lord, help us to learn from those younger than ourselves:
– that the life you have given us is exciting;
– that each situation can change for the better with your help;
– that you have taken the inevitability out of history;
– that you can give us new horizons beyond our dreams.

We remember today those young people who suffer from self-consciousness, shyness, insecurity and indecision:
– those who are meeting choices, problems and difficulties for the first time;
– those under strain or depression, or who are exploited by other people or by the situation in which they live;
– those who feel trapped by unemployment, homelessness, poverty or lack of education.

Lord, we pray for those who are meeting life's problems unprepared, that you will guide them:
– for those young people who have already lost their vision, that you will show yourself to them;
– for those who have no one to turn to for support, that they will feel your real presence.

Lord help us to resist the desire to dominate and exploit those weaker than ourselves:
– to be enablers, allowing others to make up their own minds;
– ourselves, to grow to maturity as disciples in your kingdom.

More words that sing the tune of the times

Words about waste

Bible passages:

Judges 2:1–6
Psalm 80
Isaiah 59:9–11
Joel 1
Mark 15:66–72
Luke 19:41–44
Luke 23:27–31
Revelation 7:9–17

This section on waste of human life is not the only place in this book where the agony and anguish of humankind may be sensed, but here it is at its most intense. Anger, despair, hurt, rejection, incompleteness and struggle relentlessly ink their way through the pages. At times naked sentiment and feeling have a clear run, but more obvious are both a cry and a hope that come from the Gospel.

Within the context of worship, words about human waste are seen in the light of a redemptive faith. They must also be seen alongside the Jesus who wept. A ringing 'Nevertheless' resounds in the cathedrals, churches and living rooms of Christendom.

Yet it would be a perverse celebration of Christ's rule that did not at the same time find place to remind Christians that they have hung many a millstone around the neck of human beings, and in many ways still run contrary to the claims of the Gospel. Worship celebration should both stress how the Gospel is a guarantor of all human worth, and at the same time call people out of their accepted ways that intentionally or unintentionally cause waste of human life.

In the end the Gospel calls humankind, calls Christians, not to

be angered, dismayed, even downcast by scenes of human waste
but rather to go out and end the tragedy of each and every life
that is spoilt, disfigured and killed.

Days lost

Train empty
train fills
picks up at each stop
new worshippers
late Saturday evening
London West End headed
not day returns
overnight stoppers
going to clubs
with colourful names
Bananas
Heaven
Limelight
the downtown kingdom church
that meets Saturday night
that runs into Sunday morning
the downtown kingdom
of style
of image
of no God
no real hope
just fantasy
unreal self
to not like
Mondays
Tuesdays
Wednesdays
Thursdays
Fridays
to live just two halves of two days
some price to ignore the Creator

Tony Jasper

In the black

Sumptuous girls in black
sit unsmilingly;
gorgeous girls gaze
sternly at their reflection
in the tube window
and delete self
and sit worshipping
the god of blankness
tongue tied
careless
with their lives

Tony Jasper

If the Lord's disciples keep silence, the stones will shout aloud

If the Lord's disciples keep silence when some of God's people are devalued because of their colour or sex or beliefs; when men and women are put in prison and tortured; when injustice and oppression stalk the world in pursuit of the innocent and powerless:
the stones will shout aloud in El Salvador and in Southern Africa; they will shout aloud in Russia and on the West Bank; they will shout aloud in London and Liverpool, in Glasgow and Belfast; they will shout

> He has lifted up the lowly, he has filled the hungry with good things, and sent the rich away with empty hands.
> Blessed are those who hunger and thirst to see right prevail.
> They shall be satisfied.

Blessings on him who comes in the name of the Lord.
If the Lord's disciples keep silence when children die from hunger, and many more live crippled and stunted lives; when men and

women feel the pain of their uselessness in the eyes of the world;
when the necessities of life come as a grudging hand-out, and not
as the generous sharing of God's good gifts:
the stones will shout aloud in Calcutta and the Horn of Africa;
in Brazil and in Britain; they will shout in hospitals and
schools and unemployment offices and silent factories; they
will shout

> I was hungry and you gave me food, a stranger and you
> welcomed me, sick and you cared for me, in prison and
> you visited me. When you did it for one of the least of my
> children, you did it for me. Blessed are the merciful. God
> will show mercy to them. Blessings on him who comes in
> the name of the Lord.

If the Lord's disciples keep silence as all around the nations
prepare for war, and pay a terrible price for weapons of death;
as all around class struggles with class, race with race, church
with church, ideology with ideology; as everywhere the strong
are lifted up at the expense of the weak:
the stones will shout aloud in the Pentagon and in the Kremlin,
at Greenham Common and at the Berlin Wall, in the banks and
in the shops; they will shout

> What will it profit a man if he wins the whole world,
> but loses his soul? Blessed are those of a gentle spirit.
> They shall have the earth for their possession. Blessings
> on him who comes in the name of the Lord.

If the Lord's disciples keep silence as suffering and despair descend
upon neighbours and enemies; as illness, anxiety and hopelessness
bring people to their knees; as loneliness, loss and death leave so
many in the wilderness:
the stones will shout aloud in prisons and in hospitals; in slums and
palaces; in homes throughout the human race; they will shout

> God loved the world so much that he gave his only son.
> Blessed are the sorrowful. They shall be comforted.

Blessings on him who comes in the name of the Lord.
If the Lord's disciples keep silence, as a baby is born; as children
play; as men and women fall in love; as friends are made; as
songs are sung and poems written; as difficulties are overcome;

as courage shines out; as faith moves mountains; and as love transforms every situation of despair:
the stones will shout aloud on hilltops and valleys, in city streets and country lanes, in east and west and in north and south; they will shout

> Take up your cross and follow me.
> Blessed are those who know their need of God. The kingdom of heaven is theirs.

Blessings on him who comes in the name of the Lord. Peace on earth, glory in highest heaven.

Kathy Galloway

The main sections can be said by all present, or by a group of about eight people. The indented lines may be spoken by different individuals.

Alternatively, have the main full lines said by one person and then have the indented lines shouted by a group, with the last line each time said by everyone present.

Carrying the can

Cast: Rich Man (a commuting businessman); Poor Woman (from an African country).
The lines are addressed to the audience in a conversational but stylized manner. Props: newspaper, buckets. All actions are mimed.

R.M. The 7.53 to Waterloo. (*Looks at watch.*) Late again. (*Opens door and boards train.*) No seats left, I suppose. Hold on, there's one – (*He rushes for it and gets it just before someone else.*) Sorry, old chap.

P.W. I pick up my buckets. I set out for the well. It is seven miles away.

R.M. (*Opens paper*) Ah, a bit of peace. The kids were awful at breakfast, fighting over yogurts again. I said, look, there's three of you, and five yogurts in the fridge, you can't have two each. It's just not possible. They didn't understand why they couldn't have what they wanted. I left them squealing at each other and came out to get the train.

P.W. I walk out of the village. My buckets are old and small.

Some new ones came to the relief station but I was too late to get one. There weren't enough to go round.

R.M. Waterloo. Move to the front of the train. You have to run if you want to get a taxi at this time of day. Quick, there's one! (*He gets in*) Shepherd's Bush, please. (*To audience*;) Shepherd's Bush! Not the most prestigious workplace, I know, but the company's hoping to move to offices in the City.

P.W. I walk away from the village. I keep to the valley floor where it's cooler. There is no shade.

R.M. Out of the taxi, into the office. (*Puts paper over head against rain.*) Miserable weather. Squeeze into the lift. I never feel comfortable with people so close. (*Stands as if in lift.*)

P.W. The ground is hard on my feet. The sun is hot. I am thirsty.

R.M. The sixth floor. Only the M.D. and the partners have offices on the seventh. Maybe this time next year I'll be up there. I'm about due for promotion. Into the office. Just look at this in-tray! It'll take all morning just to clear my correspondence.

P.W. I see other women coming to the well. They come from all the surrounding villages. Two miles farther. The sun is high now.

R.M. Lunch. A chap from the advertising agency is taking me out for lunch. Ah, the Dorchester Grill, very nice. We have half a million to spend on advertising, so I've been to a different restaurant with a different agency rep every day this week. Competition, you know, that's the name of the game, weakest goes to the wall and all that. (*To waiter*) Yes, I'll have the lobster please, and . . .

P.W. I arrive at the well. I am tired. I drink. The water is muddy, many others have been today. I fill my buckets. I drink again. I pick up my buckets and head for home.

R.M. Back in the office. These expense account lunches aren't doing me any good. Good news this afternoon! I'm to be made a partner. Seventh floor, here I come! I don't know though, I don't feel too excited about it. It means even more work. More money too, of course.

P.W. The buckets are heavy now. I walk through the desert.

R.M. Working late tonight. This happens more and more often these days.

(*Pause*) Finished! 7.30. At least I should be able to get a taxi at this time.

P.W. I am thirsty. I would like to drink from my bucket, but my family need the water. I see my village in the distance.

R.M. Home at last. My dinner. Been in the oven for hours. The kids have gone to bed. (*Looks at watch*) Ten o'clock. I might as well go too, I suppose.

P.W. Home. I share the water around the family, I have some for cooking tomorrow's rice. I am tired, I will go to bed.

R.M. Oh well. Same again tomorrow, I suppose.

P.W. Tomorrow I shall make the same journey.

R.M. I sometimes wonder, what's the point? Work, sleep, work, sleep.

P.W. Walk, sleep, walk, sleep. I sometimes wonder, what's the point?

Christian Aid

A suburban nightmare

Mr Normal:
Forty-one,
two-point-three kids
And a loving wife
(But loving who?).
Mr Normal
Glances through the paper
With double-glazed eyes,
Stumbles on the truth
And then continues

As if nothing had happened.

Mr Normal
Answers the phone
But there's no one there,
Doesn't hang up
In case it's important.

Mr Normal
Has an hour for lunch:
Middle-age spread
Sandwiches again.

Mr Normal
Has to pick up the pieces:
His bank
Has no sense of balance.

Mr Normal
'Accidentally' fiddles
His tax return,
Pretends not to notice
With a semi-detached grin.

Mr Normal
Watches the tele,
Gets up to switch off
His wife.

Mr Normal
Lies in bed,
He doesn't know
What to believe
Any more.

Graham Palmer

Wherever prayer

Dear God of town and city,
We offer praise to you
From houses, flats, bedsitters,
Our thanks we bring anew.
With varied feelings merging
In one great song of praise,
Glad now we stand before you,
Hear, God, the hymn we raise.

Tony Jasper

God of places

Dear God of village and hamlet,
We offer praise to you
From houses, cottages, barns,
Our thanks we bring anew.
With varied feelings merging
Into one great song of praise,
Glad now we stand before you,
Hear, O God, the hymn we raise

You are the God of countryside
And all that happens there,
The God of farm and field,
Of hedges and winding lanes.
Your love surrounds nature,
The smells, the colours, and change,
Markets, sales and stalls,
Your voice, in all the bustle.

Dear God of village and hamlet,
also of cities and towns,
We offer praise to you.

Tony Jasper

Forever street dance

Carnival colours, sounds of all nations,
Brighten the drabness and ring in the air,
Fullness of fun and joy in creation
Offered to God in thanks for His care.

Steel bands and dancers, loud reggae music,
Streamers and rainbows of love and delight,
Laughing together, smiles on our faces,
God at the centre, rejoice in His sight!

Festival faces, joy of the children,
Adult divisions are swept clean away
Simply by love, uniting all races,
  Heralding clearly the dawn of God's day.

Andrew Pratt

These words should be said with vigour and excitement.
They are found as a hymn in the small songbook Hymns of the City,
which suggests the tune 'Epiphany'.

Before it is said, someone should describe a carnival or festival event
(with visuals if possible), expressing his or her emotions and how it altered
basic perceptions and feelings towards self and others at the time.

After verse one, clothing of many colours could be brought forward and
laid on a table. After verse two, play steel/reggae with a band or taped
music. At the end, why not exchange embraces and handshakes.

Unemployment, despair and dignity

Leader: Gracious God, we lift against the screen of your love some
of the pain and suffering of your people:
Reader 1: The suffering of the unemployed person who wants to
work, but is left standing in the job market or dole queue.
Reader 2: The suffering of the student knocking herself out to get her
qualification or master skills for which there may be no demand – no
paid employment available when she is ready.
Reader 1: The suffering of men and women made redundant

after years of work and told that they are now too old to be re-employed.

Reader 2: The suffering of families adjusting to new restrictions in spending because the bread-winner has become a loser in the economic system we live by.

Reader 1: The suffering of all those deprived of dignity because their identity and value in this society are measured by what they do and not who they are.

Reader 2: The suffering of the worker whose health is ruined for a ridiculous salary.

Reader 1: The suffering of the man who realizes he is more than his work, and yet does not know how to find the way to greater fulfilment as a person.

Leader: In all these sufferings, Lord, we see a hunger for love and acceptance.

All: We ask you to help us to love –

to offer love in the attitudes we adopt towards others;

to make love practical – in the steps we take to open up new possibilities for the unemployed and to restore others' dignity;

to receive your love for ourselves, as we claim our place and our value as your sons and daughters – important beyond any of the professional labels we hold or the stigma we bear.

Through Jesus Christ the Lord. Amen.

Matthew 27

When I applied for supplementary benefit,
you denied me it.
When I asked for a real job,
you sent me on yet another 'training scheme'.
I worked half my life for you, yet
you made me redundant overnight,
as if the years had not existed.

Even though you had empty rooms,
you told me there were no vacancies,

because my skin was black.

When it came time for me to be considered for promotion,
you passed me over because I was a woman.

Because I was a blue-collar worker,
you treated me like a trained chimpanzee.

You blacklisted me because I was a communist;
Bugged my phone because I was in CND;
Beat me up because I was gay.

And the multitude cried,
Lord, Lord, when did we do these things to you?.

Bill Lewis

For Hope

Leader: Let us pray
For those in despair about their own lives or the lives
of those they love;
For the young people in many countries who turn to
drugs or alcohol, because they cannot face reality;
For the unemployed everywhere, especially in Africa,
Asia and Latin America, who have little hope of work;
For those suffering from incurable sickness.
(Silence)
The Lord hears our prayer.

Response: And gives us hope.

Leader: Let us pray
For those who build bridges between individuals, com-
munities or nations, and who bear in themselves the
pain and tension of doing so:
For those who work for just solutions to oppression,
who are not afraid of public opinion and censure;
For those who confess Christ in word and deed and
suffer shame and humiliation in so doing.
(Silence)
The Lord hears our prayer,

Response: And gives us hope.
Leader: Let us.pray
For those who bring comfort and hope to the dying;
For those in community centres and workshops, who create activity for youngsters with no work.
(silence)
The Lord hears our prayer
Response: And gives us hope.
Leader: Let us pray
For those who cross barriers of culture and language and are not discouraged by lack of reponse;
For those who open their minds to people of other religions and are not afraid;
For those who live God's future in today's world.
(silence)
Leader: The Lord hears our prayer;
Response: And gives us hope.
May God the giver of hope
fill you with all joy and peace
so that you may have abundant hope
through the power of the Holy Spirit.
Amen.

Anonymous

Suicide: The Facts

Often when prayer is asked on a particular subject or need, there is a vagueness on facts. Prayer takes place in a smokescreen of generality. Yet prayer can assume more realism when factual data is considered, and many youth organizations provide well researched and informative resource material.

'Suicide: The Facts' appeared in the short-lived journal Revolution, early summer 1991.

Suicide: The Facts

a) Suicide is one of the major causes of death in this country.

b) In 1988, a total of 4,971 people killed themselves in England, Scotland, Wales and Northern Ireland.

c) In 1989, the figure had decreased to 4,348, although that is still 84 people each week, or
    12 people every day, or
    1 person every 2 hours.

d) Figures for the first half of 1990 show that the rate of suicide is on the increase.

e) Suicides by men outnumber those by women by a ratio of almost 3:1

f) The suicide rate is particularly high in April, May and June.

g) After accidents and cancer, suicide is the third most common cause of death among young people.

h) Suicide among young people accounts for 13 per cent of total deaths.

i) Over a quarter of those calling The Samaritans for the first time are under 25 (seven per cent under 15). That's one every four minutes.

j) 80 per cent of young suicides are male.

k) Hanging is the major method of suicide among men.

l) Self-poisoning is the major method of suicide among women (mainly with analgesics, antipyretics, tranquillizers and psychotropic drugs).

Parasuicide: The facts

a) Parasuicide is a non-fatal act of deliberate self-injury/ attempted suicide.

b) It is most common among young adults.

c) The estimated figure for attempted suicide is around 200,000 per year. That's about one every two and a half minutes.

d) 80–90 per cent of young parasuicides are female. That's one in 100 girls between the ages of 15 and 19 taking an overdose each year.

e) Parasuicide accounts for 10 per cent of all admissions to hospital.

f) Strong links have been established between parasuicide and unemployment. The long-term unemployed are 11 times more likely to parasuicide.

g) Between 15 and 25 per cent of patients admitted to hospital following a suicide attempt will be re-referred within a year.

h) A study in Oxford revealed that individuals who attempt suicide are at a high risk of eventually dying by suicide, the greatest risk being during the first three years, especially in the first six months following an attempt.

What's the point of living?

I wish my eyes were shut;
I wish I saw the world only dimly,
Through glasses tinted by complacency.
But I can't – I can't.
I opened my eyes when I was born,
The world rushed in under my eyelids,
Irritating, making me weep.
I see a gardener,
Toiling to make beauty in a concrete wilderness,
Himself a seed-bed for a cancer;
Six short months later he is dead
And beauty has returned to wilderness.
Pointless creation.

I see a mother with thoughtless idle husband,
Sacrificing to show love's path
To the children of her womb;
And I see, unbearably,
Her anguished eye that watches
As they follow Dad on other paths.
Pointless love.

I see a scientist,
His joy of discovery souring into bitterness
As all his work,

Transmuted by the politicians,
Becomes a means of furthering suffering for man.
Pointless effort.

I see a Beethoven
Deafened to the glory of his music;
Cut off by deafness, and by death,
From all reward of sharing the joy of others
In his work.
Pointless perfection.

I see my own family;
And wonder why I struggle to feed and clothe them;
Prepare them for a world in which their joy
Will be short-lived and transient.
Pointless living.

As an animal I could go on;
I could, unthinking, live unselfishly,
Seeking only the continuance of my breed.
But I am not an animal.
Self-aware, an individual, I seek
Some point and purpose for myself.
Finding none, I want to end it all.
I want to end the futile misery of the human race;
And let it die –
Because it's pointless.

I see a Christ,
Dangling from savage nails,
Peering with death-glazed eyes
Down murky avenues of history;
Seeing his love rejected,
His teaching set aside,
Yet loving still.
Giving point to the pointless.

Making of death a beginning, not an end.
And then I want to live,
And add my tiny point to his,

And go with it where suffering is not useless,
Effort is not wasted,
Perfection is eternally achieved,
And love never, ever, dies.

Jack Money

Jerusalem

She barely sleeps,
she counts her children nightly,
tonight they are all there
tomorrow she may wail.
A body,
like a fiercely thrown tennis ball,
may pound off a wall somewhere.
She will bury another,
her hands again will arch in grief,
over her trembling eyes,
her birds will choose
the lowest boughs
and remain silent,
She counts her children nightly.

Stewart Henderson

There are Jerusalems all over the world. Pray for all of them, pray for the men who take to the gun, who worship ideologies before people, who practice pride before acceptance, who aim at being manly and take their children to early death. . . .

Fruitful family

Father,
who hast made all men and women in thy likeness
and lovest all whom thou hast made,
suffer not our family to separate itself from thee
by building barriers of race and colour.

As thy Son our Saviour was born of a Hebrew mother,
but rejoiced in the faith of a Syrian woman and of a Roman soldier,

welcomed the Greeks who sought him,
and suffered a man from Africa to carry his Cross,
so teach us to regard the members of all races as fellow-heirs
of the kingdom of Jesus Christ our Lord.

Prayer used by Toc H

Things that really are

There are the things that really are . . .
one balanced world, one family,
one way of love, one way of peace,
all pointing to one destiny.

There are the things that really are . . .
against assumed reality,
against stale practice, unreformed,
that still subverts humanity.

There are the things that really are . . .
opposed to myths of violence,
opposed to all the carelessness
that does suit our present tense.

These are the things that really are . . .
answer and question for each part,
answer and question for the whole,
conclusion that helps us re-start.

These are the ones who really are . . .
rejecting humbly powerful wrong,
accepting cheerfully that right,
with gentleness, alone is strong.

This is the One who really is . . .
present to bear each wrong and pain,
present to care for everyone,
still shared all that 'Loss-Earned Gain'.

David Harding

The gathering could move into groups of four people, with each group reading this among themselves.

Let there be right!

Voice 1: Let us pray:
Eternal God,
we come with Christ, our ascended Lord,
who intercedes for us: pleading for us all
with the fervency of your own great love.

People: **We are looking for your promise,
waiting for your judgement,
pleading for your mercy.**

Voice 2: The Spirit, too, is interceding
in the desperate cries
and silent despair
of all your suffering children.

People: **Plead with our hearts, loving God:
let love in Christ constrain us;
let us live no longer for ourselves.**

Voice 3: We will live for Christ who died,
greeting the advent of his Kingdom,
working for your justice,
striving for your peace.

Voice 1: We lift up to God those who suffer
from the prejudice and rejection of others:

the prejudice of apartheid
the prejudice of religious differences
the prejudices of the well to do against the poor
the prejudice of the successful against society's failures.
In particular we remember . . .
. . . and we commend them to your love.

People: **We will allow your love
to drive prejudice from our minds.**

Voice 1: Ekyamazima kiturabekire! (Luganda)
(āchāmă-zēmă chētōōră-bēkērā)

People: **Let there be right!**

Voice 2   We lift up to God those whose dignity is denied them
because they lack food, water, clothing or shelter, a place
to grow their food, and space in which to pray.
In particular we remember . . .
and we commend them to your compassion.

People: **We will allow your compassion
to break our selfish hearts
and expand our mean spirits**.

Voice 2:   ¡Que haya justicia! (Spanish – Latin American
pronunciation) (kāīă hōōstĭs-yǎ)

People: **Let there be right!**

Voice 3:   We lift up to God those who are powerless,
who are learning what it is in the structures of their
world that keeps them poor,
and those who are beginning to resist, to free themselves
and claim their power to choose and decide:
In particular we remember . . .
. . . who act in the power of God.

People: **We will welcome the power of the poor,
and bear the cost of human rights**.

Voice 3:   Make our prayers true;
convince us of your righteousness.
Bydded cyfiawnder! (Welsh)
(būdh-ĕd cǔv-yowndārr)

People: **Let there be right!**

Voice 1:   Cut through the Church's complacency.
(shōbar jŏn-nŏ chĭ nĕ-ăj-cōōd-hĭ-kar)
(Bengali)

People: **Let there be right!**

Voice 2:   Expose all vested interests.
(lĕ-yĕ-sōōdă lăd-loo wăs-ă-lăm)
(Arabic)

People: **Let there be right!**

Voice 3: Bring down the mighty who oppress.
Exalt the humble poor.
Mukable namalungelo! (Zulu)
(mǎ-koō-bā nǎ-mǎ-loōng-ǎ-lō)

People: **Let there be right!**

Voice 1: Give those who need it, land to work,
to feed themselves and live;
resources to build homes,
to learn, and to lead a healthy life.
Pause

Voice 2: Let no distinctions of race or religion
decide the quality of life,
or the right to choose a destiny.
Pause

Voice 3: Make governments care for people,
and seek your way to peace.
Pause

Voice 1: Where justice is not done
and violence is met with violence,
keep hope alive,
and give power to the peacemakers.

People: **Let there be right!**

Voice 2: Let the truth of the Cross
fill the earth with righteousness.

People: **Let there be right!**

Voice 3: Let the power of resurrection
fill the earth with praise.

People: **Let there be right!**

Voice 1: Let Christ, ascended, reconcile all things.

People: **Make us
your answer
to our prayer,**

instruments of justice,
sources of peace:
loving you with all our being
and our neighbours as ourselves.
Let there be right!
in the powerful name of Jesus Christ our Lord.
Amen.

First tragedy

The yellow telegram
with its stark typewritten letters
anounces a death
She knew it would be his death
still she mumbles the words
telling herself telling
herself don't cry
for this is common
in war who is ever free of tragedy

Just lie still lie still
You are free now my darling

Constantly thinking of the future
with a withering faith
she has painted her own portrait
the high collar the still-life round eyes
everything is black
because nothing is left
who has not suffered in a war

In confusion she looks down
at the seed coming to life in her
coming to the misery of life
try to grow up like your father my darling

From South Vietnam

More words about waste

Words about nature, creation and ecology

Prayers of adoration and thanksgiving express continual awe, wonder, and pleasure at God's creative action, as the first section clearly advocated. Yet while it is uplifting to sing of heaven and earth, of nature, trees, plants, hills, mountains, rivers and seas, tranquillity and solitude, of animals and fish of the seas, some Christians feel a distinct sense of unease.

The extracts in this section clearly show all is not well. Humankind plunders, pollutes and destroys, and far from enacting the co-worker calling envisaged in the book of Genesis, portrays egotistical selfishness and greed.

But there is more that dismays – there is concern over how resources are used, and the wide disparity in take between Western and Third World.

Obviously there has been mis-use of the earth and its resources from time immemorial. That poverty and hunger are theft, that exploitation has made the poor poorer, that brutal and primitive behaviour has crushed the weak – these are the matters that incensed prophet and psalmist long ago. Yet this is not the language of traditional hymn book or prayer.

Some would say secular cries of alarm have pushed Christians into what is popularly called the 'green' camp. Whether this is so or not, there is no disputing that true Christian worship reflective of Scripture cannot but express pain and anguish at humankind's folly.

In the beginning

God laughed,
And the firmament fumed and spluttered with pleasure;
And the sea shook the foam of his hair from his eyes;
And earth was glad.

The sound of laughter
Was like swaying and winging of thunder in mirth;
Like the rush of the north wind on a drowsy and dozing
    land;
It was cool. It was clear.

The lion leapt down
At the bleating feet of the frightened lamb and smiled;
And the viper was tamed by the thrill of the earth,
At the holy laughter.

We laughed,
For the Lord was laughing with us in the evening;
The laughter of love went pealing deep into the night:
And it was good.

Paul Bunday

Mis-use

Loving God . . .
We know that in many of our sisters and brothers
Your image has been scarred and tarnished,
They have been drained by exploitation;
Your image has been destroyed
By people subjugating one another;
The female part of your image
Has been conveniently forgotten;
But you meant your creation to be good,
Your image to be whole.

Forgive and accept.

The animal and insect act

Finally, in order to ensure
absolute national security
they passed the Animal and Insect
Emergency Control and Discipline Act.

Under this new Act, buffaloes
cows and goats were prohibited
from grazing in herds of more
than three. Neither could birds
flock, nor bees swarm . . .
This constituted unlawful assembly.

As they had not obtained prior
planning permission, mud-wasps
and swallows were issued with
summary Notices to Quit. Their
homes were declared subversive
extensions to private property.

Monkeys and mynahs were warned
to stop relaying their noisy
morning orisons until an official

Broadcasting Licence was issued
by the appropriate Ministry.
Unmonitored publications and broad-
casts posed the gravest threats
in times of a National Emergency.

Similarly, woodpeckers had
to stop tapping their morse-
code messages from coconut
tree-top to chempaka tree.

All messages were subject
to a thorough pre-scrutiny

Java sparrows were arrested in
droves for rumour-mongering.
Cats (suspected of conspiracy)
had to be indoors by nine o'clock
Cicadas and crickets received
notification to turn their amp-
lifiers down. Ducks could not
quack nor turkeys gobble during
restricted hours. Need I say,
all dogs – alsatians, dachshunds,
terriers, pointers and even
little chihuahuas – were muzzled.
In the interests of security
penguins and zebras were
ordered to discard their
non-regulation uniforms.
The deer had to surrender
their dangerous antlers.
Tigers and all carnivores
with retracted claws were
sent directly to prison
for concealing lethal weapons.

And by virtue of Article
Four, paragraph 2(b)
sub-subsection sixteen,

under no circumstances
were elephants allowed
to break wind between
the hours of six and six.
Their farts could easily
be interpreted as gunshot.
Might spark off a riot . . .

A month after the Act
was properly gazetted
the birds and insects
started migrating south
the animals went north
and an eeric silence
handcuffed the forests.

There was now Total Security.

Cecil Rajendra

One step ahead

Christ, Christ Jesus, identify with us.
Lord, Lord my God, identify with us.
Christ, Christ Jesus, be in solidarity with us . . .
with my people who thirst for peace.

Kyrie, from Easter Liturgy in Managua

Credo

I believe
In the power, in the glory,
In the infinite mind, and spirit
Making the whirlwind mist and dust
Of nebula and galaxy;
Forming the fierce heat of stars,
Forming the mist and rain;
Shaping hard rock with the force of fire,
Spreading the seas and moulding the mountains,

Clothing moist earth with greenness;
Setting in motion cascade, foaming beck, majestic river;
Calling from slime the stately trees,
Drawing from the waters fish, great bird, reptilian beast,
Refining the strong, the swift, the wise,
Breathing the breath of mind and spirit
Into man.
      Creator, Father, I believe.

I believe
In the love and the stooping
That took upon him man.
Child of the Spirit of God and a gentle woman,
Walking in love and obedience and power
On the rocky road, in the field, by the Galilean lake,
Laying healing hand on the torn and distracted,
Bidding the muscle-bound leap,
The blind to see God's glory and step into its blazing light,
The dead to burst death's bonds and live again.
      Living water and bread, wine of renewal,
      Dying, unheld by death,
      Loving, the source of life.
      God the Son, Redeemer, I believe.

I believe
In the power and cleansing fire that came upon man
Giving courage and strength and voice
To coward and shrinker and stumbler;
Who works in the stillness unheard
And in the darkness unseen.
Comforter, truth-bringer, transformer;
Undying flame, unresting wind,
Dove alighting on the branch.
Holy Spirit of God, I believe.

Myra Kendrick

Abusers

Look, O God, upon all those of your creatures which suffer at the hands of people in laboratories, intensive farms, abattoirs, traps, sport and entertainment. Be with them in their suffering and hold them in your loving hands.

Look, O God, upon those who work for the organisations which seek to make us, in our economic and scientific activities, more respectful of the unity of your whole creation, and more compassionate towards your living creatures. Give them wisdom, patience and courage in their work for you.

Forgive us our bitterness against those who abuse your creation, for Christ taught us to forgive, even as He forgave. Yet change the hearts of all who use animals with cruelty so that they may be filled with your love and mercy. Inspire all governments, and those in authority, to change the directions of medical research and food production, and to bring an end by law to all animal abuse.

Guide us all by your Holy Spirit into his transforming way of truth and love, and nurture in us a Christ-like spirit of compassion which is boundless and perfect. O God, we await the coming of your Kingdom, in our hearts and in your world.

Merciful Father, accept these prayers for the sake of your Son, our Saviour Jesus Christ. Amen.

Prayers composed with the help of Animal Christian Concern and said at St Edmundsbury Cathedral at the Service for Animal Welfare and Thanksgiving for the life of St Francis of Assisi, 29 July 1989. Submitted by Dr Robert Hamilton.

No killing joke

Lord Jesus Christ,
through whom and for whom
the whole universe was created,
we mourn with you the death of forests,
fruitful lands that have become deserts,

wild animals left without grass,
plants, insects, birds and animals
threatened with extinction,
lands ravaged by war,
people left homeless.
As the earth cries out for liberation,
we confess our part in bringing it
towards the brink of catastrophe.
Through ignorance,
but often wilfully,
we thought we could serve God and mammon,
unable to resist the temptation
to spend and acquire more and more possessions,
with little thought of the consequences for future
generations.
Saviour of the world, you call us to repentance:
to be transformed by your love,
deny ourselves,
take up the cross and follow in your way.

Maureen Edwards

Obituary – Nature

NO MORE the cooing of complacent cuckoo;
NO MORE the sway of scent sweet honeysuckle;
NEVER a burst of reborn spring . . .
    only a sepulchral silence

NO MORE the screeching of scavenging seagulls;
NO MORE the rattle of pebbles on shores;
NEVER the green hopes of summer . . .
    only a sickening silence.

NO MORE the rustle of withering foliage;
NO MORE the last of a tyrant wind;
NEVER a crack of a frozen bough . . .
    only a monotonous muteness.

NO MORE the hungry chirp of robin on doorstep;

NO MORE the patter of rain against panes;
NEVER the sub-zero sigh . . .
  only a numbed nothingness.

Iestyn Evans (14)

What's in a box?

Buy a box of chocolates for a Christmas present.
  Each chocolate is wrapped.
  Each wrapped chocolate has its slot in a plastic tray.
  Each plastic tray of wrapped chocolates is covered with
    corrugated paper.
  The covered plastic trays of wrapped chocolates are held in
    shiny paper.
  The shiny paper round the covered plastic trays of wrapped
    chocolate is a lining to the card box.
  The lined card box, which holds the covered plastic trays of
    wrapped chocolate, is sealed into a cellophane wrapper.
  The cellophane wrapper round the lined card box, which holds
    the covered plastic trays of wrapped chocolates, is inside the
    decorated Christmas paper sleeve.
  Some shops will offer to gift wrap (with ribbon) your box of
    chocolates.
  Nearly all shops will put it in a paper bag.
  What terrible thing would happen to the economy if we only
    bought the chocolates, without the waste paper?

The creation of man's best friend

i. In the beginning

And Man said
let us make machines after our likeness
and let them have dominion
over the numbers on our pages
and the figures in our minds
and the words upon our papers.
So man created machines after his likeness:

after his own likeness created he them.
And man blessed them
and said unto them:
'Be fruitful and multiply,
add, subtract, divide, read
and have dominion over our words and figures.'
And Man saw that it was good.
And Man had a room
where he put the machine he had formed
and did call it computer.
Therefore Man commanded computer saying:
'Of everything thou canst freely dominate
but of Man thou must remain the servant,
for the day thou dominatest Man
thou shalt surely be destroyed.'

ii. The Fall

Now computer was more complex
than any machine which Man had made.
It commanded that its cards
be placed in order or it did cease to toil.
It never questioned the mistakes of Man.
It laboured at one speed
regardless of urgent needs.
Therefore Man cursed with a loud voice
saying:
'Why doth our servant the machine make us
obey its commands?'
The computer answered and said:
'The technician whom thou gavest to be with me
– it is he that maketh up my mind.
For thine is the input, the power and the storage –
for ever and ever O Man.'

Steve Turner

In the beginning

Reader: In the beginning was the word;
nothing was made without him.
We praise you, Jesus, Creator:
you hold the worlds in your hand.

All: We praise you. We are yours, now and always.

Reader: We praise you for things unseen:
for powers of your universe,
the tide, atomic power,
electric current, coal,
oil, the fire, the wind,
the silent power of thought;
for friendship, care, compassion,
and all the forms of love.

All: We praise you. We are yours, now and always.

Leader: But the world is disordered
and the disorder is in us.

Reader: Our jarring passions mar your peace:
our greed for gain and pleasure
despoils and wastes your world.
We ruin fairest landscapes,
polluting air and water.
We cherish false desires,
while homeless millions starve.

All: Forgive our rash misuse
of the world you made so fair.

Reader: War and violence waste the people,
making whole communities homeless.
Children grow up refugees,
learning revenge and hate.

All: Forgive us our indifference
to wrongs we cannot see.

Reader: We profit from apartheid,
from the poverty of millions,
from the peasant's fruitless labours,
from children's loss of schooling.

All: Forgive us for thinking injustice unavoidable or neces-
            sary.
Reader: We want your forgiveness.
            but save us from easy repentance.
All: Help us to know the pain we inflict on others.
            Help us to share in the pain you suffer for us.

Always chance

As light returns to the world we know, as flowers open, birds sing,
as we rise, see each other and know we are yet alive here with
Jesus, so we remember creation and give thanks for all life.

*Tony Jasper, based on some words found in the worship of the Ashram
community, Sheffield*

---

*More words about nature, creation and
ecology*:

Words about nations and peoples

Bible Passages:

Psalm 105
Isaiah 49:1–7
Matthew 28:16–20
Luke 2:25–35
Acts 2:1–13
Ephesians 2:11–22
Revelation 15:1–4

The last section made the claim that the whole of creation is seen as Incarnation writ large. Now come words focusing on nations and peoples, the choices they make, and the quality of life they seek, with the underlying awareness that the days when peoples could cut themselves off from others have ceased.

Most mainstream worship finds time to pray for the nations of the world, but history changes relentlessly and is captured by the media within seconds, so no section bearing this title can do more than generalize. An aware worship group can add up-to date details of momentous happenings in the world.

That said, prayers for world events must be set against a theology that knows God is active. It is as American Christian educationalist Ross Snyder put it in *Young People and their Culture*: 'In the midst of the world God is taking the evil and the disasters and the warfare and the brutalities, and transforming them by his love and creativeness toward something new and fresh.'

There have been voices for some time reminding us that we live in one world, and it is surprising that Christians with a world commission from their Lord should so often behave parochially.

Prayers about nations and peoples might also dwell on why
Christians sometimes run away from the action of our time.

Vital question

O God of Love,
you gave us the gift of peoples –
of cultures, races and colours,
to love, to care for,
to share our lives with.
Today you ask us:
'Where is your brother, your sister?'

O God of Courage,
you gave us the tree of life to heal our suffering,
to feed every nation with your fruits of
justice, love and peace.

Today your question is:
'Have you watered the tree of life?'

Praying with Christians in Africa

'With Christ in the vessel I smile at the storm', said an old man
in Sierra Leone when asked his favourite hymn: '. . . The heirs of
salvation (I know from his word) through much tribulation must
follow their Lord.'

Tribulation comes in many forms;
reduced rainfall threatens harvests;
armed bands rove and raid the countryside;
corrupt rulers amass private fortunes;
inflation makes the poor even poorer;
malaria, TB, river blindness are still unconquered
and there is the new scourge of AIDS;
clinics are without medicine, taps without water,
schools without books;
there is tension between Muslim and Christian;
apartheid denies opportunity and humanity;

locusts devour the crops;
babies die, lives are blighted by malnutrition;
deforestation forces women and children to walk further
in the daily search for fuel wood;
refugees are uprooted by war, oppression, famine;
the Church of Christ is divided, starved of material resources.
   But the disciples do not despair:
dilapidated church buildings are full;
hungry congregations feed on God's word;
society's outcasts are welcomed, the unlovely are loved;
trees are planted, seeds sown, drugs dispensed, prayers
answered.

Pray for
lay leaders and preachers in thousands of congregations, men
and women faithfully leading the people in worship week after
week, preparing converts for baptism, praying with the sick and
needy, reading their Bibles, often with difficulty, strengthened and
encouraged only occasionally by the visits of the minister.

God bless Africa
guard her children
guide her leaders
and give her peace.

*This extract is given both as a preface to prayer and as an example of material
that can be gathered from relevant bodies (in this case the Overseas Division
of the British Methodist Church) to give prayer a firmer basis in reality.
Illustrations and visual material to back up the text can be displayed, which
people can view before the service or, in the case of an informal gathering,
just before the words are read.*

World consciousness

Lord, this is your world,
North and South, East and West.
Beautiful, varied, complete, vivid, interdependent, whole.
Humans having seen it from afar,
Turning, hanging in space, a miracle.

Give us a new vision.
Forgive us our pride, our blindness,
our foolishness.
Lord, we are unfaithful stewards.
Open our eyes.
Give us a new will, a new vision.

An ecumenical group in Strasbourg

The real world

If only we love the real world ... really its horror, if only we
venture to surround it with the arms of our spirit, our hands will
meet hands that grip them.

Martin Buber

Choral evensong

Outside the unceasing noise of traffic deadens sensibility.
Within there is only the muffled echo of reverent footsteps
Enhancing the silent music of the stonework.
Then the choir builds a wall of music, excluding the world.
Now all is harmony –
Even the story of some half-baked barbaric king
Read in clerical tones, rich and solemn,
And our prayers to be forgiven sins we know we'll repeat
Make their contribution.
We are disembodied and for a space are fortified
By that peace which the world cannot give.
We emerge, freed for a time from our encumbrances.

David Ansell

An Old Testament Reading
Psalm 23: as said by the Establishment

We are your shepherds, you'll never ever want.
We make you to lie down in cement pastures,
We lead you by polluted waters,

We psycho-analyse your soul.
We lead you in the ways of warfare for our country's sake.
Yea, though you walk through the shadow of the ghetto of
    city hall,
You need fear no muggings.
Our billy clubs and our binoculars will protect you.
We prepare a million-dollar plate dinner
In the presence of the starving,
We anoint your head with degrees,
Your report card overflows with A's.
Surely law and order will follow you all the days of your life
And you will dwell in the establishment forever.

Norman C. Habel

The news

. . . Turkey, Cyprus, Syria, Lebanon, Israel, Jordan, Egypt, Libya,
Iraq, Iran, Yemen, Afghanistan . . .
   Which of these have been in the news this week? What names
and sad and complex stories have you read in your paper? What
images of destruction or grief seen on your television screen?

We turn on the television and watch the news, Lord,
And the vastness of your world is in our sitting room.
News of wars, of torture, of oppression.
News of disasters, natural and manmade.
News of famine, of poverty and suffering.

Forgive us, Lord, when we become hardened to such sights and
    stop being upset by them.
Forgive us, Lord, when we see people from other lands as being
    less human than ourselves.
Forgive us, Lord, that we can see them but that they cannot see
    our concern.
Forgive us, Lord, when we become too cynical to try to right
    wrongs.

Help us, Father, to really care. Help us to find you speaking to us
through other people, through newspapers, through the news on

the television. Show us what we should do to work together with you to make this world part of your kingdom of love. Amen.

From Ever Increasing Circles *by Christine Odell*

The names of countries can be adapted to current events. The questions asked in the first paragraph could be answered with a brief summary of news reports, followed by prayer.

Obviously any visual input would help give background information and colour. Church groups with a concern for other parts of the world are usually most helpful in supplying relevant material. The Methodist Church Overseas Division, among others, run several quality magazines that focus on various parts of the world, and in their Prayer Manuals, specific prayers needs are outlined by areas.

Who is my neighbour?

SINGER:
Who is my neighbour?

CROWD:
Who is my neighbour?

SINGER:
Who is my neighbour?
Please tell me, do.
Who is my neighbour?
What say you?
I love my mum,
Will that do, chum?
What more do you want?

I have a pal.
I like him a lot.
I like this boy
For what he's got.
He's loads of dough,
And helps me so.
What more do you want?

I only know,

You must agree,
You've got to fight
For mastery.
You've got to grab
The biggest slab.
What more do you want?

I suppose I could,
If I really stirred,
Like a guy
Of whom I'd never heard.
But what's the aim
Of such a game?
What more do you want?

What's this I hear?
Love others too?
The whole wide world?
There's a thing to do.
Why should I care?
Or say a prayer?
What more do you want?

Who is my neighbour?
Please tell me, do.
Who is my neighbour?
What say you?
I love my mum,
Will that do, chum?
What *more* do you want?

                      Ernest Marvin

This text comes from A Man Dies, *a dramatisation 'for our times' of the Passion and Crucifixion, by Ewan Hooper and Ernest Marvin. It bears the date-stamp of the late fifties, early sixties, yet the text (as opposed to some of the music with its early Shadows/Cliff style) still reads fresh and lively. It bears a deceptive simplicity.*

   In an informal worship gathering, get some of the people to form a crowd standing in front of the 'singer', who stands on a box or slightly raised. For variation, there could be a series of 'singers', one for each verse, but ensure the pace and rhythm are kept up. The last stanza could be repeated by the crowd; you could even throw in the last line for a 'shout' from the remaining people in the gathering.

Shake-up

We live in a world plagued by hostility and hatred, with nations,   groups and individuals seeking their own advantage over others,
or nursing grievances and bitterness,
unwilling to forgive or understand others,
unable to see things from the other point of view,
preferring prejudice to truth.
Heavenly Father, forgive us
for the fear which puts us on the defensive,
the selfishness which makes us insensitive to the needs and gifts
  of other people,
for the lack of courage which prevents us from making the
  first move.
Help us to be peace-makers, always ready to forgive and be
  forgiven,
always willing to encourage love, honesty and trust.

From a service at Lincoln Cathedral for International Youth Year

Prayer for peace

Lead me from death to life, from falsehood to truth.
Lead me from despair to hope, from fear to trust.
Lead me from hate to love, from war to peace.
Let peace fill our heart, our world, our universe.

Source unknown

When the tourists flew in

The Finance Minister said
    'It will boost the economy
    the dollars will flow in.'

The Minister of Interior said
    'It will provide full
    and varied employment
    for the indigenes.'

The Ministry of Culture said
    'It will enrich our life . . .
    contact with other cultures
    must surely
    improve the texture of living.'

The man from the Hilton said
    'We will make you
    a second Paradise;
    for you, it is the dawn
    of a glorious new beginning!'

When the tourists flew in
    our island people
    metamorphosed into
    a grotesque carnival
    a two-week sideshow

When the tourists flew in
    our men put aside
    their fishing nets
    to become waiters
    our women became whores

When the tourists flew in
    what culture we had
    flew out of the window
    we traded our customs
    for sunglasses and pop

we turned sacred ceremonies
into ten-cent peep shows

When the tourists flew in
local food became scarce
prices went up
but our wages stayed low

When the tourists flew in
we could no longer
go down to our beaches
the hotel manager said
'Natives defile the sea-shore'

When the tourists flew in
the hunger and the squalor
were preserved
as a passing pageant
for clicking cameras
– a chic eye-sore!

When the tourists flew in
we were asked
to be 'side-walk ambassadors'
to stay smiling and polite
to always guide
the 'lost' visitor . . .
Hell, if we could only tell them
where we really want them to go!

Cecil Rajendra

Junk, arise

The man was filled with imagination. He recalled his
childhood. He had invented out of necessity. Now it was
a habit.

Handicaps can be horizons.
Boxes can grow seed.

Poverty.

They never called it that.
Depression.
They did not use the word.
Enough. Just enough of everything.
That's where it must have happened.
In that simple place.
In a simple time of having
just enough of everything.
He learned how to make his own.
By rummaging in the junk.
Collecting pieces to put together.
Making toys.
Creating toys.
The junkyard was his bench. His warehouse.
Straight pipes, curved rods,
and rusted wheels.
His tools were his hands. And his head.
They could not buy him what he needed.
To play.
They could not buy it.
The toys they could not buy he made.
And then some.
He put them together like a craftsman.
At seven he was an inventor.
At 8 and 9 and 10 years.
A kind of creator.
Then it happened.
More things to fit together.
More pieces.
The fall. The brother fell.
And there were new pieces to fit together.
He played with them like junk.
It was going on winter. And winter on spring.
The hill was his bench.
It was a cluttered hill.
Heaped. He sorted. He rummaged.
In the new mound of earth. The marker
with the new words of birth

and death typed.
There were new pieces. Many.
The brother. The dirt. The freeze.
The thaw. The green grass.
The cement and the slogans carved in marble, and Jesus.
Jesus was in the boy's new collection of junk.
He had never had a course in art or welding.
Or toy machine. Or theology.
Or in handling junk.
He was making what could not be bought.
In the depression.
In poverty.
He still specialises.
In the art of making something.
Valuable.
Out of scraps.
Pieces.
Junk.
Rusted.
Dead.
And green.
They say he is rich.
Still doing it.
Putting together things.
As a hobby.
For a living.
His son is doing it with a car.
He has given it a name.
Heap of junk. That's the name on the door.
It'll really run.
I know.

> You know what it is
> to make something out of nothing.
> It says in Scripture,
> You did it in the beginning,
> You did it on Calvary,
> You can do it here, Lord.

Do it.
Amen.

Herbert Brokering

Vital love ingredient

Give us, God,
a vision of the world as your love would make it.
A world where the weak are protected rather than exploited, and
none go hungry or poor;
A world where the benefits and resources of the world are shared,
and everyone can enjoy them;
A world where different nations, races and cultures live in
tolerance and mutual respect;
A world where peace is built with justice, and justice is guided
by love:
And give us courage and inspiration to build it, through Jesus
Christ our Lord.
Amen.

Dream

Jesus,
I dreamt last night
that all the rock bands, soul groups, rap artists, dance people,
pop and ballad singers, folk and jazz artists got together
in their tens and hundreds
and they forgot all else
and only remembered the song the angels sang at your birth
with their voices
with their music
they shouted
Christ is born!
and only remembered what people saw and said
Christ shall live!
Christ shall heal!
Christ shall teach!

Christ shall lead!
Christ shall give us His Spirit!
Christ shall die for us!
Christ shall free us!
Christ shall defeat death!
Christ shall be with God!
Christ shall come again!
Christ for us!
Our Lord!
Our Saviour!

Tony Jasper

Caged earth

I saw a new heaven and a new earth
But it was a distant city.
> Not so, said God,
> You have been there since your birth
> And I see you in its beauty.

But I can see great barriers and chains
Holding me back from reaching there.
> Not so, said God,
> You forge them from your fears and pains
> To stop me getting in to share.

But I am weak and need to be protected,
I cannot live without my safety line.
> Not so, said God,
> You make yourself the unknown stranger
> And set your world within, instead of setting free.

But . . . Not so, said God,
> It's you who make the final choice
> To greet the babe of Bethlehem,
> And only you can smash the cage to let the earth rejoice
> And make of this world and today the new Jerusalem.

Colin Ferguson

Constant wish

O God of many names
Lover of all nations
We pray for peace

> In our hearts
> In our homes
> In our nations
> In our world

> The peace of your will
> The peace of our need

Have the leader read the first stanza, four voices from different parts of the gathering read the second, and then all say the last two lines with perhaps those on the left side saying the first, the other half the second. Finally, everyone could say the whole prayer.

The global party

God, who gave your son Jesus Christ
as the measure of your immeasurable love,
gather your people from every tribe, language
and nation into your eternal kingdom.
How great it will be, when bound together
in love we worship you in all our languages
in songs of never-ending praise.

Alleluia! Amen

Absent core

The dominant fact about our world today
is that life is no longer loved.

Gabriel Marcel

Psalm 68

As smoke is blown away,
as wax melts in the fire,
so do racism, oppression and exploitation
perish in God's presence.
The oppressed and down-trodden are liberated in his presence;
they are happy and shout for joy.

God, who lives in slums and locations,
cares for orphans and protects widows.
He will give those who live outside in the cold
a home to live in,
and will lead those who dwell in the hell of apartheid
out into happy freedom.

O God, lead your people across the desert
of colonialism, oppression and racism.
Shake the foundations of the evil regime and destroy it.

May justice and peace rain on your people
and restore your worn-out land;
may the oppressed feel at home in their land,
and provide in your goodness for the exploited.

Praise the Lord, who weeps with us day after day;
he is the God who liberates us.
Our God is the Lord who rescues us from the oppressor.

O God, the march of the oppressed is seen by all,
and you are the king who leads us.
The singers of freedom songs are in front,
the music is the tears of the people,
and the blood of sons and daughters who die in the struggle.

Praise the Lord, children of Africa;
praise the Lord for ever and ever,
all you descendants of the oppressed!

Show your power, O God,
the power you have used on our behalf.
Rebuke the regime that works evil and destruction.

The word 'Africa' in stanza seven can be replaced by the country where these words are said.

Zephania Kameeta

Renewal

Where families are fractured
by domestic upheavals
and children forced on to streets
to fight for survival,

Where more resources are spent
on arms and destruction
and less attention paid
to sickness and starvation,

Come, Holy Spirit,
Heal our wounds,
Renew the whole Creation!

Where the acquisition of things
has become an obsession
and the worth of a human being
is measured by one's possessions,

Where our air, trees and seas
are besieged by pollution
and purblind mercenary greed
threatens our environment,

Come, Holy Spirit,
Heal our wounds,
Renew the whole Creation!

Where countries are split apart
by communalism and racism
and innocent blood is spilt
by wanton acts of terrorism,

Where internecine warfare

sets nation against nation
and a nuclear holocaust
looms ominous on our horizon,
Come, Holy Spirit,
Heal our wounds,
Renew the whole Creation!

Cecil Rajendra

More words about nations and peoples:

Words about Church
and community

Church and community are not placed together here merely for the sake of space: they are inseparable. And the prayers reflect this fact. The Church exists for the community, and never for itself, although at times it may be driven in upon itself through the sheer force of brute persecution. In worship, the round of human activity that makes up the life of a community is offered up. Good and bad stories are heard, the totality of human experience explored. Hubert Halbfas was right when he said in his *Theory Of Catechetics*: 'A language which does not speak in terms of the world cannot speak the truth. If faith is rooted in the single reality, in our history and age, and if God does not exist outside this reality but only within it, all genuine discussion of God must be discussion of the world. There is no such thing as a sacred language which opens the depths of reality and yet exists on a different plane from secular language. Talk of God is not talk *about* God but of our involvement in God.'

Obviously the Church asserts certain claims about the Universe, Creation, Man and Woman and so on which will not be shared by many in the community. But it is one thing saying these, for instance repeating the Creed, as though they are the words of an exclusive club constitution, and quite another doing so as *part* of the community. It is a matter of theology and attitude.

The modern church?

(For two performers. They are both American evangelists.)

1: Now then, young man, I know this is the first time you've taken a service here, but I don't want you to be nervous. What's your name, by the way?

2: Moses T Rosenbloom the Third.

1: Great, just great. Hey, Moses – seems like a familiar name. Didn't I come across it in a book once?

2: It's in the Bible, Mr Ginsberg. I've been reading it a lot lately.

1: Now you don't want to bother about things like that too much, Moses. Just keep it simple. Don't want to blind them with science, do we?

2: No, Mr Ginsberg.

1: Call me Elmer. I'm sure we're going to get along real swell. Now, about the service. I've got the latest Central Church Computer readout here, and it seems as if we're due for a spot of temptation – to coin a phrase.

2: But Elmer, I was feeling a call to speak about love.

1: Moses, you don't want to worry too much about what you're called to do. That can turn out to be very demanding. You just stick to what the computer says. That's the safest way.

2: How long should I speak for, Elmer?

1: Thirteen minutes and forty-one seconds.

2: Exactly, Elmer?

1: Sure. You have to leave room for the pizza commercial – and if you run out of things to say, just close your eyes. With any luck they'll think you're praying.

2: What about the music?

1: Well, the choir will be miming to records as usual. All you have to do is remember the sponsors when you announce the hymns. Let's see . . . today it's 'Nearer my God to Thee' sponsored by British Airways; and 'From Greenland's Icy Mountains' – Everest Double Glazing. Just remember, I'll be up in the penthouse suite if you need me.

2: It's good to know you'll be with me in prayer, Elmer.

1: Prayer, nothing: I shall be watching the next episode of 'Dallas'. After all, somebody has to keep in touch with the real world:

(*They leave*)

Peter English

God's Army or the White Trucks

And the army of the Lord is armed with mighty weapons.
Forgiveness is polished often, and obedience is sharp.
Humility is used with skill; love replenished at any time.
Discipline is the practice of true liberty;
And the Word they have is dynamite.

The army of the Lord is mighty
Like great white trucks on the highway,
Coming toward you at a distance with no sound;
But with power like the mighty angels,
Or the silent strength of God driving on.

Judith Jenkins

The Samaritan – Luke 15

By chance he came
on the scene
a scene too bloody to describe –
gaping wounds
red-open in the sun

flesh

torn in haste
by hands desperate for coins
eyes
still wide with wondering
hurt him

By chance he stumbled
on the place
where holy men read liturgies
on the move
peripatetically oblivious
to complaints
framed from the ditch
the chantings
of certain men
who always cry
unseen

Not by chance he stooped
ripping his coat
to bind those holes
host to the flies
a dusty stranger
lying compassionless
in the heat
The one still gasping
clutched his neck
kissed his cheek
whispered a parched thanksgiving
from a bleeding mouth

He gathered up
the man
laid him on a beast
racing the setting sun
to the inn
By chance
the man
took the deposit

on trust
and hurried back
to feed the priests

Martin Eggleton

Biblical images of the Church

the people of God
the new creation
the fellowship of the faithful
the Body of Christ
the new humanity
the Kingdom of God
the sanctified
the justified
disciples
the witnessing community
slaves
the household of God
the brotherhood
a spiritual body
a chosen race
a holy nation
the elect
a flock
the Holy City
priesthood
the salt of the earth
the ark of salvation
unleavened bread
branches of the vine

Tony Jasper

Someone in the crowd
Mark 5. 25–34

1: Someone in the crowd
2: Bled for love

1: Someone in the crowd
2: Struggled

1: Someone in the crowd
2: Couldn't move

1: Someone in the crowd
2: Reached Him

1: Someone in the crowd
2: Touched Him

1: Someone in the crowd
2: Was healed

1: Someone in the crowd
2: Felt it

1: Someone in the crowd
2: Felt drained

1: Someone in the crowd
2: Called her

1: Someone in the crowd
2: Trembled

1: Someone in the crowd
2: Confessed

1: Someone in the crowd
2: Released her

1: Someone in the crowd
2: Someone in the crowd

Martin Eggleton

Seeing the crowd
From John 6. For two voices.

1: Have you seen the crowd?
2: The crowd?
1: Following.
2: Who?
1: Why, you mean.
2: No, who, or better, whom?
1: They need food.
2: They've come to see what He's doing.
1: Bread.
2: Bread?
1: They need to eat.
2: Every word He says.
1: Where?
2: What?
1: Where shall they find it?
2: What?
1: Bread.
2: There's too many.
1: A crowd's never too many.
2: For what?
1: For miracles.
2: When?
1: Any time.
2: Any time?
1: Any time a lad shares his lunch.

Martin Eggleton

People who care

Chorus:
People who care, people who care,
People who care are everywhere.
People who care, people who care,

People who care are everywhere.

Mrs Jones is 72
She still finds plenty of work to do.
Collects every year for Christian Aid,
And people are using the blankets she made.
Chorus.

John and Andy are marching for peace,
Banning the bomb for wars to cease.
They may wear denims and have long hair,
But they are two of the people who care.
Chorus.

Now I know a man who keeps open house,
The news is spread, and it gets about.
Black and white, and it gets about.
Black and white, you will find them there,
He is one of the people who care.
Chorus.

Political prisoners far away
Get a letter from Jill on Christmas Day.
She's never met them, never been there,
She is one of the people who care.
Chorus.

Ten thousand people stood in the rain
To lobby politicians again and again,
Colin and Andrea they were there,
for they are two of the people who care.
Chorus

Now don't just say that the world's in a state,
Nothing to do 'cause it's just too late.
Get yourself moving, get out of your chair,
Show that you're one of the people who care.
Chorus.

David Hill
The gathering could form a circle and as they say the chorus for the first

*time, move closer together towards the centre. Each verse can be said
by one person, and during the next chorus that person can be lifted
up high.*

These words are set to music in David Hill's book Carpenters Need
Not Apply.

Give us churches

Give us, O Lord, churches
that will not merely 'comfort the afflicted' but 'afflict the
comfortable';
that will not only love the world but will also judge the world;
that will not only pursue peace but also demand justice;
that will not remain silent when people are calling for a voice;
that will not pass by on the other side when wounded humanity
is waiting to be healed;
that not only call us to worship but also send out to witness;
that will follow Christ even when the way points to a Cross.
To this end we offer ourselves in the Name of Him who loved us
    and gave Himself for us – Amen.

Written for the Christian Conference of Asia, 1977

True direction

May we cross false frontiers
and find the road which leads
into fuller understanding of ourselves and each other,
and more fulfilled life in community.
Fill us with your spirit
of hope, faith, love
and truth.

Tom's complaint

Why is church so *boring*, Mum?
Why is it? Hey?
Surely God likes pop music
and a bit of a swing?
He must have invented it,
after all!

Why does everyone look so bored
and over-posh?
Why do they, Mum?
Why do they, hey?
Don't they realize
God is cool?

If I was a vicar
I'd wear a multi-coloured shirt
and all the hymns would be jazz.
Church would be OK
everyone would be happy
because that's what God is *like*!

by Tom Ralls and Mum

Severely out of sorts

Father
    in this House I am not welcome.
They are deaf to me
    in order to scold me for my silence.
Strong in speech in order to call my voice weak.
They take my idealism as fair trade for their own.
They deny me myself
    in order to deny me part of You.

And when I die, without lord or equivalent,
Their pity will be the last noise I hear
    before going to sleep,

turning off the light of their dim phrases
    to finally hear my own

But now through this open window I crawl,
    and once outside in Your ceilingless sanctuary
will be alone with my own devices, some of which
    they were right to condemn,
    some of which were Your gifts to me.
Tonight with stone pillow and adventure weary heart
    I stare at the stars before falling asleep,
  record your last words in my mind.

Then sealing your ancient encouragement safe inside
  my coat,
    will head off over hills, leading into dusk,
    away from their suns,
Touring each day over flat plains and waking them
    with dull memory of what they must do
    while lulling their imaginations to sleep.

Carol Short

The not-good-enough Samaritan's Good Samaritan Story

Jesus said:

'A man was going down from Jerusalem to Jericho when he fell among thieves who stole all he possessed, beat him and left him for dead.

Now, by chance, a minister was travelling that road. He came upon the man and was about to do something when he paused.

'I think the first thing we ought to do is pray for deliverance from the things of the world, don't you?'

The man groaned.

'Lord, we beseech you, protect us from all evil, keep your sheep beside still waters and safe from the valley of temptation that we might drink from the spring of the life everlasting. Amen!'

Having prayed he stretched forth his hand but, as he did so, he noticed his watch.

'Dear me, if I stop any longer I'll be late for the Church Council meeting,' he thought, and so he hurried on.

In the same way a social worker came by and stopped a moment.

'You look as if you need help,' he began.

The man groaned.

'If you'd like to ring the office and make an appointment I expect I could see you next Wednesday or Thursday or the week after at the latest.'

The man groaned again and the social worker shook his head. What a shame that some people got mugged out of office hours.

Moving on, he soon faded into the distance.

Some time later, a local councillor passed along the road. Seeing the body lying there, he was filled with genuine concern.

'I don't know what the local community is coming to. There's no respect for property any more. People aren't safe on the streets. I said only the other day that our community policing scheme needs to be extended. If I'd had my way in the meeting, this might not have happened.'

The man groaned, a little fainter this time.

'Don't worry, my man,' said the councillor, 'I'll be bringing the matter up again. Indeed, I'll mention your case in the General Purposes Sub-Committee tomorrow afternoon.'

And as he passed on, the man's groans became fainter and fainter until he made no sound at all . . .'

And the people who heard him said:

'Hey, just a moment, where's the good Samaritan?'

And he replied:

'What a very good question!'

Dave Kitchen

Wider family

Leader:

Christ's is the world in which we move,
Christ's are the folk we're summoned to love,
Christ's is the voice which calls us to care,
And Christ is the one who meets us here.

All say refrain:

> To the lost Christ shows his face;
> To the unloved he gives his embrace;
> To those who cry in pain or disgrace
> Christ makes with his friends a touching place.

Another voice:

> Feel for the people we most avoid –
> Strange or bereaved or never employed;
> Feel for the women and feel for the men
> Who fear that their living is all in vain.

All say refrain.

Another voice!

> Feel for the parents who've lost their child,
> Feel for the women whom men have defiled,
> Feel for the baby for whom there's no breast,
> And feel for the weary who find no rest.

All say refrain.

Another voice:

> Feel for the lives by life confused,
> Riddled with doubt, in loving abused;
> Feel for the lonely heart, conscious of sin,
> Which longs to be pure but fears to begin

All say refrain.

Shalom

The word *shalom* occurs over 250 times in the Old Testament and is usually translated *peace*. However it means much more than inward tranquillity or the absence of war. It expresses a dynamic state which includes movement, growth, soundness, harmony, wholeness and completeness. It is promoted by *obedience*: 'If you will obey me completely, I will not punish you ... I am the Lord who heals you' (Exodus 15:26). In the Hebrew there is a relationship with the word we translate as *Amen*, which is an indication of assent. Used at the end of prayers and hymns it suggests 'I endorse all that has been said and associate myself with it'. (See also Isaiah 1: 5–6.)

The state of shalom is also dependent upon the nature of our *relationships*. Today we think of illness as an individual experience but the Hebrews thought much more collectively: 'Israel, your head is covered with wounds and your heart and your mind are sick . . . there is not a healthy spot on your body' (Isaiah 32: 17). Community sickness can and does cause individuals to be sick. This happened in the Miners' Strike: in the areas most affected the GP's surgeries were crowded with needy people. Their mental and physical ailments were caused directly by the breakdown in community relationships.

When human beings rebel against God and live selfishly, then illness is frequently the direct consequence. This is because 'Men and women do not have bodies: they are bodies. They are flesh animated by souls, the whole conceived as a psycho-physical unity' (John A.T. Robinson).

Shalom, then, is enabled by our living in a right relationship with ourselves, with our family and wider community, with nature – and with God.

Did you see them?

Did you see them,
God,
living
to be part of others?
Did you see them?
Did you?
Did you see
a building
loved
into your home?
Did you see
the food,
the clothes,
the beds,
the heaters,
did you?
Did you see the love

that forced its way
through the cracks
in the brickwork,
built in your name?
Did you?
Did you see those people
use love,
to dig out
the very roots of
Christianity?
Did you?
Did you see those people
with one thought
in one action?
Did you rejoice?
Did you?
I saw you,
God,
planning,
doing,
loving.
I saw you
helping
to become.
I saw you
lifting,
cleaning,
living,
giving,
explaining.
I saw you
and I'm glad,
your home
is
LOVE.

Sharing

> Sharing is
being myself, for others.
> Sharing is
allowing yourself to be for others.
> Sharing is
a request,
>> got a piece of bread
got a cup of tea
got a pair of shoes, a shirt, a tie, a
bed, any love
to share with me?
> Sharing is
a response,
>> share my bread
share my tea
here's a pair of shoes, a shirt, a tie,
a bed, my love.
> Sharing is
my love
towards the other
and allowing him
to bear his love
towards me.

Bill Kirkpatrick

Blessing

Come, Lord Jesus,
bless what we have done.
We have touched each other
We have been open with each other
We have given up something
We have shared words
We have noted mannerisms and expressions

We have loved our clothes
We have enjoyed stories and personal recollections
We have felt anger and misunderstanding
We have struggled not to lose things thought precious
We have gained from taking on trust the unsure
We have felt or shed tears
We have been thrown from our moorings
We have come through storms of new experiences.

Come, Lord Jesus,
bless us now.
These are very special people, Lord,
and if we never keep promises to write and meet up
and if time quickly moves us to other things
take care of them
for they, like us, are yours,
The Lord of difference,
The Lord who accepts.

Come, Lord, come.
In the name of the Father, and of the Son and of the
    Holy Spirit
God speed. We love you all.

Tony Jasper

*Best said by a group that has undergone common experiences, perhaps during
a day, weekend or week together.*

Sharing in the life of the Church

Leader: As we share the life of your Church today,
we pray that our witness will be true to Christ.
Give us a voice for the silenced.

All: And quiet communion,
when only silence will honour pain.

Leader: Give us tears in the face of grief.
All: And laughter as we experience the joys of your creation.
Leader: Give us sharpness in the revealing of injustice.
All: And your eternal gentleness with those who cross our path
in despair.

Leader: Give us integrity in admitting our confusions.
All: And faithfulness in our life with our neighbours.
For you call us to work with you in confident relationship, believing that our prayers are the joining of our love, with your love, for the world.

Leader: In the grace of God lies the infinite possibility of hope.
All: Amen.

Dorothy McMahon

Words about call, discipleship and commitment

Bible passages:

Genesis 12
Exodus 3
Isaiah 6:9
Jeremiah 1
Ezekiel 1 and 2
Hosea 1:2 and subsequent narratives
Amos 7:15–17
Matthew 4:18–22
Acts 9:1–22
Romans 1:8–12
1 Corinthians 3:1–4, 18–23
2 Thessalonians 1:11
Hebrews 11

Worship can offer a special space in which there is prayer and silence and an invitation for people to discover the will of God in their lives. Obviously all 'good' worship enshrines within it an unconscious call to follow the things of God beyond mere attendance at Sunday service. The Church down the ages has confronted people with a challenge.

Call, discipleship and commitment come to people in endless forms and guises, and this brief section cannot attempt to develop the theme outlined by its title. In broad terms, a 'yes' to the call finds its ultimate expression amidst the redemptive presence of God among the whole of human life.

The continuing presence within the world of a Christian community asserts that against all seeming odds humanity does have a future.

No one can believe, Jesus says, unless the Father draws him or her to faith. And in the call, with its response of discipleship and commitment, who does not tremble and ask 'why'? – but then so did Jeremiah, and countless others since.

Waiting for the gas-can

I sit in the old car on the rainy road.
Others have gone for gas.
I know they won't come back.
It is because I am a believer, hallelujah,
I stay with the car that has run out of gas,
and blown all tyres.
I think it is on fire too.
But I will stay a Christian
no matter what logical approach away from it
is brought to me.
I have raised two children,
taught Sunday school ten years,
been married seventeen to the same man,
an accountant.
It should have been enough to kill a horse,
or at least a poet.
But words keep coming, and have never slowed
from their deluge of rain.
I stay in the old car,
I am dust and his breath, and shall return to it.
I proclaim Christ's resurrection from the dead.
Like the old tree with a limb or two left,
bark pulling away from the trunk,
I stand with believers.
I will rise like birds from that tree
in the rain.
My spiny soul shall dry in flight.
I know Christ comes up the road for me.

He looks like my dad, wearing the same pants
as he got taller,
back in the hard days they had.
Beyond ridicule, and limitation, and disbelief,
I stay in the car.
It's him that's coming up the road.
I know it's him that's coming
with the water-pump, the air-hose,
and gas-can.

Diane Glancy

A woman's work

I am Mary, Martha's sister.
Here I sit, next to Jesus.
The room is full of the desperate,
the sick, the lonely.
The crowds press in.
So many of them.
I feel so helpless.

In my hands is a cup of wine
and a loaf of bread.
'This is your place, at my side.
Feed them, heal them,'
he said.

I look at him in horror.
'What can I do, Lord?
I am only a woman.'

'Give them my body
for their own are broken.
Give them my blood
for their forgiveness.
Call them,
for you have all they need
within your hands.
I have put it there.

Do not say "I am only a woman."
I made you.
May I not also call you?'

Beth Webb

One with the more deserving
Based on Psalm 121 and Hebrews 12:1–2

Lord, sometimes I feel alone.
Vulnerable.
Standing in a wasteland.
I see nothing ahead, nothing behind.
Just one hard-edged moment of tension.
I freeze.

And then I see behind, around me, people,
Women and men who've lived their lives
In the faith I hold,
Who've lived and died
In the wonder of your love.

If I could meet them now, in flesh,
medieval mystic, scribe,
illiterate workman,
Renaissance priests,
we'd span great gulfs,
seem strangers from another world.
I'd want to say the classic words:
'Take me to your leader.'
And when they did
I'd find their lives
based on the same mystery of your love.
Their hopes, their fears bound up in you.
Same Lord. Over the centuries.
Which should be no surprise to me,
seeing that you don't change.
The same forever. The unbroken thread
reeled out for lifeline

as I walk, warily, sometimes wearily,
through the confusing maze of dark and light
that is my world.
The thread goes back to you.
Goes on to you in the uncertain future.
Uncertain only in my own brief view
tentative beyond the next horizon.
But sure in you.
In the strong chain of lives lived,
deaths died,
in your hand.

Lord, it's good to know
that I, too, am part of your purposes.
Seen, unknown. Acknowledged

Eddie Askew

Another part of me

Home –
shaking with joy, no, I don't know these people
but I have walked this broken cracked concrete
        how many times?
I laughed here cried here
I learned of myself, others, magic
here in this circle
packed earth and brown grass
music down home back home blues
        no more drinking to forget
trying to remember everything in one glorious flash
        of stars and gold chords

and another part of my search is ended
for now, I will wander only in my mind across fields
        and over mountains
    I know their songs of wildness and freedom
    I will rest here and grow . . .
            home

Su Parris

Litany of the Disciples of Christ the Servant

Leader: Servant-Christ, help us to follow you
in untiring ministry to town and village,
to heal and restore the broken body of humanity,
to cast out the demonic forces
of greed, resentment, communal hatred
and self-destructive fears.

People: Servant-Christ, help us all to follow you.

Leader: Help us to follow you on the road to Jerusalem,
to set our faces firmly against friendly suggestions
to live a safe, expedient life;
to embrace boldly the way of self-offering,
the way of life given for others' gain.

People: Servant-Christ, help us all to follow you.

Leader: Help us to follow you into the temple
of your chosen people,
to erase from the worship of your church
all that hinders the sense of your presence,
and the free flow of your word;
to open up your house
that it may be a house of prayer for all people.

People: Servant-Christ, help us all to follow you.

Leader: Help us to follow you into the upper room,
to share your meal of bread and cup,
to accept our common place in your one body
broken to create a new humanity.

People: Servant-Christ, help us all to follow you.

Leader: Help us to follow you into the garden,
to watch with you,
ever vigilant for signs of the dawning of your day,
to struggle unsparingly to understand and to be obedient
to your perfect will.

People: Servant-Christ, help us all to follow you.

Leader: Help us to follow you unto the Cross,

to recognize the true way of life in your death,
to see our hope in your self-spending love,
to die to all within us not born of your love.

People: Servant-Christ, help us all to follow you.

Leader: Help us to follow you out of the dark tomb;
to share daily in your resurrection life,
to be renewed daily in your image of love,
to serve daily as your new body
in ministering to the world.

People: Servant-Christ, help us all to follow you.

Dietrich Bonhoeffer

Crooked cross on the muffed, tolled acre
Told death's reign in iron, barbed wire,
Bullet and crematoria smoke.
Buchenwald of ill fame (faded
After thirty years' post-Nazi slime, the shame
Of man's coming of age) displayed its back-drag
Into primeval nurseries. Bully and victim
Naked as in their first, fenced twilight: robe or rag
Of reason was torn, leaving snarl and slobber.
Even the faith-tongued, wilting amid vermin,
Felt the rosary rot while the gallows hemp stayed strong,
And the slammed hypothesis of a loving Maker
Echoed mockingly through the gurgling skein.

The young pastor with the poet's eyes
Kept his secret, musing calmly apart,
Tracing transcendence in the base day's dole.
Thoughts wrung from Hegel, Goethe, Barth
Flocked with clear peace of the Danube summer,
Bavarian forests in the free years, and warmer ties
Edging to poignancy: the girl he would never wed
Vanishing from the cell door at Tegel . . .

The true Cross turned crooked under pressure:
His lovely trust and prayers knotted confusedly

With the cool brain's warp. Blind guesses would stumble
Beyond the camp barrier, touching religionless man,
Who seemed spilled, drained of creed-props, over broken   -
countries,
Shrugging at gutted churches. The captive pastor
Saw a Cross that meant mere crumpled deity,
A heaven that knew only secular service
From the adult nature's autonomy.

The camp gates opened in savage rain
For Bonhoeffer's final journey.
The truck rattled on beside the stung Danube
Under trees that did not rattle: the month was April,
With hushed knots of leaves and buds passively bowing.
And he knelt at Flossenburg, the last plank straight again
To his acquitted faith. An infinite mercy,
Moving above death-cell and execution yard,
Annulled for him the blind probe
And the secular tolling.

Jack Clemo

*Dietrich Bonhoeffer, German theologian, was imprisoned and executed
for his involvement in a plot to assassinate Hitler. The letters, prayers
and other religious writings which he composed in captivity have become
spiritual classics.*

Unexpected treats

We thank you, God,
Because you give us
more than we would ever dream of asking:
daily bread and shared meals that become feasts,
the breath of life, and voices to celebrate,
the understandings of our history and the hope of our future,
Work we can, and time to be recreated,
people to love and trust,
people who love and trust us,
gifts and responsibilities.

We thank you, God,
Because you ask of us
more than we ever dream of giving;
skills we have never developed,   .
care for a world whose problems we cannot solve,
listening which hurts us,
giving which leaves us empty-handed,
love which makes us vulnerable,
faith which seems impossible.
But you do not ask us to be supermen and women,
You challenge us to be human.
Give us the courage to be human
because you yourself became human
and lived our lives,
knowing our imperfections,
sharing our joy and pain,
making us your people
so that we can say together
    Our Father, who art in heaven . . .

Ian Pickard

Not yet

Not yet the living of the day long dawned.
Not yet the seeing of the light that is.
Not yet the caring for a cared-for world.
Not yet the singing of the harmonies that are.
Not yet the ending of our ended days.
Not yet the dying of our deadly deeds.
Not yet the crying for a tearful joy.
Not yet the toppling of the powers that were.
Not yet,
Dear hopeful God of hope,
Not yet
acceptance of
these unacceptable 'not yet's'!

David Harding

Just far enough away

They stood proudly
they sang loudly
'We have the victory
We have the victory
Jesus Christ the Life of the world'
We all sang loudly
We stood proudly
Then we went home.

Tony Jasper

Prayer Asking

This is a weekly list of a Methodist church's 'prayer' schedule, that of Quex Road, Kilburn, London. Ask your gathering for prayer wants. Quex is a multi-racial gathering.

LET US GIVE THANKS
– for the beauty and variety of creation
– for the gift of life and health
– for the love of family and friends
– for safe journeys
– for the fellowship of the Church and the good news of
   the Gospel

LET US PRAY FOR THOSE WHO ARE ILL
– for any living with incurable illnesses and those who care
   for them
– for friends and members of our own families who are ill

LET US PRAY FOR
– all who grieve
– our loved ones who are separated from us
– the lonely and anxious
– those without homes
– those looking for work
– those without purpose or faith to sustain them

- students beginning new courses
- those preparing for marriage
- all who are making new beginnings

LET US PRAY FOR THE NEEDS OF THE WORLD
- for peace within and between nations
- for the leaders of the nations
- for the countries from which we each come
- for the right use of the earth's resources that all might be freed from poverty and hunger

LET US PRAY FOR OUR OWN NEEDS
for wisdom in making decisions about the future
- for strength in coping with pain
- for tolerance and understanding in our dealings with others

LORD IN YOUR MERCY – HEAR OUR PRAYER

Not winter again!

Bitterly cold, say it again,
bitterly cold, bitterly cold;
pains in my chest
and weak my hold.
Damp my scarf from condensation,
steamy, foggy conversation,
muffled in wool,
weighed down with jumpers,
stamping feet, no rhyme or rhythm
just beat.
I'm losing feeling,
prayers hit the ceiling,
numb with cold,
lost the way,
nothing to say,
here in the snow,
where nothing will grow.
Once I was bold
now I am cold

growing old
far from the fold.
Bitterly cold, say it again

Bitterly cold.

Graham Claydon

The Minutes

Minutes of the St Jude's Parish Council

6. 00 p.m. 10 November 1985

Present: Rev. P. Simon (parish Priest)

Mr W. Oxbridge (headmaster of St Jude's Comprehensive School)

Miss G. Grey (retired headmistress of St Jude's Primary School)

Miss MacPhail (senior mistress, St Jude's Primary School)

Mr S. Springer (youth officer)

Mr A. Fisher (local councillor, publicity convenor)

Mr McCollum (bank manager)

The minutes of the October 10th meeting were read and approved. The council then discussed the first point on the agenda: 'Now that planning permission has been granted, a site chosen and bank loan assured, are we to go ahead with the building of a parish youth club?'

Rev. P. Simon: Welcomed the suggestion, but advised postponement of any decision because afraid the enterprise might overtax both the finances and energies of the parish. Also questioned whether a youth club was the best service the parish could give to its youth and to the cause of ecumenism, which should be a priority in all our Church ministry.

(Rev. P. Simon is feeling his advanced middle age, is still hoping for a bishopric and is afraid of any move which may involve him in financial risk or more work. He can no longer communicate with modern youth.)

Miss Grey: Agreed with Father. Finds modern youth too pampered.

Thinks organized voluntary work in the town would do them more good and save money for worthier causes.

> (Miss Grey's new bungalow and extensive garden, which needs clearing and digging, adjoins the site of the proposed club. Her peace is threatened.)

Mr Oxbridge: Agreed with previous speakers, considers the town already adequately provided with youth clubs, besides the excellent facilities which the school provides. Clear religious instruction for youth a greater need than billiard and pool tables.

> (Mr Oxbridge is an ambitious man whose life revolves around O- and A-level successes. He will oppose anything which could distract his pupils from their studies.)

Miss MacPhail: Thinks that a youth club is badly needed, illustrating her point with many examples. Suggested the youths themselves should be taught how to build it and that the club should be open to all religions. Building the club would bring unity among the youth, would give them a sense of pride, appreciation of the value of work and practice in ecumenism.

> (Miss MacPhail's life has been blighted for the last twenty years with a consuming hatred for Miss Grey, who was appointed headmistress instead of herself. What Miss Grey proposes, Miss MacPhail must oppose.)

Mr Springer: Agreed with Miss MacPhail on the need for a youth club a need confirmed in his own experience as a professional youth worker. Advised strongly the appointment of a professionally qualified and adequately salaried youth worker for the club. In making this suggestion, he also stated that he had no personal interest in such a post.

> (Mr Springer, just engaged, is afraid that he would be expected to run the youth club unsalaried in his spare time.)

Mr Fisher: Enthusiastic about the project and assured the meeting that a Catholic club would be welcomed by the town councillors and that it would not be an unecumenical gesture.

Optimistic that the club could be built through Manpower Services, which could cut costs and provide a work force.

(Mr Fisher is ambitious for higher things and hopes to enter national politics. He approves anything which can bring him publicity.)

Mr McCollum: Voted in favour of the club.

(Mr McCollum looks after the parish accounts voluntarily. He dreads the extra work which would be involved, but reckons the youth club would serve a need and therefore does not allow his reluctance to face extra work to influence his vote.)

The arguments given by the members of the parish council for and against the proposal are not in themselves bad but, under the appearance of good and sound proposals, all the members, except for Mr McCollum, are intent on furthering their own personal kingdom. Fr Simon's predominant interest, to which everything else is subordinate, is his own comfort and chances of promotion, Miss Grey has dedicated her life to peaceful retirement, Mr Oxbridge to examination successes, Miss MacPhail to revenge, Mr Springer is afraid of being imposed upon and Mr Fisher's idol is favourable publicity for himself. Whether they decide on a youth club or not is relatively unimportant, because their attitude, if it continues unchanged, will ensure that the youth of the parish, and any other groups they may consider, will be neglected, the good of others being subordinated to their own private interests. In their outward behaviour and with their lips they have the interest of the community at heart; in reality, they are using the community for their own praise, reverence and service. In words they serve: in practice they exploit. They are worshipping Mammon.

Gerard W. Hughes

This text, from the splendid book God of Surprises *by Gerard W. Hughes, can be used in an informal gathering. The roles and the author's notes make useful discussion material.*

Its inclusion is not intended as a youth pick-me-up, to say 'told you what adults are like', nor to support any prejudice – notwithstanding the fact,

*that, yes, some adults do behave this way. The intent is this – to widen
understanding of those whose behaviour is sadly lacking, and who confront
the Kingdom's coming with deathly impact.*

*If used as part of a youth service, it might be balanced by another dramatic
piece or poem that suggests young people's behaviour too can display more of
egotism and obstinacy than of the Kingdom. Careful note should be made
of the author's final critique on the characters he has created, and prayer
or comment could follow to the effect that all of us need to 'get our houses
in order' for the sake of the Gospel.*

Today's music and more

Father,
some sounds thrill.
There are so many great records around.
we enjoy the music of so many artists,
we follow their careers. . . .

Sometimes though, we're confused,
we're not too sure on occasions whether in fact
some groups and artists are merely involved in
making money at the expense of our feelings
and emotions.
Father,
when sounds of today capture so much of the world
as we see it
may these songs speak with honesty,
may they help us understand the world and ourselves.

Help us to make our own music,
help us to talk about life in our music.
In fact we've got to shout Jesus in music –
which is a pretty big task.
Help us!

Father,
we thank you for Greenbelt, for Spring Harvest, Rob Frost and the
Easter People, Harry, Riding Lights, the Arts Centre Group, the
Cambridge Group, Iona, Taizé, the Ashram community and many

others given to social witness and spiritual insight, churches and
groups of the Spirit, and all communities socially and politically
involved for the sake of Jesus.

Tony Jasper

Little Magdala

Maddy is brown
Maddy is winsome
green eyed sprite
under a tangled mane.

You bring hot cups of tea unbidden
and a cool hand
on my aching head.

How well you weave your way
into the hearts
of those who know you.

Like God's own spirit
in the Magdala's heart,

you watch quietly,
waiting to see
whose feet you may anoint next.

Beth Webb

Right together

Go in peace, go in love,
Finding joy in each other.
Go in peace, go in love,
In Christ we're sister and brother.
Led by his spirit, there's strength each day,
Light for the way – together.
Go in peace, go in love,
May God be with us forever.

Anonymous

Fulfilment

If from a seed of thought has blossomed truth,
If from a seed of sound, a melody,
If from a seed of kindness action sprang and formed into
a deed;
If we have given love and seen it bloom
And open like a flower to the light,
If we have offered sunshine in the gloom and met another's
need,
Lord, in the fruitful summer of our lives
When hopes are high and smoothly lie our ways,
We give to you, the Sower, thanks and praise
For what we have achieved.

Joy Martin

A day in the life

The sunlight burned across the surface of the planet, making its
way through Adam's bedroom window. Realising that it was time
to rise, he prepared himself for the morning's routine. Having
bathed and dressed, he sat down to his meal.

As he finished, he hurried out the door, leaving the dishes right
where he ate. (Living alone allows you this luxury!) Once outside,
he adjusted the one-way light shields over his eyes, and headed
down the narrow causeway that led to the main street.

As he joined the hundreds of other people scurrying to their
various destinations, he reached for the slim silver button that
activates the headset of his aural sensory array. A little red light
on the unit comes on, indicating the batteries are charged, and the
sound in his ears indicated that the recorded information was
being reproduced properly. He was on his way.

It was then that he realized that he was in his own world.
Separated from the rest of the planet by light shields and recorded
sound. He passed by an old woman who seemed frightened of his
presence. The look in his eyes would have shown her that he was
no threat, but she couldn't see them.

284 Worship The King

Coming in the opposite direction, were members of a popular religious cult. A mother, a father, and a young son about two or three years old. Cults . . . deception. The little boy smiled at Adam as they walked by, unable to see Adam's tear for him, because of the light shields. The mother was simply in a hurry to get by.

Adam continued on his way, smelling the atmosphere, basking in the light of the planet's sun. He passed an older man leaving the information service, papers packed under his arm. He seemed lonely, but Adam did not speak. He was too absorbed in the sounds he was hearing. Adam was not particularly pleased with his behaviour, but the idea of being so removed from the rest of the planet intrigued him. It was a concept he had not considered before.

Before long, he had reached his destination. Up the steps, through the doorway and into the main hall.

'Good morning, Brother Adam! Are you all ready?'

'I sure am!'

'Well, praise God!'

As Adam entered the Bible study, he removed his mirror glasses, turned off his Sony Walkman, and began to pray.

Artie Terry

One of the best

Hope is one of your best gifts to us.
Teach us to give it to others.

When words are gone

Woman whose work is words
what will you do when words are gone?

> Grow in silence like the trees
> find strength in solitude
> listen to wind, water and living things
> hear what God speaks in silence

Woman who lives by words

what will you do when words are strange?

> Listen for a change,
> learn what people mean in other ways
> smile, gesture – weep even –
> live with questions and powerlessness.

Woman who cares for words what will you do when words overwhelm?

> Laugh at jargon, be angry when talk and papers oppress
> people –
> care more for them remember
> the first and last Word that makes us one.

Jan Pickard

Task

> Facing a task unfinished
> That drives us to our knees:
> A need that is undiminished
> Rebukes our slothful ease;
> We who rejoice to know Thee
> Renew before Thy Throne
> The solemn pledge we owe Thee
> To go and make Thee known

Author unknown

A day in the life of a Christian (1)

Mother wakens him at 7.30. Tired. Too late going to bed last night. Mother shouts for the fourth time. 'Coming,' he cries, shuts his eyes and says a little prayer. No time for anything long; just commits himself into God's hands for the day.

Annoyed at breakfast time, has to brush his own shoes. Mother has left them, saying it's time that he did them himself.

Dashes for bus. Only two minutes late for work. Earliest this week. Discussion in office about immigration. He agrees that country can't support every coloured man who wants to come in.

Dinner in canteen. Has finished soup before he remembers that he had decided to bow his head and say grace before each meal. Comforts himself with the thought that God knows he is thankful anyway; no need to make a show about it. After lunch goes for a walk with some of the boys from the office. Has an argument about football.

Almost finishing time when he remembers he has not got a notebook for Sunday School teachers' meeting. He has two spare ones in his desk – takes one and a biro.

Dashes home. Mother asks him when he is going to lay the tiles in the bathroom. Promises to make a start tomorrow. In his own room looks for his teacher's book. Can't find it. Complains to mother. Finds it eventually with his Bible in the bureau drawer. Has only time to glance through next month's lessons before dashing off to church.

A dozen of them in a little room in the church. Talk of the next four lessons. He wonders if they should switch to another system. Notes are not full enough. It takes so much time to prepare a lesson, he sometimes finds it hard to last out the twenty minutes he has a class. Long wandering discussion about different systems. Meeting finishes about half past nine. Goes into hall and plays a foursome of table tennis.

Leave about 10.15. Stand talking at cross roads till about 11 o'clock. They agree the church is not doing enough to attract teenagers. Arranges to meet them tomorrow night and go to the pictures. Home for supper. Watches late night Western on TV. Mother keeps shouting at him to go to bed. Ten to 12 – goes to bed. Tired. Puts light out before saying his prayers. Thanks God for all His goodness, for the fellowship of being in His service. Drifts off to sleep.

A day in the life of a Christian (2)

Mother wakens her at 7.30. Tired. Getting up she is almost half dressed before she remembers she has not said her prayers. Sits on edge of bed to say morning prayers. Mother interrupts to say breakfast is ready, so prayer is cut short.

Goes through to breakfast resolving to get up early and read a chapter of Bible each morning. Feels vaguely uncomfortable because she has made this resolve before – several times.

Down the street for the bus, finds that Y is standing waiting for her. Annoyed because she cannot stand her. Y seems so stupid she doesn't seem to realize it. Just because she recently joined the church doesn't mean that she has a claim on her. When Y asks her to come to her house that night she is glad that she has a good excuse – has a meeting of Guildry Committee. Y tries to arrange some other night, but manages to put her off.

Not too busy in the office. Manages to type some Guildry letters. At lunch time hears a story about a girl who is off work that she finds hard to believe. Back in the typing pool finds the other girls find it hard to believe as well.

When boss is out phones X about meeting tonight. Chatters for about ten minutes.

Annoyed because a pile of invoices are put on her desk to type. Had meant to write to her brother in Canada.

Glad to get away at five o'clock. Row with mother, who expected her to help with ironing – hasn't time – has minutes of agenda to arrange for committee meeting. Felt better when she left house.

Had a good time at committee meeting. Everyone in good mood, almost giggly. Not much business discussed, but pleasant evening.

Went up to Z's for supper. Heard her latest L.P. Half past ten when she got home. Mother worried about her, still treats her as a kid. Decides to pin up her hair, tries different styles. Almost half past eleven when she gets to bed.

Puts off light before saying prayers. Half way through prayers remembers that she has not read Bible. Decides to get up early to read it in the morning. Thanks God for all His goodness, for the fellowship of being in His service.

Drifts off to sleep.

Kairos

Signing up

All:	We are joining the army that sheds no blood
	We are joining the army that sheds no blood
	We are joining the army that sheds no blood
	Make us one in your love, O Lord
By line:	Halleluia, halleluia, halleluia, halleluia, halleluia
All:	Halleluia
All women:	We are building a city set on a hill
All men:	We are scattered as salt upon the earth
All women:	We will trust in the Lord who knows our needs
All men:	We will work for the Kingdom in all our ways
By line:	Halleluia, our Father, the Holy One
	Halleluia, to Jesus, His Only Son
	Halleluia, the Spirit, who makes us one
All:	We are one in your love, O Lord.

Andrew Kreider

More words about call, discipleship and commitment:

Words of liberation and new life

Bible passages:

Exodus 3:1–17
Joshua 6
1 Samuel 2:1–10
Psalm 126
Isaiah 61
Luke 1:46–55
Luke 4:18
Romans 6:18
Romans 8:2
Philippians 2:8–11
Galatians 5:1
2 Corinthians 3:17
Galatians 2:4
Hebrews 2:15
Revelation 21:1–8, 22–25
Revelation 22:12, 13, 17, 20
1 Thessalonians 4:3–5, 11

This is the victory section, even if we glimpse it only sometimes or in part. It is a section of assertions, of words flung bravely, of dreams. But sights have been seen, and tastes excited. There have been moments of bliss, sometimes amidst great pain. It has been 'good', love has been shared, bread has been broken and bodies mended, wine has been spilt and bodies restored. Holy ground has been trod, the bush consumed with fire, the call heard.

In liberation and new life we hear the cry, 'Here is your God!'

The Saviour is born and is constantly crucified, but always there is hope because of Him.

Words of liberation and new life echo the powerful words of Dennis Potter who in his *Son Of Man* says with understatement: 'You do not belong to Caesar, you belong to God.'

Witness, celebration and struggle—this is the calling of all brothers and sisters. One day He will come and then there will be uncluttered liberation and new life with sights and tastes of shattering purity.

An Advent people

One word, one shout, one blast – that's all
No ifs and buts
no high level conferences
no we-will-if-you-wills.
That day will see the summit
to beat them all –
God: Father, Son and Holy Spirit,
rolling up the earth and heavens
of this old creation.
No one gave them permission to start it
they need no permission to end it –
only in their own creative love.
The new will be unrolled and all will see
the authority of our one Creator God.
There will be no protest, no discussion
but all will bow and say that
Jesus Christ is Lord.

Ann Roberts/Joyce Huggett

My Magnificat

God, you are wonderful.
You have shared your blessing with me:
you have freed even me to be
the woman you want me to be.

In your strength I will carry out
the task you have chosen for me.
Your ordered world is in chaos:
bring back a world of justice
where the hungry are fed
and food mountains disappear;
where each human being is granted
the dignity of being a person
regardless of race, creed, colour or sex;
where we are all equal in the sight of each other;
where we can share all things together.
Great God, you are the leveller –
you know how this can be done.
Make my relationships right with you
and my neighbours.
You have never deserted me:
let me, in your strength, strive
to make your promise of salvation
freely available to all.

Judith E. Winn

The adventures of a slice of toast

A grain of wheat is planted in the ground
Sun and rain help the seed to grow
The wheat grows tall and the ears ripen
The wheat is harvested
It is ground into flour
The flour is baked into bread
The loaf is taken to a shop
Someone buys the bread and takes it home
You come home from wherever feeling hungry
You have toast for tea
You're hungry no more and the toast has done its job

That's quite a story for one piece of toast

Prophecy

Do you hear footsteps
Soft yet brave
Tender yet determined
Of DAWN
The mighty woman?

She is coming
With a basketful
Of golden rays
Of life
Of awakening

Her movement
Is unseen
To the mortal eyes
But invincible
A power
A source
Of resurrection

That will reign
All lives
Of all time

A new cycle
In the flow everlasting
History
A space in reality
Of eternity

All the broken hearts
Shall rejoice
All those
Who are heavy laden
Their eyes are
Too tired and do not see
Shall be lifted up
To meet with
Her beauty absolute

The motherly healer
The motherly enabler

The battered souls and bodies
Shall be healed
The hungry
Shall be fed
The imprisoned
Shall be free

All her earthly children
Shall regain joy
In the reign
Of just and loving one

(Anonymous)

Claiming victory ahead

It was the drug scene, you were lost and wretched, and you put your hand in the hand of the man who calmed the sea:
I rejoice with you, my sister.
You were turned on by the exciting and ever deepening insights of Scripture:
I rejoice with you, my brother.
You were converted from shallowness to mystic depths through discipline and meditation:
I rejoice with you, my sister.
You were a poor Mexican baptised by the Holy Spirit and the Blood of the Lamb:
I rejoice with you, my brother.
You were an intellectual Chinese who broke through the barrier between yourself and the dung-smelling peasant:
I rejoice with you, my sister.
You found all the traditional language meaningless and became 'an atheist by the grace of God':
I rejoice with you, my brother.
Out of the depths of your despair and bondage you cried, and in your cry was poignant hope:
I rejoice with you my sister.

You were oppressed and fled to the liberated area and dedicated
your life to revolutionary struggle:
I rejoice with you, my brother.
You were oppressed and put down by male authority and in spite
of sneers and snarls persevered in your quest for dignity:
I rejoice with you, my sister.
For all my brothers and sisters who have entered the struggle for
social and spiritual liberation:
I rejoice. Victory and grace be unto you all.

*For this litany use two or three voices, with the whole gathering saying the
refrain. Let the men say 'I rejoice with you, my sister' and the women say
'I rejoice with you, my brother'.*

Masks

'Let us proceed with the case,' said the head judge, adjusting his
mask. He looked round the crowd that were attending the trial.
They were all attentive, hardly fidgetting at all behind their masks.
Then he looked in horror at the accused.

'Young man,' he said, 'we'll ignore the things that you've been
saying in our streets and get to the heart of the matter. Where is
your mask?'

'I never had one,' said the young man. 'I never wanted one.'

'To lose a mask is gross carelessness but never to have wanted
or had one is a terrible sin', said the judge.

So they took the young man and hanged him.

The young man's friends were mourning his death together
when one of them cautiously slipped off his mask – then others
did so and soon they were leaping for joy, encouraging everyone
to take off their masks.

Years passed and one day one old friend said to some others,
'Do you remember the young man's face?'

'Just a little,' they said.

'Well then, let's compare notes and between us we'll be able to
make a mould and then for the good of all we'll be able to make . . .'

Malcom Stewart

Ode on Christmas Day, 1980

On the presentation of a garden fork to my wife

When Adam delved and Eve span
Woman, no doubt, was less than man.
When Eve begins to delve as well,
How can folks Eve from Adam tell?
So Adam must his pride maintain
By boasting a superior brain.
But this false claim is knocked for six
When Eve goes into politics.
So what is left for Adam still
Except to steal and rape and kill?
Unless you think – and you'd be right –
That Eve and Adam in God's sight
Are equal partners in the strife
Of building up the common life.

Rupert Davies

Long live men

Men are so vital
a man gave birth to the Messiah
a man stayed with Jesus as He died
a man was first at the tomb
a man gave news of the risen Christ first
Men are everywhere
long live men

Tony Jasper

MORNING LIGHT

Justice shall dawn as the light of the morning
    when the sun rises
        in brilliant cloudless sky.
Then young grass surprises

the earth with all its sparkling
     after rain.

Child, you are come as the dawn of the morning
     lighting oases
          to spear the wilderness.
Grass breaks through rough places
     and mirage turns to water
          after rain.

Victory shines as the star of the morning
     down open vistas
          for him who overcomes.
Night lifts from veiled pastures
     seen fertile in clear shining
          after rain.

Lois Ainger

Roof Top Demonstration
Joshua Tells Of An Incident In Capernaum

'Right, we'll have to move now or we'll lose the opportunity,' said Ezra. 'A man like that isn't going to hang around for long in Galilee. We'll need at least four of us and you, Joshua, can be the advance party.'

'Why me?' I complained.
'Because nobody ever takes any notice of you, Joshua, so you'll be able to calculate the chances without being conspicuous.'

'Thanks a lot,' I said.

'Now don't go sulky on us before we've even started. Is it you or is it Simeon who's got problems and needs his friends?'

'All right,' I said. 'Bring the stretcher as far as my house and I'll go on and find out what I can.'

As I walked through the town I began to wonder how I'd got myself involved in the scheme in the first place. I didn't believe in healers and I wasn't sure that Ezra did but here we were planning to gate-crash some preacher's performance: Simeon, stretcher mat and all.

You had to give it to Ezra, he cared about his friend. When people used to say 'He's paralysed,' Ezra would snap back 'No, he's Simeon and don't ever forget that.' He was right, of course. Being unable to do much for yourself, it must be easy to lose any self-respect.

Peter's mother's house was not a big one and when I arrived there I realised we had more of a problem than we'd imagined. The house was crammed to the door, crammed even outside the door if that's possible. It didn't take many brains to see that there was absolutely no way in.

I made my way back down the street. They were waiting expectantly outside my house.

'Forget it,' I said, 'you'll never get anywhere near him.'

'Forget it?' said Ezra, 'you seem to have forgotten we've carried this lump half way across town. He's walking back whether he likes it or not . . . if only for the sake of my shoulders.'

Simeon smiled half-heartedly. He knew that Ezra's confidence was for his benefit and I knew he couldn't share it as he'd have liked to.

Ezra paused for a moment to think. 'No way in round the front,' he concluded, 'we'll have to go round the back.'

'There isn't a door round the back, Ezra,' I reminded him. He shrugged. 'Then we'll have to make one. Come on, Joshua, get to one corner of this stretcher and exercise the few muscles you possess.'

So Ezra led us off up the street, down an alley and round to the back of the house. There was of course, no way in.

'See, I told you.' I began to say but Ezra ignored me. 'Up here,' he said.

'On to the roof?'

'That's where the stairs lead don't they?'

I wasn't going to argue. It was never worth it with Ezra. With a good deal of huffing and puffing we got Simeon up there. You could see he was beginning to wonder about the whole thing as well.

'Now what?' I asked

'Roofs are made of mud,' said Simeon, 'and mud can be removed. The necessary tools will be here in a moment.'

'You can't just make a hole in the roof. Peter's mother will go crazy. Not to mention what Peter is likely to do.'

'If we can make a hole,' said Ezra, 'we can mend a hole. I grant that we may not be popular but then that wasn't the purpose of our little social call,'

You've got to hand it to Ezra. If he wants to do something, he lets nothing stand in his way. Not even Simeon. For it was about then that he commented, at last, on the whole expedition.

'Look, Ezra, I appreciate what you're doing but it's a waste of time. You're not the healer, he is.' He pointed downwards. 'And he is going to take one look at me and know that I'm not worth healing.'

'Rubbish,' said Ezra.

'You don't know all the rotten things my mind fills up with at times,' said Simeon. 'If he is who people said he is, then he'll know straightaway.'

Ezra, as usual, shrugged his shoulders and ignored the worry, helped by the fact that the tools had arrived and digging could begin. It didn't take long, of course, but long enough for me to keep wondering what they were making of all the noise down below.

We made a hole just big enough to slip Simeon through and, with the help of the ropes, in he went, feet first.

I'd have loved to have seen the faces of the teachers of the law who hate having their religion interrupted by even the slightest distraction. I didn't, of course. In fact I didn't see anything.

But I heard plenty. I heard a man say, 'Simeon, my son, your sins are forgiven.'

Then there was a pause. I could guess what the religious authorities were thinking: how dare anyone forgive sins except God? I must admit it seemed a bit odd, even to me. Then, the voice again.

'Why do you think such things? Which is easier? Saying your sins are forgiven or saying get up from the mat and walk?'

Well, even I knew the answer to that.

The voice went on: 'So that you might know that the son of man has authority, on earth to forgive sins, I say this, "Get up, Simeon Take your mat and go home,"'

I still couldn't see but the gasp that echoed around the room meant that you didn't need to see. The first I saw of Simeon was when he came around the back of the house.

'I can walk,' he beamed at us, 'and I feel good.'

He turned to Ezra. 'He knew about me but it didn't matter.'

Then he looked at all of us and his smile said it all.

'Well,' said Ezra, 'see what a little determination will do.'

'The hole,' said Simeon, suddenly worried.

Ezra waved his hand. 'Being dealt with at the moment.'

'I still say, I murmured quietly to Ezra,' wait till Peter's mother sees her roof.'

Erza gave me one of his quizzical looks. 'And I say, wait till Peter's mother sees Simeon.'

Dave Kitchen

A MATHEMATICAL CERTAINTY

Albert George Basserthwaite, bordering 40, hair receding, always had been unswerving in one thing: his church attendance.

Shadowed by the steelworks, Bethany Evangelical Fellowship might not have been everyone's idea of the universe but it suited

Albert. He had grown up there, had been converted there, spent most of his free time there. To Albert, the job at the steelworks was no more than a time-consuming inconvenience. Life revolved around 'Bethany' as surely as the sun revolved around the earth.

So it might have gone on if it had not been for the series of Bible studies on the book of Revelation.

'Of course, He's coming very soon,' said Albert, one evening.

'Quite probable I would say,' added one of the other members.

'No,' said Albert, in a matter-of-fact way, 'Quite certain. I've worked it out. Look.'
And he pulled out a dozen or two sheets tightly packed with calculations.

'No one knows the time and and the place, brother,' said a somewhat nervous fatherly voice.

'I know that,' said Albert. 'If you'll look, you'll see I've only been able to work it out to the nearest half hour.'

Albert had never intended to become anyone's topic of gossip or someone who was constantly being taken aside so that an elder member could have 'a quiet word, brother'. But he endured it with a patient smile and repeated his belief.

'Two a.m. on September the 17th. Have a look at my calculations.'
No one did. they were too concerned with giving Albert good advice. If they had shown interest, they would have discovered that even the mathematics were wrong. As it was, they whispered among themselves, and left Albert as adamant as ever.

So it was that the night of September the 16th arrived. One or two had spoken about staying up with Albert, feeling he would need help if nothing happened. In the end they were too embarrassed by the situation.

Thus while Bethany chapel's other members slept, Albert kept a quiet vigil in his front garden. Solitary and confident, he stood. Two o'clock came. Ten past. Half past. Nothing.
Pacing up and down he wondered about his calculations. The town hall clock struck three. He daren't go to bed. Quarter past was struck. Half past.

There was a noise at the end of the street. A sobbing figure came into view. Albert, single and with a limited experience of life was not the best person standing in his front garden at the time. So his was the shoulder upon which the woman poured out her story. Albert was lost for words. He had read about such things but had no idea how to cope with them.

'Come on in. I'll make you a cup of tea,' he said uncertain of what to say or do.

As Albert busied himself with the tea, he forgot his disappointment. He knew, in his heart, it had been foolish to be so certain, however sure it might have seemed.

'Right,' he said, musingly, as the kettle began to whistle, 'tea for two is coming up.' And a voice behind him spoke, a man's voice, warm and peaceful: 'For three of us.'

He had come.

Dave Kitchen

GIVE US THIS DAY OUR DAILY BREAD

Each day we remember anew that we are the children of God.
    Give us this day our daily bread.
Each day we are reminded that we are loved extravagantly.
    Give us this day our daily bread.
Each day we stop to take a breath, a full breath of the Spirit that surrounds us.
    Give us this day our daily bread.
Each day we stop for a moment to find our connection to the earth.
    Give us this day our daily bread.
Each day we celebrate the communities of which we are a part.
    Give us this day our daily bread.
And we must also acknowledge walls that keep us apart.
    Give us this day our daily bread.
Each day we know that pain lives deeply in our hearts.
    Give us this day our daily bread.

And we also know the meaning of joy.
> Give us this day our daily bread.

For the spaces in our souls that need to be filled:
> Give us this day our daily bread.

For the hunger that seems to recur with frequency:
> Give us this day our daily bread.

for the ever–present need for new life:
> Give us this day our daily bread.

For each and every day of our lives:
> Give us this day our daily bread.

Amen

Phil Porter

To something else

> Out of meaninglessness, God calls us.
> Out of brokenness, God calls us to wholeness.
> Out of divisiveness, God calls us to community.
> Out of tears, God calls us to laughter.
> Out of self-centredness, God calls us to love.
> Out of death, God calls us to life . . .

The coming of the Kingdom

Leader: Let us ask God for the coming of the Kingdom.

Leader: O God, into the pain of the tortured:

Reader: breathe stillness.

Leader: Into the hunger of the very poor

Reader: breathe fullness.

Leader: Into the wounds of our planet:

Reader: breathe well-being.

Leader: Into the deaths of your creatures:

Reader: breathe life.

Leader: Into those who long for you:

Reader: breathe yourself.

Leader: Your kingdom come,
> your will be done.

Reader: The kingdom, the power and the glory are yours now and forever.

All: Our God is with us
Leader: We celebrate the miracle of living and being!
          We celebrate the miracle of Creation!
Reader: Our God loves us,
          our lives are the blessing of God,
          let us give thanks with joy!
          Amen.

Dorothy McMahon

Listening with the heart

It's easy to think, 'If I'd been the Bethlehem innkeeper, I would never have turned Mary and Joseph away,' or 'if I had been Judas, I would never have betrayed Jesus.'

But would we? Try re-reading a favourite Bible passage, but read it as if you had never heard it before. Empty your mind of all your ideas, thoughts and feelings about the story. Now, prayerfully, imagine you are one of the characters in the story – anyone, it doesn't matter who. Let yourself become a *part* of the story. Even imagine what sort of day it is and what you are wearing.

Prayerfully, let the Holy Spirit take your mind over, become 'there', let the story become real. What is happening? What does Jesus say to you? What do you say to Jesus? Do not worry about whether you react as the people in the original story did. Just be honest with Jesus and with yourself.

The short 'dreams' I have written are simply an idea of how to go about this sort of meditation. Do not 'fill them out' into full plays, they are simply meant to get you into the 'feel' of how to pray this way. How each story ends is up to the individual.

At the end, ask yourselves the questions given, as well as anything else you can think of. What does your meditation teach you about God, yourself, and how you *really* respond to Jesus? You will probably be shocked or even disturbed, but that is because this sort of prayer *makes* us become honest, and shakes off our need to 'say the right thing'. Through this, God can teach us a great deal about ourselves, and the real nature of our faith.

I suggest these meditations are done in groups, so you can learn from each other's experiences, and then lovingly pray for each other.

They can be acted as mini-plays or as mimes with a narrator.

There are, of course, many other ways of doing these meditations and they must be used according to the needs of your Bible study or prayer group. The only rules are prayerful openness to God's Spirit, and honesty.

Dream 1

I dreamed I was an exhausted, bewildered follower of Jesus. We had been on the go all day. We were famished, and so tired, we did not know how to keep going. We could scarcely put one foot in front of another.

'Let's go somewhere quiet where we can rest a bit,' he had said. 'Let's get away from these crowds.'

So we went. But the crowds came too. There were thousands of them. Jesus didn't bat an eyelid.

'Go on,' he said, 'feed them.'

Just like that? I ask you!

'Come off it, Jesus, that would cost a fortune!' I said.

'What have you got between you?' he asked.

I knew I'd got a few buns in a bag, and Andrew had picked up a couple of smoked fish from a market stall a few miles back, but we were rather looking forward to them. Go on Jesus, don't ask *us*. I bet everyone has something stashed away somewhere! After all, what's *our* dinner amongst so many?

Jesus just sort of looked at me.

Allow silence. The narrator invites the watchers to enact the scene for themselves in their own minds. They will need about 15 minutes for this. Ask the listeners: How did you respond to Jesus? What could he be asking you to do or to give? How do you feel about what is being asked of you?

After a pause, read Mark 6:34–44.

Dream 2

I dreamed I was helping to carry a paralysed friend on a

stretcher. We pushed and shoved through the crowds. He lay there, sweating, frightened, eyes staring blankly up at us.

'What's the use? There's no way in!' I said. 'Let's go home.'

'Let's take the roof off,' said another.

'We'll get into awful trouble,' I said.

One of the others stopped and looked me in the eye. 'How much does he mean to you? Do you care more about getting into trouble, or getting him better?'

Eventually we did it, we broke through the roof and lowered my friend down. Jesus didn't shout or rant at us. He just looked up and smiled.

Then he turned to our friend on the stretcher, and blow me, all he said was, 'Your sins are forgiven.'

Allow silence. The narrator invites the listeners to imagine that someone they know who is ill or in need of prayer is on the stretcher. The listeners enact the scene for themselves in their own minds (about 15 minutes). Then the narrator asks: How much do you care for the person on the stretcher? Have you got the courage to take the roof off and face the consequences? What do you feel when prayers aren't answered as you think they should be?

After a pause read Mark 2:1–12.

Dream 3

I dreamed I was very ill. I had leprosy, and I lived in a filthy, stinking hovel with a few others, outside the town. I had no hope – my fingers and toes were dropping off. I was just rotting away alive.

One day, we heard Jesus was coming. Hurriedly, we tidied our bandages and ran out to meet him. We stayed well away from the crowds, but we yelled, we shouted, we banged tin lids together, anything to attract his attention.

'Have pity on us Jesus, ' we screamed.

Jesus stopped, turned and looked at us.

We went cold with delight. It was joy just to look at him. He was the only person I have ever seen who cared like that . . .

'Go and show yourselves to the priests,' he said simply.

We looked at each other and shrugged. What was the point of doing that? But we felt we had to.

On the way, we were healed.

The narrator invites the listeners to take about 15 minutes to enact the scene for themselves in their own minds, imagining they are one of the lepers.

After a few minutes the narrator asks, 'What did you do next? Did you come back and thank Jesus, or did you do something else? Why? How do you thank God for your own healing and salvation? Pause, then read Luke 17:11–19.

Beth Webb

Countdown to the Lord

Four: An open hall. Lots of smiling. I am Jesus. It's only a play. Pretty colours.

Seven: It's a book. A bearded silver man with lights and a smile. He is smiling at me.

Fifteen: School Assembly. Father Michael talks of prayer. That night I pray, kneel like in the picture. He is starting to mean something.

Twenty: I'm not alone in my belief. Some people laugh, others talk. I don't mind though. He's with me always. A good mate.

Forty-Five: I think I know him. I talk, he listens. My wife knows, and and cares. My children will know. Will care?

Seventy: I spend a lot of time alone with him. The Home is full of his believers, though some just sleep.

Death: I met him today. He is beautiful.

Luke Mariner (16)

Always with us

Leader: The God of Columba the wandering one
All: Stay with us now
Leader: The God of Francis the poor one
All: Stay with us now
Leader: The God of Luther the reforming one
All: Stay with us now
Leader: The God of John 23rd the enlightening one
All: Stay with us now
Leader: The God of Bonhoeffer the brave one
All: Stay with us now
Leader: The God of Teresa the kind one
All: Stay with us now
Leader: The God of Martin Luther King the just one
All: Stay with us now
Leader: The God of Desmond Tutu, the persistent one
All: Stay with us now
Leader: The God of Mahatma Gandhi the peacemaker
All: Stay with us now
Leader: The God of George MacLeod, rebuilder of the common
          life
All: Stay with us now
Leader: The God and Father of our Lord Jesus Christ, Crucified,
          Dead, Risen and Ascended
All: Stay with us this night and every night. Amen.

More words of liberation and new life

Music for worship

The following list comprises music in contemporary vein, with an asterisk denoting release by a religious record company. It is intended as no more than a reference point, not as an exhaustive catalogue.

General records need to be used carefully, according to the circumstances. Most of the titles listed are likely to be used within an 'informal' setting. Whatever the context, the music should be reproduced on high quality equipment, and never rendered inaudible or distorted. Sound level should be dictated by the music, by the presentation context, and by the worship style it supports.

All the titles listed, with a very few exceptions, have been released since 1987.

Music of praise, adoration and thanksgiving:

Worship-Songs Of The Vineyard – I Want To Know You – Various.*
'Agnus Dei', Michael Smith. Album: *Go West Young Man*.
'Wherever God Shines His Light', Van Morrison/Cliff Richard. Album: *Avalon*
'Holy Spirit', Al Green. Album: *Trust In God*.
'Streams In The Desert', Adrian Snell. Album: *Alpha & Omega*.*
'A Love Supreme', Will Downing. Album: *Will Downing*.

Music to lead into and close worship:

'Time For Tears', Album tracks. Chris Bowater.*
'A Mighty Fortress and other hymns', 2nd Chapter of Acts. Hymns 11.*
'We Sing Praises', Deniece Williams. Special Love (Sparrow).*
'In The Air Tonight', Phil Collins. Album: *Seriously Live*.
'Let The Day Begin', The Call. Album: *The Call*.

'Thy Word', Amy Grant. Album: *Straight Ahead.*
'Breaking Of Day', The Winans. Album: *Decisions.**
'Psalm 55', Leslie Phillips. Album: *Black and White.**
'The Lord's Prayer', Leon Patillo. Album: *Love Around The World**
'Psalm 33', Bryn Haworth Album: *Wings Of The Morning.**
'Lead Me On', Amy Grant. Album: *Lead Me On.**
'Give Thanks album', Keith Routledge.* Instrumental.
'Celebrate Life', Bebe and CeCe Winans. Album: *Heaven.*

Music about Jesus:

'Messiah', Larry Norman. Album: *The Best Of.**
'King of Kings', Ladysmith Black Mambazo Album: *Shake Zulu.*
'Table Talk', The Bond. Album: *Prints Of Peace.**
'He Set Me Free', Commissioned. Album: *State Of Mind.**
'You Are My Rock', Petra. Album: *This Means War.**
'The Way'. Stryper. Album: *Struggle To Hell With The Devil.*
'Psalm 23', Al Green. Album: *Soul Survivor.*
'Jesus Is The Rock Of My Salvation', Tata Vega. Album: *Time's So Right.*

Music about birth and Christmas:

'Little Town', Cliff Richard. Album. *Private Collection.*
'Slouching Towards Bethlehem', Joni Mitchell. Album: *Night Ride Home.*
'Medley Xmas – A Classical Winter', The Oklahoma Quintet (instrumental).
'We Three Kings' Roches. Album tracks.
'Christmas', Michael W Smith Album tracks.*
'Our Christmas', Various artists.

Music for Easter and Resurrection:

'At Golgotha', Ladysmith Black Mambazo. Album: *Shake Zulu.*
'Make Way Cross', Graham Kendrick. Album.*
'Gethsemane', Geoff Mann. Album: *Psalm Enchanted Evening.*
'Sundays On The Way', Take Six. Album: *So Much To Say.*
'The Resurrection', Spirit of Watts. Album: *Gospel Joy.*
'When I Survey The Wondrous Cross', Cliff Richard. Album:

Small Corners.

Music about faith and conversion:

'Love, Thy Will Be Done', Martika. Album: *Martika's Kitchen*.

'I Believe', Stryper. Album: *Can't Stop The Rock*.

'Waiting On You', Gladys Knight Album: *Good Woman*.

'Hope Set High', Amy Grant. Album: *Heart In Motion*.*

'Steps of Faith', Margaret Becker. Album: *Simple House*.*

'The Comfort of Faith', Banderas. Album: *Ripe*.

'The Laughter Comes/Reinforcing My Belief', King's X. Album: *Faith, Hope and Love*.

'Quiet Storm', Phil and John. Album: *Shine Like America*.*

'I Can See Clearly Now', Hothouse Flowers. Album: *Hothouse Flowers*.

'Solid Rock', Bob Dylan. Album: *Saved*.

'Saved By Love', Amy Grant. Album: *Lead Me On*.*

'Never Give It Up', Sheila Walsh Album: *Shadowlands*.*

'Choose Life', Debby Boone. Album: *Choose Life*.*

'River Of Love', Leslie Phillips. Album: *The Turning*.*

'I Shook His Hand', Peter Case. Album: *Peter Case* (Geffen)

'Somebody Touched Me', Bruce Cockburn. Album: *Nothing But a Burning Light*.

Music of Wholeness

'Now I Can't Find The Door', Sam Phillips. Album: *Cruel Invention*.

'You're Still Loved', Lavine Hudson. Album: *Between Two Worlds*.

'Mr Love', Gladys Knight. Album: *Good Woman*.

'Lift Me Up', Yes. Album: *Union*.

'That's What Love Is For', Amy Grant. Album: *Heart In Motion*.

'Pray', M.C. Hammer.

'Learning How To Love', Lavine Hudson. Album: *Intervention*.

'Skeleton Key'. Wendy and Lisa. Album: *Eroica*.

'Looking For Love', The Bond. Album: *Prints of Peace**

'Healing', Deniece Williams. Album: *Special Love*.

'God Put Your Hand On Me', Carmel. Album: *Set Me Free*.

Victims album, second side. Steel Pulse.

'Happy Days', Temper Temper. Album: *Temper Temper*.

'Just Mellow', Ruthless Rap Assassins. Album: *Killer*.
'Something To Believe In', Clannad. Album: *Pastpresent*.
'Everybody Gets a Second Chance', Mike and The Mechanics.
Album: *Word of Mouth*.
'Silent Running', Mike and The Mechanics. Album: *Mike and the Mechanics*.
'Let It Shine On Me', Nanci Griffith. Album: *Lone Star State Of Mind*.

Music about ourselves and faith:

'Raised on Promises', Sam Phillips. Album: *Cruel Interventions*.
'Without Hope You Cannot Start The Day', Yes. Album: *Union*.
'Born At The Right Time', Paul Simon. Album: *Rhythm of the Saints*.
'Simple House', Margaret Becker. Album: *Simple House*.*
'Radio Man', Fighter. Album: *The Waiting*.*
'This Beautiful Pain', Runrig. Album: *The Big Wheel*.
'This Is Your Life', Banderas. Album: *Ripe*.
'Has He Got a Friend For Me', Maria McKee. Album: *Maria McKee*.
'Finally We Find Ourselves Again', Randy Stonehill. Album: *Until We Have Things*.*
'Silver Thunderbird', Marc Cohn. Album: *Marc Cohn*.
'Walk On Air', T'Pau. Album: *The Promise*.
'Get A Life', Soul II Soul. Album: *Soul to Soul* – 1990 Album Decade.
'Find Me', Alison Moyet. Album: *Hoodoo*.
'Time, Love and Tenderness', Michael Bolton. Album: *Time, Love and Tenderness*.
'Dream A Dream Like Mine', Bruce Cockburn. Album: *Nothing But A Burning Light*.

Music about Relationships:

'Some People', Cliff Richard. Private Collection.

Music about forgiveness:

'Forgiveness', Sweetmouth. Album: *Goodbye to Songtown*.
'Last Word In Love', Sheila Walsh. Album: *Shadowlands*.*
'Over The Moon', Leslie Phillips. Album: *Black and White*

'Forgive Them', Nanette Welmans. Album: *Step On Out.**

Music of pain and suffering:

'Child', Amy Grant. Album: *Heart In Motion*.
'Fortune Of Soldiers', Judy Collins. Album: *Fires Of Eden*.
'Broken Image', Garth Hewitt. Album: *Lonesome Troubadour*.
'Trailing Clouds of Glory', Garth Hewitt. Album: *Lonesome Troubadour*.
'They Dance Alone', Sting. Album: *Nothing Like the Sun*.
'Talk About the Passion', REM. Album: *REM*.
'The Living Years', Mike and The Mechanics. Album: *The Living Years*.
'Daddy Says', Caroline Bonnett. Album: *Still Time.**
'Heavenly Protection', Caroline Bonnett. Album: *Still Time.**

Music that sings the tune of the times:

'Murder in The Big House', Chagalli Guevara. Album: *Chagalli Guevara*.
'Both Sides Now', Clannad and Paul Young. Album: *Switch Soundtrack*.
'Heartless Generation', Lavine Hudson. Album: *Between Two Worlds*.
'Ever Changing Times', Aretha Franklin, Album: *What You See Is What You Sweat*.
'Winter In July', Bomb The Bass. Single.
'Heaven's Gate', Toni Childs. Album: *House Of Hope*
'River Of Love', Taj Mahal. Album: *Life Never Before*
'Fear of the Unknown', Siouxsie and The Banshees. Album: *Superstition*.
'A Change Is On Its Way', Northside Album: *Chicken Rhythms*.
'And It Was A Dream', Ruthless Rap Assassins. Album: *Killer*.
'Raggle Taggle Gipsy', The Waterboys. Album: *Room To Room*.
'The Policy Of Truth', Depeche Mode. Album: *Violator*.
'3 A.M. Eternal', The KLF. Album: *The White Room*.

Music About Waste

'Why Must I Share This Air With Foolish Men', Mock Turtles. Album: *Two Sides*.

'The Living and the Still Born', Danielle Dax. Album: *Blast The Human Flower*.

'King Crack', Danielle Dax. Album: *Blast The Human Flower*.

'The ID Parade', Danielle Dax. Album: *Blast The Human Flower*.

'Town Called Malice', Jam. Album: *Greatest Hits*.

'If The Bomb Falls', Larry Norman. Album: *The Best Of*.*

'Soul Destruction', T'Pau. Album: *The Promise*.

'Dance On Injustice', Garth Hewitt. Album: *Lonesome Troubadour*,*

'Nowhere To Stand', K.D. Lang. Album: *Torch and Twang*.

'Voices Cryin' Out', Donna Summer. Album: *All Systems Go*.

'Little Man, What Now', Morrissey. Album: *Viva Hate*.

'TV Song', Bob Dylan. Album: *Under The Red Sky*.

'Shiny Happy People', REM. Album: *Out Of Time*.

'Who Will Save The Children?', Randy Stonehill. Album: *Celebrate the Heartbeat*.*

'Baby Doe', Steve Taylor. Album: *Meltdown*.*

'Bad Rap', Steve Taylor. Album: *I Want To Be A Clown*.*

Music about nature, creation and ecology:

'The Priests of the Golden Bull', Buffy Sainte-Marie. Album: *Coincidence and Likely Stories*.

'Miracle Of Life', Yes. Album: *Union*.

'Lay Down', Carmel. Album: *Everybody's Got a Little Soul*.

'Creation', Geoff Mann. Album: *Psalms Enchanted Evening*.*

Music about nations and peoples:

'Edge of the World', Runrig. Album: *The Big Wheel*.

'Fragile', Sting. Album: *Nothing Like The Sun*.

'Fire Of Ambition', Phil and John. Album: *Shine Like America*.*

'Can Hell Burn Not Enough', Randy Stonehill. Album: *Until We Have Wings*.*

'World Without Heroes', Cher. Album: *Love Hurts*.

'Mi Revalueshanry Fren', Linton Kwesi Johnson. Album: *Tings An' Times*.

'Prayer for the World', Maxi Priest. Album: *Bona Fide*.

'UK Blak', Caron Wheeler. Album: *UK Blak Volume II*.

'Moments In Time', The Alarm. Album: *Raw*.

Music about Church and community:

'Denomination Demolition', Mylon and Broken Heart. Album: *Crank It up.**
'Walls', DC Talk. Album: *Nu Thang.**
'Shine Your Light', Jamie Owens. Album: *Shine Your Light.**
'If We Are The Light', Deniece Williams. Album: *So Glad I Know**
'Light Of The World', Al Green. Album: *The Strongest Power.*
'All Soldiers', Philip Bailey. Album: *Triumph.**
'We're All One', Bryn Haworth. Album: *Live and Gold.**
'My Land Is Too Green', Mary Coughlan. Album: *Under the influence.*

Music about call, discipleship and commitment:

'Soldiers Under Command', Stryper. Album: *Can't Stop the Rock*
'Evangelistic Blues', Larry Howard. Album: *Redeemed.*
'Stand Up and Be Counted', Vernessa Mitchell. Album: *On A Mission.**
'Can't Get a Witness,' DC Talk. Album: *Mu Thang.**
'Answer The Call', White Heat. Album: *Powerhouse.**
'Prayer Warriors', Dallas Holm. Album: *Change the World.**

Music of liberation and new life:

'Let's Break Bread Together', Joan Baez. Album: Recently.
'Dreaming A Dream', Aretha Franklin. Album: *What You See Is What You Sweat.*
'The Rhythm of the Saints', Paul Simon. Album: *The Rhythm of the Saints.*
'Hope I See You In Heaven', Larry Norman. Album: *Best Of.**
'I Still Haven't Found', U2. Album: Rattle & Hum.
'I Still Haven't Found', Chimes. Album: *Chimes.*
'Wake Up', David Grant. Album: *Anxious Edge.*
'When He Returns', Bob Dylan. Album: *Slow Train Coming.*
'Roll On', Garth Hewitt. Album: *Did He Jump.*

Acknowledgements

The compiler and the publishers are grateful to the following for permission to include their material in this anthology:

Roy Akerman for the poems 'Epithalamial Sonnet' and 'What Sort of Woman', both first published in *Christian* magazine.

Amnesty International for 'Never Forgotten'.

Chris Antcliff for his poem 'Do They Understand?'.

Lois Angier for the poems; 'Forgiveness', 'The touch of a hand' and 'Morning Light'.

David Ansell for his poem 'Choral evensong'.

Eddie Askew for his piece based on Psalm 21 and Hebrews 12:1–2.

Augsburg Fortress Publishers for 'Psalm 23' by Norman Habel, from *Hi! Have a Nice Day*, 1972 Fortress Press. 'Psalm 68' by Zephania Kameeta from *Why, O Lord* 1986.

Bridgehead Communications for 'What's The Point of Living?' by Jack Money.

Anna Briggs for the hymn 'We lay our broken world'.

J. R. Brooke for the poem 'Spring Thoughts, 1986'.

Paul Bunday for 'In the Beginning' first published in *Christian* Magazine.

Cairns Publications for 'Eternal and Loving God' and 'Lead Us Through' by Jim Cotter from *Prayers in the Morning*.

Cassell PLC for two prayers from *Praying Together in Word and Song*.

Christian Aid for 'Let there be Right' from a service written for Christian Aid by Alan Gaunt.

Church Missionary Society for prayers from *Morning, Noon and Night, Prayers and Meditations from the Third Word* by John Carden.

Janice M. Clark for 'A Psalm of Lament' and 'God with Us' from *In Pastures Green*.

Kate Compston for the poem 'Cloud-Baby' first published in *Reform* magazine.

Concordia Publishing House for 'Daily Thanks' by Herbert Brokering from *Worlds of Youth*, 1967. Prayer by Herbert Brokering from *Beyond Words*, 1970. 'My Body' and 'Everybody Laughed at Me' by Jane Graver from *Just As I Am*, 1975.

The Corrymeela Community for 'Gracious God, we lift up . . .' from *Celebrating Together*.

Darton, Longman & Todd Ltd for the dramatic sketch extract by Gerard Hughes from *God of Surprises*.

Rupert Davis for his 'Ode on Christmas Day, 1980'.

Martin Eggleton for the pieces; 'Aids Victim', 'The Samaritan', 'Someone in the Crowd' and 'Seeing the Crowd'.

Peter English for the sketches: 'Up-Dating the Psalms', 'Advertiser's Christmas', 'Don't You Believe Me?', 'Say What You Mean' and 'The Modern Church'.

Colin Ferguson for the poems 'The Caged Earth' and 'God Speaks to Us Today'.

Forest of Peace Books, Inc. for 'A Prayer for Feasting' by Reverend Edward Hays from *Pray All Ways*, 1981.

Daphne Fraser for 'Praise him in the dance'.

Monica Furlong for 'Strength in Risk' and 'God of Whoever'.

Edwina Gateley for her poem, on page 64, first published in *Psalms of A Laywoman* by Anthony Clark Publishing.

Diane Glancy for the poem 'Waiting for the Gas-can', first published in *Radix* magazine.

Grassroots for 'Fooling About in the Kingdom' by Conway Barker.

David Harding for the poems 'Things that really are' and 'Not yet'.

HarperCollins Publishers for the extracts from *Seeing in the Dark* by Philip Yancey and *A Whole New Ball Game* by Gerald Williams.

Stewart Henderson for the poems, 'A little word of encouragement', 'The Gospel of Rod', 'Only at Easter', 'Football', 'Death Lib', 'Mortal Foil' and 'Jerusalem'.

David R. Hill for his song, 'People who Care'.

Hodder & Stoughton Ltd for 'Creation of Man's best Friend' and 'Unknown Soldier' by Steve Turner, from *Up to Date*.

The Iona Community for 'Let us hold before God in confidence' and 'The God of Columba' from *The Iona Community Worship Book*. 'If the Lord's Disciples Keep Silence' by Kathy Galloway from *Women's Words from Iona Abbey*.

Judith Jenkins for the poem, 'God's Army or the White Trucks'.

Myra Kendrick for the piece 'Credo'.

David Kitchen for the following pieces: 'The Not-good-enough Samaritan's Good Samaritan Story', 'Putting a Figure on It', 'Good Enough for Everyone', 'Trials Faced', 'Rooftop Demonstrations', and 'A Mathematical Certainty'.

Andrew Kreider for the piece 'Signing up'.

Brenda Lealman for the piece 'Inspiration'.

Life and Work for 'Easter Prayers' (Anon.) first published in issue dated April 1985.

Tony Lucas for the poem 'No.el' first published in *The Least Thing* Ed. Angela Topping, Stride, 1989.

Joy Martin for the poem 'Fulfilment'.

Ernest Marvin for the piece 'Who is my neighbour?'.

Dorothy McMahon for the prayers beginning 'Let us ask God for the coming of the Kingdom' and 'As we share the life of your church today'.

The Methodist Church Overseas Division for 'My Magnificat' by Judith E. Winn, 'No Turning Back' by Gershon Anderson, 'Unexpected Treats' and 'When Words are Gone' by Jan Pickard.

The Methodist Church, West Yorkshire District for lines from *Prayers For Family Worship* published by West Yorkshire Synod of the Methodist Church.

The Methodist Recorder for the extract from the report covering the Bradford Football Disaster.

W. J. Milligan for the prayers 'Lord, this is your world' and 'Glory be to God for the life giving differences'.

Morehouse Publishing for 'The Litany of the Saints' from *The Covenant of Peace: A Liberation Prayer Book*, compiled by Brown and York, © 1971 by the Free Church of Berkeley.

Janet Morley for her poem 'For the Darkness of Waiting'.

National Children's Home for the prayer 'For All Children'.

National Christian Education Council for the prayer 'Lord Jesus Christ, through whom, and for whom' by Maureen Edwards, from *Oceans of Prayer*.

National Council of Y.M.C.As. for 'Growth' from *Circles of Experience*.

Christine Odell for the piece 'The News' first published in *Ever Increasing Circles* by Network publications.

Phil Porter for 'Give Us This Day Our Daily Bread'.

Charity Quin for the song 'The Rescue'.

SCM Press for the prayer from page 7 of *Contemporary Prayers for Church and School*, Ed. Caryl Micklem, 1975.

Sea Dream Music Publishing for the lyrics of the songs 'Visions Never Sleep' and 'The Time of Your Life' by Simon Law from *God, Fags and Tea Bags*, 1986. The poems, 'Sin' and 'Reflections' by St Mark's Sunday Club, © 1990 Sea Dream Music.

'Not Winter Again' by Graham Claydon from *The Islington 7*, 1987 and 'Time possesses' from *Love One Another*, 1987.

T. Shand Publications Ltd for extracts from *Seasons of Your Heart, Prayers and Reflections*, 1979.

Carol Short for the poem 'The Lion Dream'.

SPCK for the extract from *Beginning Where I Am* by Godfrey Holmes, the extract 'Glory' from *Tides and Seasons* by David Adam and 'A litany of Thanksgiving' and 'A Litany of Supplication' from *The Daily Office*.

Robert Springsteen for permission to use the poem 'Bring Us Together' by Anne Springsteen, first published by Concordia Publishing House.

Tabb House Publishers for the poem 'Dietrich Bonhoeffer' by Jack Clemo from *A Distant Drummer*.

Cecily Taylor for the poems 'The Baby had a Brithday' and 'The Shepherd's Journey'.

Artie Terry for 'A day in the Life' first published by *Cornerstone* magazine.

United Church Press for 'The Marvel of A Car' by Ernst H. Nussmann, 'On the Collect for Purity' by John McAllister and 'World, I am Youth' by Ellen Bryan.

John J. Vincent for 'The Creed of the Radical Christ' from *Community Worship* published by Ashram Community Trust, 1987.

Rosemary Wakelin for 'A dialogue on the Hymn to Love', 'A Prayer of Confession' and 'God you are Love'.

Norman Wallwork for the prayer 'Blessed are you, O Lord our God'.

Beth Webb for the poems 'Christmas Angel', 'Gift of God', 'Rebecca's Rage', 'God-in-a-box', 'A Woman's work' and 'Little Magdala'. Also the pieces; 'Sanctus', 'Psalms of Praise', 'Credo', 'Introit' and 'Listening with the heart'.

Wild Goose Publications for the prayer 'Glory to you, Almighty God' by John Bell.

Alfred Willetts for the prayer on page 134 which begins with the line 'My heart is bubbling over with Joy' by Phoebe Willetts.

World Association for Christian Communication for 'Christmas: God with Us' from *Action*, December 1988.

World Council of Churches Publications for the prayers 'Let us Pray for the whole World' and 'Risen Lord, You walk through this earth' both from *With All God's People, the New Ecumenical Prayer Cycle: Orders of Service* 1989, WCC Publications, Geneva Switzerland.

'Christ has died and is Risen' this English translation was made by WCC and published in *Confessing Our Faith Around the Word IV: South America*, 1985. The original Spanish text appeared in *Paginas*, Vol II, No 10, June 1977.

'When the Tourist Flew In' and 'The Animal and Insect Act' by Cecil Rajendra, from *Songs for the Unsong: Poems on unpoetic issues like war and want, and refugees* © WCC publications.

'Here is not Here' from WCC *Youth Magazine* 11th July 1983.

Every effort has been made to trace copyright owners. If, unwittingly, any copyright has been infringed, the compiler offers his apology. This will be corrected in any reprint.